Praise for Frances Greenslade and SHELTER

"A page-turning novel. . . . Once you get caught, you find yourself caring about these characters, wanting to know what they will do next, how they will survive."

The Globe and Mail

"From the very first page, this eloquent, evocative book crept into my heart and wouldn't go away. I think it will linger inside me for a long, long time—like a powerful dream or one of those take-your-breath-away kind of tales that someone tells you in childhood and years later, still haunts you. *Shelter* is an unforgettable novel about love, loss, family and what it means to go home."

Mira Bartók, author of *The Memory Palace*

"Greenslade has a real gift as a teller of stories, and she tells them in the clearest, most accessible prose, so that they flow one into the other. Once I started reading . . . I was so engrossed that I couldn't stop. Before I knew it, an entire afternoon had flown by."

Sharon Butala

"The longing for a lost mother has rarely been expressed so soulfully. The yearning of these two vulnerable young sisters for their mother, who has disappeared, is palpable. I was entirely absorbed in their precarious situation and their desire to find her, yet aware that their mother's gift was the resourcefulness they needed to survive. Greenslade is a fresh new voice that you are sure to hear again."

Bobbie Ann Mason, author of *The Girl in the Blue Beret*

"This book casts a strong spell—the landscape is so vividly rendered, it is a character all on its own, and sisters Maggie and Jenny are unforgettable in their resilience. Greenslade depicts the battle between different types of love with harrowing intensity and quiet compassion. *Shelter* shows us how wilderness can be a safer haven than a home with four walls, but also how love, despite its heartbreaking unpredictability, remains the shelter we desire most."

Jamie Zeppa, author of *Every Time We Say Goodbye*

"Reminiscent of great Canadian writers like Ann-Marie MacDonald.... By capturing the place so perfectly, Greenslade allows you to disappear into a story with a clear, visceral beauty of its own."

Penticton Western News

"Greenslade weaves tales of mythology into her meditation on her experience, contrasting timeless and universal beliefs with contemporary bizarreness surrounding mothering. It's lovely, thoughtful and ultimately uplifting."

Toronto Star

SHELTER

ALSO BY FRANCES GREENSLADE

A Pilgrim in Ireland: A Quest for Home

By the Secret Ladder: A Mother's Initiation

FRANCES
GREENSLADE

SHELTER

A NOVEL

VINTAGE CANADA

For David, who told me stories.

VINTAGE CANADA EDITION, 2012

Published in Canada by Vintage Canada, a division of Random House of Canada Limited, Toronto, in 2012. Originally published in hardcover in Canada by Random House Canada, a division of Random House of Canada Limited, in 2011. Distributed by Random House of Canada Limited.

Vintage Canada with colophon is a registered trademark.

www.randomhouse.ca

Grateful acknowledgement is made to the following to reprint on page 347:
"I've Been Everywhere"
Words and Music by Geoff Mack

Library and Archives Canada Cataloguing in Publication

Greenslade, Frances
Shelter / Frances Greenslade.

ISBN 978-0-307-36032-8

I. Title.

PS8613.R438S54 2012 C813'.6 C2011-902233-8

Text design by CS Richardson

Cover photograph: Philip and Karen Smith
Cover design: R. Gill

Printed and bound in the United States of America

2 4 6 8 9 7 5 3

FOOD

[ONE]

Jenny was the one who asked me to write all this down. She wanted me to sort it for her, string it out, bead by bead, an official story, like a rosary she could repeat and count on. But I started writing it for her, too. For Mom, or Irene as other people would call her, since she abandoned a long time ago whatever "Mom" once meant to her. Even now there was no stopping the guilt that rose up when we thought of her. We did not try to look for our mother. She was gone, like a cat who goes out the back door one night and doesn't return, and you don't know if a coyote got her or a hawk or if she sickened somewhere and couldn't make it home. We let time pass, we waited, trusting her, because she had always been the best of mothers. She's the mother, that's what we said to each other, or we did in the beginning. I don't know who started it.

That's not true. It was me. Jenny said, "We should look for her." I said, "She's the mother." When I said it, I didn't know the power those few words would take on in our lives. They had the sound of truth, loaded and untouchable. But they became an anchor that dragged us back from our most honest impulses.

We waited for her to come to get us and she never did.

There was no sign that this would happen. I know people always look for signs. That way they can say, *we're not the type of people things like that happen to,* as if we were, as if we should have seen it coming. But there were no signs. Nothing except my worry, which I think I was born with, if you can be born a worrier—Jenny thinks you can.

Worry was stuffed into the spaces around my heart, like newspaper stuffed in the cracks of a cabin wall, and it choked out the ease that should have been there. I'm old enough now to know that there are people who don't feel dogged by the shadow of disaster, people who think their lives will always be a clean, wide-open plain, the sky blue, the way clearly marked. My anxiety curled me into myself. I couldn't be like Jenny, who was opened up like a sunny day with nothing to do but lie in the grass, feel the warm earth against her back, a breeze, the click of insects in the air. *Soon, later, never*—words not invented. Jenny was *always* and *yes.*

As I say, there was no sign of anything that might go wrong in the small, familiar places that made up our world. The bedroom Jenny and I shared was painted robin's egg blue and the early morning sunlight fell across the wall, turning it luminous, like an eggshell held to the light. I watched how it fell, and after a while tiny shadowed hills rose up and valleys dipped in the textured lines of the wallboard. Morning in that land came slow and slanted with misty light, waking into the glare of day.

Our house in Duchess Creek had a distinctive smell that met me at the front door: boiled turnip, fried bologna, tomato soup, held in the curtains or in the flimsy walls and ceiling or the shreds of newspaper that insulated them. It was a warm house, Mom said, but not built by people who intended to stay. The kitchen cupboards had no doors and the bathroom was separated from the main room by a heavy flowered curtain. Electricity had come to Duchess Creek in 1967, the year I turned seven and Jenny eight. A saggy wire was strung through the trees to our house a few months later. But we had power only occasionally, and only for the lights.

The small electric stove had been dropped off by one of Dad's friends who found it at the dump in Williams Lake. It was never hooked up and Mom never made a fuss about it, though her friend Glenna asked her about twice a week when she was going to get the stove working. Glenna said, "Hey, aren't you happy we've finally joined the twentieth century?" Mom said that if she wanted to join the twentieth century, she'd move to Vancouver. Glenna laughed and shook her head and said, "Well, I guess you're not the only one who thinks that way. There's people who like it that Williams Lake is the biggest town for miles and miles in any direction."

In the Chilcotin, where we lived, there were the Indians, the Chilcotins and the Carriers, who had been here long before the whites came. Their trails and trade routes still criss-crossed the land. And there were the white settlers whose histories were full of stories about pioneering and ranching and road-building. Then there were the late-comers, like our family, the Dillons.

Dad had left Ireland in 1949 for America and ended up in Oregon, then had come north. Others came to avoid marching into wars they didn't believe in, or ways of life they didn't believe in. Some came from cities, with everything they owned packed into their vehicles, looking for a wild place to escape to. They were new pioneers, reinventing themselves following their own designs. Dad had a friend named Teepee Fred and another named Panbread. When I asked Dad what their last names were, he said he'd never bothered to ask.

Mom didn't care much about the electric stove because she had learned to cook on the woodstove. She cooked out of necessity, not pleasure, and stuck mainly to one-pot stews that she could manage without an oven. We didn't have an electric fridge, either. We had a scratched old icebox where a lonely bottle of milk and a pound of butter resided.

There was a pump in the backyard where we got our water. Someone before us had made plans for indoor plumbing. There was a shower and sink in the bathroom, and a hole in the floor, stuffed with rags, where a pipe came in for a toilet, but none of these worked. We pumped our water and carried it in a five-gallon bucket that sat on the kitchen counter. We had an outhouse, but at night we set a toilet seat over a tin pot and Dad emptied it each morning.

Just at the edge of the bush behind the house, Dad had rigged up a heavy, old claw foot bathtub especially for Mom. Underneath he had dug a hole and in that he'd make a small fire. He ran a hose from the pump to fill the tub. The water heated nicely and Mom sat in there on a cedar rack he'd made so she wouldn't burn herself. Some evenings we'd hear her out there, singing to herself, her voice lifting out of the dark on the steam that rose from behind the screen of fir boughs he'd wound through a piece of fence. Sometimes I sat on a stump beside her, trailing my arm in the hot water. Bats wheeled and dipped above us, just shadows, a movement in the corner of the eye. Stars grew brighter and as thick as clouds of insects while the water cooled. I thought that if she needed any proof that Dad loved her, that bathtub was it.

There must have been a time when I sang myself awake, trilling up and down a range of happy notes as a beetle tracked across the window screen and cast a tiny shadow on the wall. But I don't remember it. I can't remember a time when I didn't look at the world and feel apprehension chewing at the edges. It wasn't our mother I worried about, though. I felt lucky to have a mom who took us camping, wasn't afraid of bears, loved to drive the logging roads and what she called the "wagon trails" that wandered off Highway 20 and into the bush. We found lakes and rotting log cabins and secret little valleys; it felt like we were the first people to find them. Our measure of a good camp was how far from other people it was. "No one around for miles," Mom would say, satisfied, when the fire was built. She was the constant in our lives, the certainty and the comfort. It was Dad I worried about.

He had to be approached like an injured bird, tentatively. Too much attention and he would fly off. If he was in the house, he was restless. He would stretch, look around as if he was an outsider, and then I'd feel the sting of disappointment as he went for his jacket by the door.

Sometimes he whistled, made it seem casual, putting his arms into the flannel sleeves. Then he'd go outside, chop wood for a few minutes, like a penance, then disappear into the bush. He'd be gone for hours. Worse days, he'd go to his bedroom and close the door.

I listened with my ear against the wall of my room. If I stood there long enough, I'd hear the squeak of bedsprings as he turned over. I don't know what he did in there. He had no books or radio. I don't think he did anything at all.

When he came back from his working day in the bush, he liked to sleep in the reclining chair by the oil drum that was our woodstove. I wanted him to stay asleep there. If he was asleep, he was with us.

But sometimes he pulled the chair too close to the woodstove. One afternoon, I tried to get him to move it back. "Don't worry, Maggie," he said. "I'm not close enough to melt." And he fell asleep with his mouth open, occasionally drawing a deep breath that turned to a cough and woke him briefly.

I wasn't afraid that he would melt. I was afraid that the chair would burst suddenly into flames, as the Lutzes' shed roof once did when Helmer got the fire in the garbage bin burning too high.

At the counter, my mother stood slicing deer meat for stew. I watched, waiting for his eyelids to sag, flicker, and drop closed again. Mom peeled an onion, then began to chop. Jenny and I had our Barbies spread on the sunny yellow linoleum. Jenny's Barbie wanted to get married and since we didn't have a Ken, my Barbie had to be the husband. I tucked her blonde hair up under a pair of bikini bottoms. Mom turned to us. Her eyes streamed with tears. For some reason, we found her routine with the onions and the tears very funny. We put our hands over our mouths so we wouldn't wake Dad. Mom never cried. Maybe that's why we found it so improbable that something as ordinary as an onion could have this power over her.

She moved to the woodstove. The sweet smell of onions frying in oil rose up and then Mom dropped the cubes of deer meat into the pot. A pungent, wild blood smell that I didn't like filled the house. But it only lasted a minute, then the meat and onions blended to a rich, sweet fragrance and Mom sprinkled in pepper and reached for a jar of tomatoes.

She struggled with the lid and turned to look at Dad to see if he was awake. She wouldn't wake him. She wouldn't break the spell of all of us being there together by asking him to open a jar. Instead she got out a paring knife, wedged the blade under the rim and gave it a twist.

Smoky fall air spiced the room, drifting in through the kitchen window that was kept open an inch whenever the woodstove was going. The warm yellow linoleum heated my belly as I stretched out on the floor and Mom stood solidly at the counter, her auburn hair curled in a shiny question mark down the back of her favourite navy sweater. She wore her gingham pedal pushers, though it was too cold for them, and well-worn moccasins on her bare feet. Her calves were strong and shapely. Something about the knife and the jar made the easiness radiating through me begin to crumble. Mom had tacked up cloth decorated with brown Betty teapots under the sink to hide the drainpipe and garbage. This became part of my worry, the flimsiness of it. Maybe it meant that we didn't intend to stay, either.

Near the woodstove, black charred spots marred the washed yellow of the floor. Jenny teased me whenever I rushed over to stomp out the embers that popped from the stove when the door was open. Dad would tell her not to bother me about it. "Mag's like me," he'd say. "Safety first."

Dad worked with Roddy Schwartz on a Mighty Mite sawmill near Roddy's cabin. Roddy had brought the mill in from Prince George on a trailer. It had a Volkswagen engine that ran two saw blades along the logs and could cut almost any tree they hauled out. They usually spent a few days felling and limbing trees, then skidded them out to where the mill was assembled. Dad didn't like the skidding, because they couldn't afford a proper skidder. Instead they had an old farm tractor with a chain that they wrapped around the logs to pull them out of the bush. Dad worried about the logs snagging on something and the tractor doing a wheelie.

I had listened to him talking to Mom about the work one evening when they were sitting out on the porch.

"I don't trust Roddy when he's hungover," he'd said. "He gets sloppy like. Says I'm bitching at him. Like an old woman, he says. Claims he knows the mill inside out, could do it with his eyes closed. I keep telling him, it doesn't matter how many times you've done it. You let your guard down, one of those boards'll take your fingers off so fast you won't know what hit you."

"Oh, Patrick," Mom shuddered. "Don't even say that."

"I know, but he's a law unto himself. Cocky bastard, that's what gets me. These are thirty foot trees we're fooling with."

"Don't remind me."

"You don't need to worry about me." Dad raised his voice a little when he saw me standing at the screen door. "Mr. Safety," he said, and winked at me.

It was Dad's nickname. It wasn't just our family who called him that. His friends did too, irritated by his careful checking and rechecking of his guns, his gear, his methodical testing of brakes before descending the Hill to Bella Coola. The Hill had an 18 percent grade and a reputation for turning drivers' legs to rubber. The local habit was to fuel up with liquor before making the attempt. But Dad was disgusted by that.

"You can't rush Mr. Safety," his friends teased, lighting another cigarette to wait while he put an air gauge to each tire in turn.

Now as he slept in his reclining chair by the stove, I went over to hold my hand flat against the green vinyl. It was almost too hot to touch. I didn't know which I wanted more: to have him stay asleep and with us or to have him wake up and get out of harm's way. I stood behind his chair watching the whorl of his red hair quiver as he breathed. At the crown where the hair parted, a little patch of ruddy scalp showed.

I pulled a kitchen chair over to the counter and got down the biggest glass I could find. Then I scooped water into it from the bucket and, as Mom watched me, took a little sip. I carried the tall glass of water over to the chair where Dad slept and I stood on guard.

A few minutes passed calmly as I pretended to be interested in the top of Dad's head. Suddenly he drew one of his deep ragged breaths and his whole body went stiff, then jerky, with his hands pawing the air and choking sounds rising from his throat.

"Mom!" I called as she dropped her knife and whirled.

"Patrick, wake up," she said. She knelt by his knees and took hold of his hands. He cried out then, making the most un-Dad-like sound I'd ever heard. Like a baby. Like a cornered animal.

"Patrick!" Mom said again, then, "Give me your water, Maggie."

I handed her the glass and she brought it to Dad's lips. "Take a sip, Patrick. Have a drink. It's nice and cold. There you go, there you go."

He opened his eyes and coughed as he swallowed.

Mom said, "It's okay now, girls, he just had a terror."

"I had a terror," Dad said. That's what they called them, these fits of Dad's. Apparently, his father had had them too—seizures of fear that took possession of his whole body when he was on the edge of sleep. He drank down the water and shook himself awake. His messy red curls were damp with sweat.

"Don't look so worried, Mag," he said and pulled me onto his lap. "Nothing's going to happen to me. I'm Mr. Safety, remember?"

Dad smelled of tobacco and woodsmoke and the outdoor tang of fall leaves. I began counting the freckles on his arms.

"Do you think I have as many freckles on my arms as there are stars in the sky?" he asked.

"Maybe more," I said. It was what I always said and it was what he always asked. As long as I was counting his freckles, he was my captive.

Nothing bad had happened. It was only a terror. Still I worried.

—

As I walked to the school bus each morning, shuffling my boots along in the fresh snow to make my own trail, Jenny already a powder blue beacon by the power pole at the highway, I worried about leaving Mom at home alone, about the wild way she swung the axe when she was splitting kindling and the way Dad nagged her to be careful. One of these days she was going to chop off her own foot, he said. And when we got off the bus at the end of the day, just before we rounded the final bend by the bent pine tree and our little house came into view, I worried that I'd see it engulfed in flames, or already a smoking heap. And each time it stood blandly, paint peeling to grey, smoke rising from the chimney pipe, I felt my tight muscles loosen and I broke into a run.

We were a normal family; that's our story. Our days were full of riverbanks and gravel roads, bicycles and grasshoppers. But you think a thing, you open a door. You invite tragedy in. That's what my worry taught me.

[TWO]

THERE WERE FAMILIES IN Duchess Creek who knew trouble like their own skin. Things went wrong for these families as a matter of course, and they were the subject of kitchen table conversations over the pouring of coffee and the dipping of biscuits. The Lutzes were one of those families. They lived a couple of miles from our place in a half-built house with plastic stapled over the windows and tarps on the roof to keep the rain out.

"It always comes in threes." Glenna was having tea with my mother at the kitchen table. Her spoon rang against her cup, punctuating the authority of this remark. She let it sink in. Glenna worked at the nursing station in Duchess Creek, so she had the inside story on most of the tragedies in the area. "First the twins, then Peggy's cancer treatments, and now this."

"Poor Mickey," Mom said.

Mickey Lutz was my best friend in Duchess Creek. Mom would let me go to their house for sleepovers only if Helmer was away on one of his hunting trips with his buddies. "On a tear," was what Mom called it. The house smelled like baby piss and sour milk. Dirty dishtowels hardened into place littered the living room, and balled-up socks, chewed baby toys, and drifts of dog hair. The Lutzes had a little white and brown dog named Trixie. Trixie was going grey around the mouth, like an old man, but she was so faithful she would run alongside Mickey and me on our bikes, limping to keep up. When we stopped, she'd curl up in the gravel on the side of the road, exhausted. But as soon as we made a move again, she'd force herself up on her rickety old legs and start running.

The bed Mickey and I slept in was always coated with white dog hair, and I would try to discreetly brush it off before I got in. Once, before bed, Peggy gave me an orange that smelled like a dirty sock. When I peeled it, the segments were dried out. I ate it anyway, because Mickey was eating hers and didn't seem to notice. For breakfast we had crackers and orange pop.

"The Lutzes all came in together," Glenna continued. "Just showed up at the nursing station like a pack of wolves with their injured. Helmer was hanging off Peggy's shoulder, poor thing; she could barely hold him up, and him dragging this bloody foot across the floor. Little Mickey had the baby."

When Glenna came for coffee, she would bring her own packets of Sweet'N Low. She bought them in big boxes at the co-op in Williams Lake. It allowed her to count calories, so she said. It seemed to be her only gesture towards trying to lose weight. She tore open the Sweet'N Low packets as Mom refilled her cup and then, two at once, poured the powder into her coffee. She stirred, staring into her cup, giving Mom time to ask the questions to which she'd have the answers.

"Poor Peggy," said Mom. "How did he do it?"

"He was hunting."

They both laughed at this. I knew it was because Helmer's idea of hunting was sitting on the tailgate of his truck in the sun, drinking beer and waiting for game to wander by. "You know Helmer," Glenna said, "if there's trouble, he'll find it. He forgot the rifle was loaded? Who knows? Took off the whole big toe and part of the next two."

Their heads moved left to right, slowly, in unison. It was pity, sincere, but with just a hint of self-satisfaction. I don't think it's fair to call their talk gossip, though. If they could have, they would have set Helmer up with a regular paying job. Driving truck would suit him, Mom said, doing deliveries town to town, up and down Highway 20, something not too challenging that would keep him out of the house and Peggy and the kids in groceries.

Still, there was always that underlying confidence that things like this couldn't happen to us. Glenna and Mom had husbands who knew better than to carry around their rifles with the safety off. They themselves knew better than to stay home pregnant with twins, like Peggy had, well past the due date.

"I don't know why she didn't get him to drive her to Williams Lake," Glenna still said every time she came to visit, though it had happened months ago now and she'd heard all of Helmer's excuses. I'd heard Mom say Glenna kept talking about it because she felt guilty since one of the babies died on her shift, and Peggy herself had nearly bled to death in the nursing station and had to be rushed to the Williams Lake hospital.

As for the cancer, the talk was that Peggy had never taken good care of herself. She spent too much time inside, she didn't get enough fresh air. They didn't eat properly either. Everyone knew that when Helmer got his welfare cheque, Peggy would stock up on TV dinners. I'd seen her myself in the store, wearing that defiantly ashamed face as she stacked the counter with the flat boxes. Then when the money ran out, the Lutzes lived on Wonderbread and jam.

"He's a dead weight around Peggy's neck," Glenna said, stirring. "She'd be better off without him. Best thing that could happen to that family, Helmer isn't paying attention, gets airborne out over the canyon."

"He's got horseshoes up the whazoo, that guy," Mom said. "He should be dead by now."

"He should be dead three times over. Listen to us. I take it back, God," Glenna called to the kitchen ceiling.

"Yeah, well," muttered Mom. "More coffee?" She glanced at me and Jenny playing checkers in the patch of sunlight by the woodstove. I suppose Mom thought that her conversations with Glenna were part of our education.

—

Mickey stayed with us the night her mother lost one of the twins. She stayed with us again when her mom found out she had cancer and had to fly to Vancouver for treatments. And she stayed with us the night after her dad shot off half his foot with his 30.30. Mom had bought the new *McCall's* magazine and Mickey and I sat cross-legged on the bed cutting out the Betsy dolls. I could hear Mom at the kitchen counter, getting down pans, then the crash as they all slid to the floor.

"Sorry!" she called, to no one in particular. She began to hum "Sweet Caroline." Something else clattered to the floor.

She was making meatloaf following a recipe that allowed her to use the roasting pan on top of the woodstove. Mickey's and my feet were dusted with breadcrumbs from running through the kitchen looking for scissors and tape. Mom called to me to bring her a piece of toilet paper—she had grated her finger along with the carrots.

"Let's pretend I'm the dad," said Mickey when I came back. She said it like "lepretend," which irritated me. She wasn't a baby. She should speak properly.

"Lepretend I just bought a new truck. Like it?" She drove her paper doll along the edge of my bedspread.

"What colour is it?" I asked.

"It's red," she said.

Her games bored me, but I played along because I knew that this was the Lutz family story about how one twin died.

Helmer didn't drive to Williams Lake that night because he didn't think his truck would make it. He always kept a couple of cans of transmission fluid in the back so he could top it up every few miles, all the while complaining about how he needed a new truck.

Mom had fumed about it for days when she'd heard.

"Slouching around with his guilty, hangdog look," she said. Hangdog was the word Mom used to describe the kind of men who treated their families so badly in the privacy of their own homes that when they went out, they couldn't look anyone in the eye. Especially other women. Guilty conscience, that was the hangdog look.

"Lazy son-of-a-bitch," Mom had said. "Cowardly, lazy son-of-a-bitch. Blames it on his truck."

Dad had laughed.

"What?" Mom demanded.

"Oh nothing, nothing," he'd said, smiling.

"Tell me what's so funny then. You think losing a baby and almost dying yourself is funny?" She was really mad. "She'd be better off without him. At least then she could keep the welfare cheque for herself and the kids. He's useless. Like a baby, only he's bigger and he eats more."

"Lepretend you're the mom and you're going to have a baby," said Mickey.

Mickey always wanted to play these improved-version-of-reality games. Even though they bored me, usually I said,

"Okay and my baby is the next king of the empire and we have to protect him from the kidnappers who are hiding in the hills nearby." And that way we were both happy. But not today. Today I made my Betsy doll say, "I don't feel so good. I think I'm going to have my baby."

"I'll drive you to the hospital," Mickey's doll said.

"No thanks. I have my own truck," I said. I couldn't help myself.

Mickey stared at me, at a loss for a minute.

"My truck's not new," I said. "But it works fine."

"Let's go outside and play," said Mickey.

That night, lying with Mickey's feet near my head and Jenny whistle-snoring in the next bed, I listened as the coyotes started yipping. One began it, a full-voiced, forsaken wail, long and high. Then others took it up, and the dogs from the nearby Indian reserve joined in, their unburdening ringing in the night.

At the other end of my bed, Mickey was crying. I could hear her, though she tried to stifle it.

I felt sorry for Mickey. But more than that, I was glad I was not her.

[THREE]

Nights when I couldn't sleep, when I worried about the fire in the woodstove and whether it would get too hot and set the roof on fire and we'd lose everything like the families whose kids had to come to school wearing their neighbours' too-big and too-small cast-offs, I would tiptoe to our bedroom door and peek out.

"I'm thirsty," I'd say. And if Mom or Dad nodded, I padded across the warm floor, past the stove, brushing my hand across the back of Dad's chair as I went. I couldn't keep glasses of water on the dresser. Mom had an obsessive knowledge of the habits of mice. She knew, for instance, that though they only needed tiny amounts of water to survive, they did need water, and so each night before bed she made sure that cups and glasses were tipped bottoms up and the water bucket was covered with a board. One time, she had wakened to the sound of something rustling through the wastebasket and found a mouse going after the hardened flour and salt play-dough that Jenny and I had been rolling into cakes in the shower stall, then dropped in there. She slapped a piece of cardboard over the top of the basket and woke the whole house as she carried it out to the front yard, dumped it and smashed at the mouse with a shovel, her nightgown flapping in the moonlight. Dad, in his pyjama bottoms, stood at the door laughing sleepily. "Just let it go," he called.

Her obsession worked to my advantage, since it meant I had to stand at the counter and drink down the whole glass of water, dry the glass and return it, bottom up, to the cupboard. That meant I could linger within the safety of Dad lightly snoring in his chair and the snap of Mom's game of solitaire on the table.

Sometimes I would find Mom and Dad playing cards together, with the table pulled close to the woodstove and the kerosene lantern burning between them. I'd drink my water and watch them, absorbed in their hands, shifting cards, teasing each other. Those rare nights I was content to go back to bed and listen to their muffled game and the sporadic victory shout from Mom, followed by Dad's low laughter.

But usually, if I couldn't sleep after the drink of water, I followed up with a tiptoed trip to the tin pot in the bathroom, shivering in my nightgown, because the bathroom never warmed up. Sometimes Dad noticed and said, "Can't sleep?" and he pushed himself out of his chair and came to sit on the edge of my bed with me. He'd tuck the blankets close around my chin. "Imagine we're out in the bush and we're building a lean-to shelter," he'd say. "We're setting some long sticks and fir boughs against the ridgepole. The clouds are building up for a good, hard storm, but we have to be patient. We want to be able to build a fire in front of the lean-to that's protected from the wind. One branch after another, weaving them into each other so they hold together. Make a nice, firm mat against the wind. You keep laying down the boughs, Maggie, and I'll make the fire. Then you gather up some leaves to put inside so it'll be nice and soft. Here comes the rain. We're just in time."

I was glad to be in my bed then, and I could feel myself drift into the safety of sleep.

In the late summer and fall Dad would take me into the woods almost every weekend. Jenny never came on these outings and I never wondered why. She was off with her friends, playing Barbies or riding bikes down to the river for picnics and to play house in the forts they built. I figured she wouldn't have wanted to come. Dad and I never went very far, maybe an hour or so from home at most. Sometimes we went fishing in one of the small lakes. If there was an abandoned canoe or rowboat on shore, and often there was, we took that out, cast into the green softness of the early morning, mist rising up, the plop of a fish going for a fly. Once we built a raft ourselves, spent most of the day at it, cutting poles and lashing them to two floater logs. Then we paddled across the lake to an island where we made a fire and stayed until the moon rose. Sometimes we looked for mushrooms or berries and we brought a feed home to Mom and Jenny. But my favourite thing was when Dad showed me how to build a shelter for real. He knew how to make lean-tos, teepee style shelters, or natural shelters that already provided protection from the elements, like an overhanging rock that formed a cave and just needed some insulating leaves tucked into it for added warmth.

"I want to show you the place I found, Maggie," he said one Sunday when I was nine.

Little lakes dotted the land around Duchess Creek, and roads led to many of them. Some of the roads were logging roads. Some had been made by homesteaders who'd put up cabins in the woods, made a go of it for a while, hand-logging or doing odd jobs, then moved on and left the cabins to the raccoons and the mice, shells of hand-chinked logs and caved-in roofs, mouldy newspapers, dusty shelves and canning jars. I liked to imagine what these cabins would be like at night, with the wind whistling through the empty window spaces and the dust kicking up where the door used to be and moonlight falling on rusted bedsprings.

It was fall. Dad kept the window open a crack; a sharp tangy breeze freshened the cab. As we followed the rutted road deeper into the woods, we slowed and the sun on the windshield warmed my face. The truck bounced over rocks and tree roots, rocking me to sleepiness.

"Warm in here, eh?" Dad said. He wore his blue flannel jacket; his red hair curled over the collar. "Hold the wheel for me?"

I scooted over and held on while he took off his jacket. The steering wheel jerked like something alive in my hands.

"You want to drive?"

"Yes, please."

Dad gripped the wheel again then braked to a stop as I crawled under his arm to sit in the little triangle of seat between his legs. He put his hand over mine on the gearshift and helped me find first. We lurched forward then stalled.

"That's okay," he said. "Try again, Maggie."

Once we were riding along in second I relaxed a little into Dad's warm chest. His freckled arms, and his scent of sweat and tobacco, made a protective circle around me.

I drove until the track petered out into grass, then Dad took over again. The woods closed around us, a lit tunnel of yellow, orange and red. Aspen leaves whipped the truck windows and caught in the mirrors; trees scraped along our sides; a branch with brilliant yellow leaves caught in the windshield wipers and fluttered there like a butterfly trying to free itself. Then the canopy of trees opened into a clearing by a small turquoise lake and Dad parked the truck. A peeling, overturned rowboat lay half-hidden in reeds.

"Here we are."

We got out. A crisp wind rippled across the lake, sending up a faint song from the reeds and grasses.

"See this tree?" Dad said. It was a big old gnarly fir with a solid branch that curved out from the trunk about eight feet up. "I'll show you how to make a double lean-to shelter from this tree. You go find a long sturdy branch, one that'll go from the crook here to about here."

I went off into the bush. Leaves dropped from above like large snowflakes, sailing gently down to land on the spongy forest floor. I stood and watched them, the whole woods gently raining dying leaves. Underfoot, the ground felt hollow, a shell of earth covered in dead leaves and fragrant burnt orange pine needles. Below, the tunnelled homes of insects, ants and beetles, then below that, the hollowed bones of animals, layer upon layer, then rock then coal.

I picked up a branch. It felt hollow in my hands and when I cracked it against the side of a tree it flew into pieces. Deeper in, I came across a tangle of deadfall. I took up an aspen limb, thick enough, and pulled it from the tangle. It was about twelve feet long, still greenish, not brittle. A high wind rose and shivered through the trees. I turned and looked for the lake. Through the leaves, sun glinted on water.

When I got back, Dad was sitting on the hood of the truck smoking, his red curls fluttering like the fall leaves.

"Good job, Maggie," he said. "That's perfect." He jumped down from the truck, put out his cigarette and put the butt back in the package.

"A lean-to is one of the easiest shelters to build. But this one has an extra wall," Dad said. "We don't need it to be very big, so we'll put the ridgepole right about here. Now what are you going to look for?"

"The sun. Face the door east for the morning sun."

"That's right. You want that warmth to hit you as early as possible." Dad set the ridgepole tightly into the V of the tree. "But we're going to make it a little more to south so we can look out at the lake. Now what else?"

"Make sure there's no overhanging dead branches and we're not near any landslide danger."

"Anything like that around here?"

"No."

"Right. This is a perfect little spot at the edge of this clearing here. The bush behind us, the lake in front, but not too close. We don't want animals stumbling over us on their way to get a drink."

Dad placed one of the branches he had gathered against the ridgepole. "It doesn't matter if they stick up," he said. "It makes it stronger." We worked quietly in the autumn sun, laying branches to make the walls of the shelter. After a while, a cold wind blew up and drummed at our bare hands and faces. When I went to get more branches, I squatted for a minute against the lee side of a pine out of the wind, the sun on my face and the sweet warm spice of bark and forest rising up around me.

I couldn't wait to be done the shelter and climb inside away from the wind. But Dad was methodical and, even though we were only building the shelter for this afternoon, he would make sure it was near perfect.

"Know why I came to this country?" he said, as we worked.

"You'd had enough of Ireland."

"Yes, but I could have stayed in the States. I got a job

logging in Oregon. I made pretty good money. For Christmas I went to Portland to spend some of it. In a little bar I heard a musician named Pete Seeger, singing about the draft. I'd read in the paper that they were going to call up fifty thousand young men for the army. That was the Korean conflict. I didn't leave Ireland to get caught up in someone else's war.

"When I went back to work, I met a fellow who told me his grandfather had been a chief of one of the great tribes near Bella Coola. They were like the kings and queens of the land back then. So much wealth, they gave it away just to show how wealthy they were. But the government came along and outlawed all that, their language, their religion, their old songs and dances. I told him it was just like in Ireland.

"His mother had married into the Ulkatcho band. He said if I went almost straight north of where we were in Oregon, and just kept going, I'd find the place where he grew up. There was a network of trails the people had made over hundreds of years, from Bella Coola to Williams Lake, and they moved along those trails following the food and the seasons. You never had to go hungry as long as you knew what you were doing. As long as you had your freedom, you could find game, berries, fish. It was a land of plenty. Make your way to the coast and you've got nature's grocery, free for the taking: cockles and clams and salmon. So I came. I listened and I watched. That's how you learn to do it."

When he felt satisfied that the pine bough walls would repel a light rain and heavy dew, if not a downpour, he said, "Let's try her out." We backed into the opening, one of us on either side of the supporting tree, until just our heads were poking out.

"If you ever get lost, this is what you do first. You build yourself a little shelter. Don't forget."

I couldn't forget. He told me the same thing every time we went into the bush.

"And oh, I almost forgot." He took a bottle of Orange Crush from inside his jacket and handed it to me. Then he brought out a beer for himself. He fished deeper in his inside pocket and brought out a package wrapped in a dishcloth. "Then you eat your chocolate biscuits."

—

Some people believe that a person knows when he's going to die. Even if he's not sick, even if death comes out of nowhere like a deer on the highway. I don't know about that. But sometimes I think about it when I remember this afternoon with my father.

The pop chilled me, but I drank it, shivering, because he'd brought it for me. Dad cracked open his beer and had a few slow sips as we watched the lake rippling in the wind. He said, "You know, Maggie, I'm not fond of talking. You know that, don't you? Nothing I think about seems worth saying when I think twice about it. Your mother doesn't understand that."

He took a sip of beer and smiled at me. The right fish bait to use, the name of the bird trilling an unfamiliar song, these were the things Dad usually told me. I didn't know if I was supposed to say anything or not.

"You know on a sunny afternoon when we sit outside against the house and the sun is warming us? I look at her and she looks lit up. Her skin, her hair and everything. And then I feel it. Like a little fish flipping on the bottom of the boat. It makes me want to celebrate. I want to get a cold beer and forget about the rest of the day. Make a toast, to her.

"And if I could just spit it out, the way I see her. But I never do. The words just don't seem good enough. And when I go and get a beer, I spoil everything. You know that look she gets?"

He took a long swallow.

"She never says anything, bless her. I can tell she's trying to keep the smile on her face. And I know I'm going to spoil everything, but I can't help myself. Now why is that?"

Did he want me to answer? I held the Orange Crush to my lips, took a gulp, and studied the backwash as it foamed into the bottle.

"My father, your grandfather, he was the same. No, he was worse. I swore I'd never become a drunk like him. And I never did. I'm my own kind of drunk."

He tipped the neck of his beer at me, and said "cheers." I clinked my Orange Crush bottle into his, the way we always did.

I had never seen Dad drunk like Helmer, laughing loudly at jokes that weren't that funny, then turning weepy, then suddenly mean and the other men trying to calm him down. My mother hated that maudlin weakness in a man and I suppose if Dad had been that kind of drunk, she wouldn't have married him. "It goes from funny to pitiful to mean pretty quick," she said.

But there were those nights when Mom went to bed without him, after her low, pleading voice came through our bedroom wall and his turned insistent: "I'm just enjoying myself here, Irene." I could hear Mom's anger in the slam of a dresser drawer, the rattle of hangers in her closet. I wondered what kept him sitting there by the stove all by himself, sometimes singing "Goodnight Irene" softly. His shaky, whispery voice made me smile, but it didn't have that effect on Mom.

When he started in on his Irish songs it made Mom cry. Once I heard her say, "You remind me of my dad." I didn't see why his singing would make her cry. I was mad at her for leaving him alone and for being angry at him. Why wouldn't she sing with him and have fun, like he wanted?

And there was the day when Dad, his friend Panbread and Mom were playing darts against the side of the house. I could hear Dad teasing Mom about something. Next thing I knew, Mom was telling Jenny and me to get our shoes on because we were going for a walk. She went in the house to get us some apples for the road and baseball caps to keep the sun off.

Dad called after her, "Aw, come on Irene, finish the game at least."

I heard Panbread say, "Let her go, Pat. That's women for you." Then they both laughed, too hard and too long, and I was glad that Mom was in the house and couldn't hear them.

Mom set a blistering pace through the woods, then slowed as we picked our way up a dry creekbed. I stopped so often to pick up smooth rocks that Jenny was way ahead of me, out of sight, and Mom was a long way past her. The sun burned down on the creekbed. I caught glimpses of hummingbirds hovering over orange Indian paintbrush. A woodpecker drummed against a tree. The sun, the hollow drumming reverberating through the firs, the soft clacking of my running shoes against stones wrapped me in a cocoon. Some part of me was looking down at myself, moving along the creek. A narrow trickle of water wove its way through the stones. When the tips of my running shoes turned dark from the water, I raised my eyes and there were trembling Saskatoon bushes, bright white daisies and turquoise sky. I felt as if I had wakened from a dream.

Then I heard Mom calling me. "Ma-ggie!" the two-note fee-bee, like a chickadee. "Ma-ggie! Come on. We're over here."

I followed a skinny deer path through the brush and over a little rise. There was Mom, up to her neck in a clear green-blue lake. Jenny was jumping up and down with excitement in the mud, naked except for her baseball cap, her long red hair sticking out from under it.

"Guess what?" Mom called.

"What?"

"It's not deep!" and she threw her arms up and burst splashing from the water like a jumping fish. It was only waist-deep on Mom who was naked too, her clothes dumped in the grass beside Jenny.

"Hurry up!" Jenny yelled at me, and laughed as she ran into the water with her baseball cap still on.

I remember that sweet, bone-tired exhaustion we got from playing in the water for hours. We had to duck under the water to escape the horseflies. We held contests: chasing each other in the shallows, our hands in the mud pushing us along; who could stay sitting upright on a floating log the longest; who could hold her breath longer; who could spring out of the water and into the air higher. We dried off on a big boulder in the sun, with the warm stone under our cheeks, then back into the water again to cool off, yelling at Mom to watch from where she was lying on our clothes in the grass, her smooth hip curved into her waist and one brown-nippled breast resting against the other.

By the time we dragged ourselves within sight of home that evening, the summer sky had darkened to purple. Our legs felt like rubber from the long walk and we couldn't stop giggling, because we were all tired and scratching in fits at ourselves. Along with mosquito bites, we'd got some kind of swimmer's itch from the lake.

"We'll have to have baths," Mom said. "Then we'll put some calamine lotion on."

Jenny led the way to the front step. "Dad," she said, and

stopped. She'd nearly stepped on him. He was curled up on the grass at the foot of the steps with a toppled kitchen chair beside him.

"Go in the house," Mom said.

"Is he all right?' Jenny asked.

"Go on in the house, Jenny, Maggie. Go on!"

Jenny and I went inside, but we stood near the door and watched.

Mom had him half off the ground, hauling on him to get him up. But he slipped through her arms and slumped back to the grass.

"For Christ's sake, Patrick! Come in the house."

It was one of the few times I heard my mother swear and it scared me. Though we only went to church at Easter and Christmas, she considered herself a good Catholic and God-related curses were strictly forbidden in our house.

"What's the problem, Irene?" my dad said, suddenly awake.

"Get in the house. Go to bed."

"Calm down, calm down. I was just getting some air." He shook free of her and waltzed into the house, winking at Jenny and me as he went by.

Mom let him go. She sat on the step, her back to us.

"I'm itchy," Jenny said after a few minutes.

Mom pushed herself up and went to pump water for our bath.

[FOUR]

One morning in June, when I was ten, Mom called Jenny and me to the door to watch the Indians from Duchess Creek Reserve heading to Potato Mountain, where they'd camp and harvest wild potatoes.

"Used to be a lot more of them," Mom said, leaned against the door, watching. "Big caravans, like you'd imagine crossing the desert. When I was a kid they used to take the trail right behind our cabin. When my dad saw them headed to Potato Mountain, he'd get antsy. He wanted to go up there, too. The Indians used to move around more back then, for fishing and hunting."

It still seemed like a lot of people to me, more than I ever saw when we rode our bikes around the reserve. Where had they all come from? They had their horses loaded down with packs and tools and bedding. Some of the horses had five-gallon cans strapped to their backs. These were to bring back the potatoes they would dig. A long string of dogs trotted along behind the horses. A team pulled a Bennett-wagon, made from the frame of an old car, with old folks and kids riding in it, some of them holding even littler babies.

When Mom raised her hand to wave, a woman left the group and came walking up the driveway. She was about Mom's age, with long hair as shiny black as a crow's wing and wearing a purple-flowered print dress over her pants. Even with the pants, I could see her legs were thin and a little bowed. But she walked like I imagined a ballerina would walk, graceful, her toes touching down first, lightly, on the gravel.

"Agnes," Mom acknowledged.

"Brought your moccasins," the woman said. She had a soft whispery voice and a way of cocking her head, like she was shy. Jenny, sitting next to me, pinched my arm as a warning. When I looked up at Agnes's face, I gasped. Her lip had a mashed gap in it that joined her nose in what looked like an open wound. She smiled at Jenny and me kindly and I felt my face flush in embarrassment for reacting.

"You remembered," my mother said. She took the moccasins from Agnes, a large pair made of soft moosehide, beaded with blue and orange and white beads. Dad's birthday was coming. "Get my purse, Maggie."

I realized that Agnes was the woman Glenna sometimes talked about. "I feel so sorry for the poor thing," I'd heard her say. "She says no one will marry her because of the harelip. And you know she's probably right."

Mom never agreed with Glenna about Agnes. "I think she does all right. There's something about that woman that's made of steel."

I'd also overheard Glenna talking to my mom about the time Agnes came to the nursing station with bruises on her face. "And with that harelip. What a mess!" The man who had promised to marry Agnes had done it. My mother called it rape, a word I didn't know then, and she and Glenna had argued about the word. "But can you call it rape?" Glenna asked, and my mother had gotten angry.

As for me, I had not understood how something so minor as a harelip, which I had pictured as a kind of soft mustache, could have such an impact, and I thought this was something maybe peculiar to Indian men, this dislike of hair, like some of the other traits that they were supposed to have, like never allowing themselves to be rushed, or spending money as fast as they got it.

I brought the purse back and handed it to Mom, deliberately looking in Agnes's face to let her know I wasn't bothered.

"Bring back potatoes for you girls," she said, as if she was telling us a secret, and she smiled again.

"Thank you," Jenny and I said.

We watched her go. Her long hair swung gently down her back as she picked her way carefully along the road to rejoin the caravan.

"Some years Dad would get up to Potato Mountain," Mom said then. "He went looking for cattle but he stayed to race horses." She rarely talked about her parents. Her mom had died when she was little, and her dad wanted to be a cowboy, not a father, that's what she said. "Mom went with him once. They joined the Indians camping one night. She said she'd never seen so many wildflowers as she did in the meadows they passed through on the ride up: Indian paintbrush and yellow balsamroot and blue mountain lupines covering the hills. And then at the top, the blankets of white potato flowers. She only went that once, but she talked about it as if she'd gone every year. She would say, 'I remember that mountain covered in little white flowers.'" Mom made her voice wistful, teasing: "'And the berries. So many you couldn't pick them all. Dik. That's what the Indians called them. We ate dik and wild potatoes, this big, the size of my thumbnail, and deer meat cooked over the fire. And at night the stars were so thick. As thick as the white flowers covering the hills. We slept outside under the stars. I say slept. The music and singing and dancing all night, who could sleep? You couldn't imagine all the stars.' And then when she got fed up with us, with the snow, and being trapped in the cabin all day, she used to say, 'I wish I could go to Potato Mountain. I want to see those wild flowers one more time before I die.'"

"And did she?" I asked.

"No, she never did get back up that mountain."

"I wish I could go to Potato Mountain," Jenny said. "Instead of going to school. All those kids are skipping the end of school. Lucky ducks."

"I don't think I'd like it now. I used to want to go," Mom said, still watching the caravan, the horses' hooves sending up little puffs of dust. "Too much drinking now, from what I've heard." She looked away and to the house, then added, "That might not be true. That's just what people say."

That night I had a dream that Mom, Jenny and I were getting ready to go up Potato Mountain. We were outside packing the car, even though in real life you couldn't get up the mountain in a car. We came in and out of the house with our suitcases and blankets while Dad sat in his green vinyl chair by the stove.

"Isn't Dad coming?" I asked Mom.

"No, he's not strong enough. He'd never make it up that mountain."

I felt so sorry for him. Mom was right; he was only a little boy and he'd hold us all back. I looked at him sleeping in the chair. Then it hit me: he was not sleeping at all—he was dead. The shock of it woke me up.

A bright half moon shone in our bedroom window, washing our bedspreads with ghostly blue light. Our clotheshorse cast the shadow of a hunched old woman on the wall. I listened to Jenny's gentle breathing and felt my own heartbeat clipping raggedly along. I sat up and looked at my sister for signs that she was actually awake. My feet touched the cold linoleum. Even in summer, our floor was cold at night. I bent over Jenny and she mumbled a bit then went back to snoring.

She really was asleep. She'd be mad at me if I woke her up. I had the uneasy feeling that someone was outside watching me and so I forced myself to look out the window.

I thought of Agnes and her harelip and imagined her walking gracefully in the moonlight, along the road to Potato Mountain. Shadows crisscrossed the grass and driveway. Something black darted across the yard, a bat probably. No wind at all, not a shiver.

I went to Mom and Dad's room and stood at the door. It was open about a foot and I listened to them breathe, Dad making a choppy, whistling sound. He was fine. I turned sideways and slipped into the room without a sound. On the dresser, Dad's jackknife gleamed in the moonlight. He kept it in his pocket all the time, pearl-handled and decorated with a moose and the words Beautiful British Columbia printed on it. He used it to cut twine, thread, fingernails, fruit. I picked it up and held it in my hand, and then took it into my room. I sat down on my bed and opened the blade. I turned it and watched it glint. I looked for something to test its sharpness. I didn't think it would cut the doubled edge of the sheet's hem, but when I ran the blade along it, it sliced through the fabric easily. Mom would be annoyed. When I went to snap it closed, the blade sliced my finger. A dark drop of blood spread on the sheet. I had to pad through the dark of the house to the bathroom for a piece of toilet paper to wrap my finger in. I fell asleep holding the knife in my hand.

When I woke up, Dad had already gone to the sawmill. I fished around in my blankets for his knife. I found it near the bottom of the bed, twisted in the sheets.

"Isn't that funny," I heard Mom say from her bedroom as Jenny and I were eating breakfast.

"What?" Jenny called.

"Oh, your dad was looking for his jackknife this morning and he couldn't find it anywhere and here it is on the dresser, where he always leaves it."

"Weird," said Jenny, bent to her cornflakes. After a minute she raised her head and looked at me.

I felt guilty then, but it was nothing like the guilt I felt later, when we suddenly became a family like the Lutzes, our grief unfolding at the nurses' station for everyone to see. I pictured Dad that morning, looking for his knife and not finding it in its usual place, checking and re-checking the dresser-top, his pants pockets from yesterday. How many times that morning had he thrust his hand in his pocket to finger the smooth imitation pearl and not found it there?

I was the one who saw Roddy's truck at the nurses' station as we went by on the school bus that afternoon. Both cab doors were wide open and I thought of saying something to Jenny, but she was laughing with her friend Josie, and the two of them always made fun of anything I said. So instead, after we got off the bus, I yelled, "Race you" and ran up the road ahead of Jenny with the worry boiling into panic.

"Why is Roddy's truck at the nurses' station?" I burst out as soon as I saw Mom. So in a way, it was me who brought the bad news.

"What?" I could see her fear was instant.

"The cab doors were open."

"Stay here." She grabbed the station wagon keys from the hook near the door. "I'll be back in a few minutes."

"Mom? What's going on?" Jenny asked, trailing into the house.

"You two stay here. I'm going to the nurses' station."

"Why?" said Jenny, but Mom was already out the door. We watched her drive off, dust flying up as she turned onto the highway.

Jenny says I didn't speak at all after Dad died. I don't remember not speaking, though I remember Mom crouched in front of me, holding my shoulders, looking into my face. "Say something, Maggie," she begged. I wanted to, for her sake. But what did she want me to say? I understood now how Dad had felt. There was absolutely nothing in my mind that seemed important enough to put into words. I heard Mom in the bedroom whispering with Glenna. Their whispers went on and on, crescendoed into anger, then fell back almost to silence, a soft mumbling like chickens settling in their roosts at night. What could they possibly have to say so much about?

I remember physical sensations—smell, hunger, heat and cold. I sat in Dad's green vinyl chair by the woodstove and I smelled him. Sawdust. Tobacco. Motor oil. Sweat. And something else. Warm, musty, spicy. Not really spicy. Not musty either. Like the top of his head, a familiar skin tang. I could smell it too if I went into Mom and Dad's room and stood there.

Women came with casseroles and tubs of stewed rhubarb and home-canned salmon and I watched them bend to try and find room in the icebox. I watched their strong legs—a hot spell had settled into the Chilcotin and the women wore the first shorts of the season. Their legs were rosy from the weeding they'd done under the noon sun. How could legs hold you up without you even having to think about it? But somehow there was something in your brain that kept them working and it could let go all of a sudden too, like Jenny's and Mom's had that afternoon when we found out what happened to Dad.

Mom had barely been able to stay standing when Glenna and Ron brought her through the door, each one holding her up by an elbow.

"Mom?" Jenny had said, then without even hearing a word, she folded like a lawn chair whose old aluminum legs have finally given out. Mothers don't have to be held up between two people unless the worst thing you've imagined as you sat staring out the window, waiting for the station wagon to appear at the end of your road, has actually happened.

"There's been an accident, girls," Glenna said.

I hated her for saying it. I hated her instantly and ever

after, the sight of her and her self-satisfied sympathy, as if she had immunity, and her a nurse who should know better.

"Is Dad dead?" Jenny managed through her tears.

Mom said simply, "Yes."

They say that when you get food poisoning, you'll never again eat the last thing you ate before getting sick, even if it was something else that poisoned you. I had the feeling that Dad died because I'd taken his jackknife. Later, I would learn that a pile of logs had rolled loose and knocked him flying. I would learn that Roddy had carried him like a baby into the nurses' station. Why this detail? Why 'like a baby'? But that's what people said, and so it made it hard to blame Roddy; people could go on liking Roddy if they wanted and not hate him for living when Mr. Safety had died.

The wake went on for four days, during which time a constant stream of food flowed into our little house. A big aluminum coffee pot bubbled on the stove. Someone's white coffee mugs were arranged in a row on the counter. Glenna even brought her Sweet'N Low. I watched her set out a little margarine tub of packets beside the mugs. I watched her tear them, two at a time, shaking the powder into her mug as the candle for Dad burned beside his photo. Her routine, at least, would not be broken, not even by the death of her best friend's husband. She was counting calories.

When there was no more room in the icebox, someone got the idea to dump ice into the unused shower and store the food there. Mom grumbled about this after everyone had gone home for the night. The ice had melted and she had to try to find room in the icebox for the pots of potato salad and plates of Nanaimo bars.

"Why all this eating?" I heard her saying to herself.

That's what I wanted to know, too. But I realized the food wasn't really for us. It gave each person who walked through the door something to say. "I brought a rhubarb pie," was something at least. "Is there any room in the icebox?" was something else and "I'll make another pot of coffee" was something else again. And so the talk went on and the ache and the anger and the fear burned like the candle, endlessly.

Dad himself was nowhere to be seen, except in the framed photo that sat on top of a tall shelf that Glenna and Ron had brought over. I heard some adults whisper that there would be no viewing of his body because of the heat, and another corrected authoritatively that it was really because of the accident. I didn't know what either of these things meant.

After the funeral, as the reality of Dad's death descended, Jenny's grief gathered and built like a summer storm. Her crying spells piled on top of each other, majestic and furious, then died to small, helpless sobs as her body collapsed on her bed, beyond the ability of her mind to call it back together and stand and walk. Jenny's grief drew people to her. Glenna and the other women brought cups of chicken noodle soup to her bed and later came out with the cup saying, "She took a little more than half," or, "She barely touched it."

For me, where Dad had been there was a hole now, gaping with the memory of him. I couldn't find a way to put it into words. But each night Jenny talked to Mom, who sat with us until Jenny wore herself out with questions.

"Are we going to be poor now?" Jenny asked. "Like the families who have to wear other people's hand-me-downs?"

"No, sweetie, that's not going to happen."

"Did Dad love me?"

"Of course he loved you, don't be silly."

"Why did he always take Maggie to the woods and not me?"

"Oh, Jenny. I don't think he ever knew you wanted to go. He thought you preferred girly things. He brought you Barbies from Williams Lake, didn't he?"

"Maggie's more of a tomboy, I guess. No offence, Mag."

In this way, her storm began to calm.

After a few days, two of Jenny's friends came and took her outside. They would sit on a blanket in the sun with their Barbies, dressing them up in different outfits and combing their hair with little pink combs and brushes. They went on picnics, with their lunch in a cloth sack. I watched them disappear into the trees, three sets of legs pale against the rich green of the woods, their ponytails swinging softly down their backs. Hours later I saw them reappear on the road, coming from the other direction, blurry in the heat haze rising from the highway.

—

After the hot spell, the rain came. The noise of it woke me early one morning, the hollow ping ping on the stovepipe and a gentle steady pattering on the roof like small pebbles were falling. It picked up force as I lay there listening, until it hammered down in a roar of water. Mom got up to close her window, then went out to the kitchen and closed those windows, too.

Jenny opened her eyes and lay there blinking at me. I pictured the rain soaking the road, the patchy lawn around our house, our vegetable garden, and the scented, springy earth beneath the spruce outside our window. The roaring abated a little, like an engine gearing down, then rose and rose and rose to a thunder of water, as if the sky had cracked wide open and an ocean of rain poured on Duchess Creek.

I felt the creep of worry. A steady dribble of roof run-off twisted in a finger-sized stream across our bedroom window. It wasn't that. Mom clattered in the kitchen and the leak trickling in by the stovepipe drummed into an aluminum pot. It wasn't that, either.

After breakfast I put on my rubber boots and went outside to crouch under the limbs of the spruce. The rain continued, a steady slanting volley.

"In a pinch, you can always find natural shelter," Dad had told me the fall day we'd built the lean-to by the lake.

"Like under the spruce tree at home," I'd said.

"That's right. If you just need something temporary, there's almost always something you can use. But you might as well build yourself a shelter. It helps you think, keeps you from panicking until you're found."

A puddle seeped into the thick bed of needles under the spruce and crept closer to my rubber boots. If I was going to camp under here, I would need to dig a trench to catch the runoff and a trough to carry it away. I realized that what I was worried about was the lean-to by the lake that Dad and I had built the fall before. I hoped it was still standing. And if someone was in it, I hoped the rain was not seeping in through the branches.

After the rain started, we were left alone with our grief like a family in quarantine. For a time, even Glenna seemed to be avoiding my mother.

"If this rain keeps up, I'm going to have get up there and fix that leak," Mom said as she made lunch in the dull light of another rainy afternoon.

"Why don't you ask Glenna to get Ron to do it for you?" Jenny said.

Mom looked at her for a minute, thinking. "I guess I've never really fit in in Duchess Creek," she said. She didn't seem regretful or upset. She spoke as if this was a fact she'd only just learned. "I was more at home on the ranches where my dad worked. I could go into the hills for hours and never see anyone. I even preferred the coast, where I didn't know anyone.

Though I hated the rain," she continued, to herself, it seemed, more than to Jenny.

Late in the afternoon, the sun came out and shone on the puddles and brightened the leaves and grass. Mom got the wooden ladder from under the front porch and asked me to hold it for her as she climbed onto the roof.

"Maggie, Jenny you've got to come up here," she called, as she looked out over the land. "Jenny, you hold the ladder for Maggie."

I scrambled onto the wet roof where Mom was straddling the ridgepole. She held out her hand and guided me up to sit facing her, one leg on each side of the roof.

"Look how far you can see." She pointed with her hammer out beyond the glistening highway and across the meadows that ran down to the valley. I was still not talking and I knew Mom was doing her best to unlock whatever had a hold over me.

"Things look different from up here, don't you think?"

I smiled at her. Jenny climbed up and joined us.

We watched as a white pick-up truck slowed and took the turn at our driveway. I could see into the box: a cage with chickens in it, a stack of two-by-fours, some buckets. The truck stopped below us and the door opened and a blonde woman in overalls and a white T-shirt got out.

"Need any help up there?" she called. "I saw you from the road."

"Know anything about roofing?" Mom yelled.

Her head appeared above the eavestrough. She had long braids and bangs cut evenly across her forehead. "Is there room for me? It looks like a party up here."

It turned out that the woman, whose name was Rita, knew quite a bit about roofing, and a lot of other useful things, too. I liked the way she helped without taking over. She showed Jenny and me how to place the shingles we'd found in the shed and then watched as Mom nailed them into place. After that job was done, Mom made coffee and they sat on the damp step in the sun and drank it. Mom leaned back against the warm wall of the house like she always did and I saw her relax. Rita talked about the deer that had been eating from her garden, a young one who came by herself. No tin plates or bars of soap could keep her away.

"I finally just planted some lettuce and spinach for her," Rita laughed. "She seems to know that's her part of the garden. She doesn't eat from the main one anymore." I wanted to ask if she'd given her a name, but I didn't. The sun lit Rita's pale bangs; the sharp smell of coffee and rank mud rose up from under the step.

"Does she have a name?" Jenny asked.

"A name?" Rita turned to Mom. Her eyes shone very green, like cats' eyes, and they were lazy, too, like a sleepy cat. "Yes I have. I have given her a name. And the name I have given her is Fond. I call her Fond."

"Fawned?" said Mom. "Like pawned?"

"Sure. Like pond. Fond. F-O-N-D, because she's a fawn and I'm fond of her, you know."

I liked Rita.

Later that night, Mom came to our bedroom. Jenny was already sleeping and Mom whispered to me. "You know Rita lives out on Nakenitses Road all by herself. She has a nice little place with a house and sheds and a small barn. She keeps chickens and she delivers the mail. I was there once, a long time ago. She can fix anything. She fixes her own truck. She built her shed and her barn. She doesn't really need anybody."

When I didn't say anything, Mom smiled and kissed my forehead. "I'll tell you a little secret." She waited again. She smoothed my eyebrows. "I hope Rita will be my friend. That's my secret. I like the way she can take care of herself, don't you?"

I nodded. Mom tucked the blanket up under my chin and I let her, though the night was warm.

"I have a present for you," she said. And she uncurled my hand and in it placed Dad's jackknife. "I want you to be able to take care of yourself, too."

I should have said something then. She left the room. I wanted to call her back. She had never mentioned the sharp cut in the hem of my sheet or the stain my bleeding finger had left. Yet she must have seen them both and wondered. Maybe she was waiting for me to admit that I was the one who had taken the knife and left Mr. Safety vulnerable.

[FIVE]

I RODE MY BIKE DOWN to Bull Canyon, where I could sit on a ledge of land overlooking the Chilcotin River. On the bank, wild roses were in bloom; pine needles baked in the sun. The river hurried past, turquoise and swift with mountain run-off. I took up a pine branch perfect for a walking stick, dug Dad's knife from my pocket and began to shave off the bark. Aspens trembled in the slightest breeze and the stink of cow parsnip floated past. The air shivered with the whir of hummingbird wings. No one here. But it seemed like someone was, someone high in a tree watching or hidden just out of sight around the bend, listening. It was the feeling I always had in the woods, not troubling, but teasing.

I was sleepy, listening to the river. I sat down, leaning against a crumbling pine log and stretched out my legs in the sun. Again I had that cocooned feeling, moving away from myself and observing from a distance. The air thickened and grew very still and then the aspen leaves began to shiver and turn like little hands waving. A twig cracked and I sat up. A little girl, about three feet tall, stood looking at me. She had a face of bark and hair of lichen, decorated with yellow balsamroot flowers. She wore a skirt of purple harebells. Her feet and hands were twigs.

"Who are you?" Her voice was funny, not child, not adult either.

"Maggie," I said.

"Where do you come from?"

"From up the road."

"Up the road." She laughed. "What tribe do you belong to?"

"I don't have a tribe," I said. "I have a mother and a sister."

"No tribe? But you must have a tribe. Who keeps you safe at night? Who does the hunting?"

"My father is dead."

"Dead, is he? Maggie's father is dead. Would you like to belong to our tribe? You have to climb through a hole in the curved tree to get to our land. Follow me. I'll show you. Can you run fast?"

She smelled of pine pitch and wild roses and her twig feet barely scratched the earth as she ran. I followed, dodging trees and leaping deadfall. She disappeared and then I heard her voice, a chatter shivering through the trees. "This way!" Her head came down from the crook of a gnarled pine. "I'm a fast runner, aren't I? I'll help you up."

I reached for her twig fingers and they closed around mine.

"Shut your eyes and when you open them again you'll be in our territory."

I did as she said.

Soft blue-flowered hills, bathed in lemon light, rolled away to the edges of dusky blue mountains. Down in a shady valley, a jade-green river sparkled in the light. Smoke rose from fires beside the river and small figures moved near them. Across the lemon hills, herds of mountain sheep ran, turning as one like a flock of birds.

"Let's go swimming. Our river is so sweet and cool. I have ten sisters and they'll play with us." The twig girl ran through the field of blue flowers, trailing a shadow of a path that undulated in the wind, leading me down to the river flats.

"Oh dead, dead, dead," she sang. "Maggie's father's dead!"

Her sisters were twig-girls, too, their dresses made of different wildflowers, orange Indian paintbrush, yellow buttercup, blue forget-me-not, white violet, blue chicory, purple foxglove, and the prettiest, on a tiny little girl, delicate red columbine that drooped below her knees.

"Swimming! Swimming!" they shouted to me and dropped their dresses in the grass. I stripped off my shorts and jumped in after them. Cool water closed around me like a skin. The heat of the pinewoods slipped away.

The girls gathered in a circle in the river. One threw a white hollow bone to another and they sang, tossing it around the circle:

Maggie's father, hair of red
Right as rain when he went to bed
Went to work, so they said
Now Maggie's dad is dead dead dead!

"Join in, Maggie!" they called. The water splashed and rolled off my skin, the drops travelling down my fingers, my arms, spilling down my sides and the twig arms of the girls sprayed glistening droplets through the air.

Maggie Dillon out to play
Fell asleep on a sunny day
Knock knock knock. Go away!
Maggie isn't dead today.

We swam and I dove with my eyes open, parting tall weeds with my hands and gliding by, watching the sun cut through water and shine on the deep rocks and glimmering sand bottom. I shot back to the surface and swallowed great gulps of air and the girls sang until the sinking sun turned the water red-orange.

I climbed out and sat on a rock. I watched the water bead on my legs. As the hills shadowed and changed, I felt a sudden chill pass over me. Night must be beautiful here, the hills bathed in moonlight, but I wouldn't wait for it; it was too lonely and I felt cold now.

"I have to go home," I told the twig girl.

"I guess you do," she replied.

I pulled on my shorts and took her hand. When I opened my eyes I was standing by my bike near the side of the road. The sun had not yet begun to set and it was still hot. My walking stick was peeled clean and lying on the ground. I picked it up. I felt for my pocketknife. Still there, nestled in my pocket, smooth and cool. Beneath my shorts, though, my underpants were cool and wet with river water and the bottom of my T-shirt was damp.

I felt very hungry. I wanted hot deer stew, salted tomatoes, a whole saskatoon berry pie. I fastened my walking stick onto my handlebars with a shoelace and hopped on the bike. My legs burned as I rode towards home.

I felt hungry all the time then, a constant gnawing in the pit of my stomach. Two things filled me the longest: our neighbour Mrs. Erickson's homemade bread, which she brought over to our house two loaves at a time, wrapped in dish towels, and the mountain potatoes Agnes brought back for us.

Agnes came up our road one day in July. She was carrying a burlap sack. I sat on the step and watched her come. She stopped in front of me, then opened the sack and let me look inside. The fresh earth smell of the potatoes wafted out.

Agnes smiled at me. "Take you with me next year," she promised.

Next year seemed a very long time away, but I did feel a small thrill at the thought.

"Your grandpa used to go," she said. "My grandpa and him were friends. Used to round up the wild horses together, take them up Potato Mountain for the races." She stood there and we looked out at the road as if we might see them riding by.

"Ask your mom to take you to the bush," she said. "You'll start to feel better." She held my gaze for a minute, then Mom came out on the porch.

"Agnes," she said.

"Irene. Heard about what happened to your man." They disappeared into the house and shut the door and the low chicken mumblings began again.

That night Mom boiled some wild potatoes and put a pat of butter on them and salt and pepper. We ate them along with a jar of salmon someone had brought and early green beans from Glenna's garden.

"We're going camping," Mom announced. "Get out of this quiet house. It's driving me crazy. We'll leave in the morning. I have a place I want to show you girls."

Over and over I have dreamed of that meal, the crisp green beans, the salty, oily salmon, and the sweet little potatoes hot with butter. My grandma had wanted to see the wildflowers of Potato Mountain again and I want to eat that simple meal again, with my mother and sister around the table.

[SIX]

"WE'RE HITTING THE Freedom Road," Jenny said as she carried her sleeping bag past me to the car. It was something we said whenever we went west on Highway 20. The night before, Mom had begun packing for our camping trip and Jenny was trying to get me excited. Freedom Road was the name the locals had given the highway in the 1950s when they had chopped the route from the coast to the interior, without the help of government, so they could get out with their own vehicles. "Or die trying," Mom said. The steep drop to the valley was sometimes called Courage Hill. Like Dad had, Mom scoffed at the idea of fortifying herself with alcohol to drive it. "People think liquor makes them better drivers. Idiots. It just makes them care a bit less about going over the edge."

It had rained during the night and when we got out on the highway, Mom opened her window. A fresh rain scent drifted in; the road steamed in the morning sunshine. "Pour me some tea, please," she said to Jenny, who sat beside her in the passenger seat. I was in the back. These were our usual places. Dad had rarely come with us when Mom took us camping. He had hardly been in the station wagon at all. It was Mom's car, and ours, a tan-and-white 1963 Chevy Impala with creamy white seats and brown dashboard and trim. Mom loved the car. She kept the seats clean and had a little garbage can on the hump that she emptied, along with the ashtray if it had been used, each time we stopped at a gas station. She kept good tires on the vehicle, checked her own oil and fluids and wrote her oil changes in the owner's manual, which she kept neatly tucked into the glove compartment. "But it's a car," she'd say. "And cars are made for driving. I'm not going to baby it." That meant she would take it down most any road where we had enough clearance and there were no sharp rocks that could pierce a tire.

Driving like this, the three of us, it felt like nothing had changed. Jenny poured the tea from the thermos and I settled into my job, which was to watch for wildlife. I didn't have to be so vigilant at this time of day; dusk was when the deer came out and grazed the open spaces along the highway. Mom's strong hands held the steering wheel. Jenny leaned into a pillow propped against the door. A sense of safety filled the car. I think we all felt it. Nothing could go wrong and there was no such thing as trouble coming in threes.

"Roll me a cigarette, sweetie," said Mom.

I smelled the spicy tobacco as Jenny opened the pouch, then the sulfur flare of the match as she held it for Mom. Mom only smoked when she drove or when we were camping, and only hand-rolled cigarettes. Sweet, light smoke perfumed the air like incense, like every other trip we'd taken in the safety of that station wagon, with Mom at the wheel.

When we entered the Redstone Indian Reserve we could see the mountains in the distance ahead.

"I want to stop," I said. My voice sounded rusty and odd even to me.

Mom's eyes met mine in the rearview mirror. Jenny whirled in her seat and put her arms out, as if to hug me. "Maggie, you're alive!" she said.

"This is near where Dad took me last fall," I said.

"Okay." Mom said it almost cautiously, as if the spell of ordinariness could break again at any minute. "Where do you want to stop, Maggie?"

"The road's just past here."

Mom slowed the station wagon and made the turn. The track cut straight and flat through a meadow, then entered the woods, the way I remembered. The trees grew thicker, their branches tangled above us.

"Are you sure, Maggie?"

"This is it," I said.

For a moment, when we came out in the clearing by the lake, I was disoriented. The water was in the right place, but everything else looked different: green reeds piercing the surface of the water, grass grown up where there hadn't been grass before, trees leafed out and obscuring the entrances to the paths. But then I saw our lean-to, tucked into the shade of some aspens with the entrance facing the lake.

"There it is," I said, and I jumped out of the car. Mom and Jenny followed, stretching and yawning. Someone had made a fire pit in front of the lean-to with a circle of rocks. Charred logs, mostly burnt, lay in the pit.

"Did you and Dad find this?" Mom asked.

"We built it," I said.

"You built it? What's it for?"

"You sit in it," I said, leading the way. "It's a shelter. We built lots of different ones. We can all fit in if we squish." I backed in feet first, leaving my head and shoulders in the opening, then Jenny followed. Mom wriggled her hips to squeeze between us. She was as supple as a girl; the muscles in her thighs showed when she moved, even through her blue jeans. Her forearms, too, exposed to the sun beneath her rolled-up shirtsleeves, were tanned, freckled and muscled. She wasn't afraid of anything, either; anyone could see that.

The sun shone full on our three heads poking from the opening. Mom rested her forehead on her arms and closed her eyes. The lake lay dead calm, the only movement made by clouds of insects moving in unison above the reeds. In the warm sunshine, Mom was soon asleep. Like Dad had said, the way the sun landed on her hair, she was lit up. Jenny traced a stick through the sandy soil, writing her own name in curlicue letters. I watched for horseflies looking to land on Mom's bare arms and flicked them away when they did. The lean-to seemed even more solid than the day Dad and I had built it, and I wondered if someone had reinforced it, made it more waterproof. The ground underneath me felt dry, even after a night of rain. Maybe someone had even spent a night in it.

"Dad never took me out to build things," Jenny whispered. Her voice was matter-of-fact; I didn't hear any bitterness in it.

"Maybe he thought you wouldn't like it. I'm the tomboy, remember?"

On the lake, we caught sight of a heron standing near the shore.

"Yeah," she said. "I guess that was it."

After Mom's nap she drove us back to the highway, then west. "Rocks!" I warned, and Mom swerved the car just as a small avalanche came tumbling down the rock face beside the road. One pinged off the bumper.

"It's like Maggie has ESP," Jenny said. "She knows things are going to happen before they do."

This wasn't new. Jenny liked to say this about me. It gave her the creeps, she said.

"She just pays attention," Mom said, trying to nip Jenny's Maggie-is-weird theme in the bud. Jenny could warm to it, and she sounded so persuasive that I started to believe it myself and didn't even mind hearing her say it. But I did pay attention and I couldn't relax, like Jenny did, her bare feet up on the dashboard, or sometimes sticking out the window in the breeze.

We began the precipitous descent down the Hill, the famous 18 percent grade. Mom pumped the brakes so they wouldn't get too hot, but even so we could smell the linings. On the north side of the road the rock face rose up sharply, but on the south a clipped ledge crumbled then dropped, tumbling thousands of feet through jack pine and rock to the bottom of the canyon. When I had the guts to look over, I saw only empty space and treetops. Were there rusted-out bodies of cars down there, those whose brakes had failed or whose owners had bitten off more than they could chew and lost their nerve for just a second? I pictured them, sailing out into clear blue sky, then the moment of pure wonder before they dropped, bounced, once, twice, and rolled, over and over to the canyon floor.

It was dusk when we got to the fir forest, the place Mom wanted to show us. Usually, Jenny and I were boisterous as we settled into a new campsite, abandoning the gear we hauled from the car to run off and explore. Tonight was different. The fir trees around us were giant and unmoving. A thick carpet of moss and needles spread out cleanly beneath them. It was very quiet, very still and the slam of our car doors echoed unnaturally. Even though it was evening, the air felt warm, heavy with the rich piney fragrance of the forest.

"This looks like a good place to put the tent," said Mom,

walking off a square in a flat area among several large firs. Jenny and I stood beside the car, watching her. She looked up. "Do you like it?"

Jenny asked, "Did you used to come here with Dad?"

"No, I found this place myself. Quite a long time ago. Before I even met him. This is an old forest. You can feel it. Bring the tent, girls."

Jenny and I lugged the heavy canvas tent from the station wagon as Mom laid out the poles and began fitting them together. I liked the familiar oil smell that rose from the canvas as we unfolded it. Mom moved confidently; she knew exactly what she was doing here.

Even before we had the tent all unfolded, we knew where the door was by the patch in the canvas over a hole from a hot ember. "There's the patch," said Jenny. "Which way do you want to face?"

"The sun will be coming up over here. Let's face that way," said Mom.

She had to turn the flashlight on before we were finished. Pale light still washed the sky above the trees, but didn't reach the forest floor where we clattered around with our supper dishes and frying pan.

"I could make a fire," said Mom. "But it's so warm, maybe we should just make our wieners on the Coleman stove?"

When we didn't answer she got the stove from the car and began pumping it up. I put our lawn chairs in a semi-circle and Jenny lit two candles in mason jars and set them in the crook of a rotted log. We sat mesmerized by the barely moving candle flames and listened to Mom stir the beans and wieners in the frying pan as the stove hissed gently. She handed us the steaming plates then closed the valve on the stove and the blue flames died.

Our human noises barely made a ripple before the quiet folded in again, like a thick liquid we were moving through.

"Sure is still," said Jenny, bending her head back to look up at the treetops.

"No coffee for me tonight," Mom said. "I'm beat. There's a creek over that way, girls. We'll find it after we eat."

The wieners and beans were smoky and delicious. My eyes followed the progress of a beetle making his way up the side of one of the mason jars as we ate.

"Look at that," Jenny said, reaching for my arm. "It's pitch black over there."

When we were done, Mom picked up the wash basin and led the way into the dark with the flashlight. Just a few yards from camp a sandy bank sloped down. We could hear the creek before we saw it, the gentle trickle of slow water flowing over rocks. Mom splashed her face and neck and ran her wet hands over her hair. Jenny and I did the same. Then Mom plunged the basin into the water and let it fill. We stood on the sandy bank watching the creek flowing in the dark.

"What are those little lights in the water?" Jenny said.

"Where?" Mom and I said together.

"Look. Watch carefully. There."

"It's starlight!" said Mom. We turned to the open sky above the creek, where a wide path of stars fuzzed the night sky.

I still remember the feeling of falling asleep that night, sunk deliciously into my sleeping bag like I had no bones, like our tent was floating in a still, warm sea, the baked canvas smell enveloping us like a cocoon. Some time in the night I woke to the sound of an owl's low hoot. Owls were supposed to be harbingers of death, but even that didn't disturb me. Its call was clear and reassuring. I didn't move my sleep-heavy limbs but let the peace of this place and the soft breathing of my sister and my mother on either side of me carry me back to sleep.

Bees darted among the wild raspberry bushes as Jenny and I filled our pails in the sunny clearing by the creek after breakfast. The raspberries were firm and juicy; we raced to see who could fill her pail fastest. When we were done, we sat by the creek eating them one by one.

"Have you ever heard of Chiwid?" Jenny asked.

"The old lady who lives outside?"

"Yeah. People see her all over the place, camping out. They say she doesn't sleep in a tent or anything. Even in the winter. What she does is she makes a little fire in a hole in the ground, then she scrapes out all the ashes and she sleeps in there. The heat keeps her warm till morning. Pretty good idea."

"I've seen her," I said.

"You have not," said Jenny.

"I saw her once when I was with Dad. She had all these bundles of stuff she was carrying alongside the road. Dad said he'd offer her a ride but she didn't like strangers, especially if they were white. He said if we stopped she'd run away."

"Cool," said Jenny. "I heard she has a lot of money and she hides it all over the place, like in swamps and stuff. I bet there's some hidden around here."

"I doubt it. Where would she get money?"

"Josie's grandpa knows her and he says she gets money from somewhere. She hardly needs any, living out like that, so she hides it. Josie said maybe she gets the money from her husband because he feels bad for what he did to her." She looked at me as she said this, as if she wasn't sure she would tell me what it was he did. She put a handful of berries in her mouth.

"She doesn't have a husband," I said. "Dad said she's on her own, even though she's an old lady. Some people say she's part coyote, that's what Dad said."

"Maybe she is. But she used to have a husband. She used to be normal. Live in a normal house and stuff."

I couldn't hold back anymore. "So what happened?"

Jenny looked at me intently and hugged herself. "This is true. You can ask anyone. But don't ask Mom because she'd kill me for telling you."

"Okay," I said, but now I wasn't sure if I wanted to hear it.

"Her husband was really mean. Josie said she heard her grandpa talk about him. He once saw Chiwid's husband take a harness and whip a horse with the metal bit, in the head and everything, till the horse kicked him in the stomach. He thought it was funny. He didn't care who saw. Sometimes he'd say he was going to shoot Chiwid. He'd hold the rifle to her stomach and then their kids had to go running off to get help."

"She has kids?"

"She used to, a long time ago. Like I said, she used to have a normal life. Anyway, one time her husband was so mad he took a chain, one of those big ones for logging, and he beat her with it. She was beautiful, too. Well, she's old now, but once she was beautiful. Some people say he was jealous. He didn't like how other men looked at her and that's why he did it. He choked her with that chain and almost killed her. That's when she ran away and she never went back to living with people. It is like she's a coyote, because she's spooked like that. She's afraid to come near people now."

"What about her kids?" I said.

"I don't know," said Jenny.

Dad had said that Chiwid was happy. "She likes sleeping out," he'd said. "Some people say she's a bit crazy, but she's right as rain. She's lived this long. She must know what she's doing."

Mom had come down to the creek. She slipped out of her shorts and T-shirt and waded into the water. I put down my berry pail. A chickadee was singing on the other side of the creek.

Jenny took off her runners and tossed them, one by one, beside a stand of willow. "Let's go wading," she said, pulling me up by the arm.

Mom sat on a rock with her feet in the water, and as the sun grew hotter, Jenny and I stretched out and let the cool current bubble over us. I thought of Chiwid alone in the bush sleeping in her little warm spot in the ground. I couldn't decide if I pitied her or envied her.

Night dropped again as suddenly as it had the evening before, and with it the light breeze that had been sifting through the firs fell calm. Mom built a fire, her rustlings and twig-snapping echoing in that strange silence. Worn out, Jenny and I drew our legs up in the lawn chairs with a shared blanket over our knees and watched the heat curl bark into orange embers that leapt into flame, grew and twisted.

"What a perfect day," said Mom, settling into her own lawn chair.

"Are you ever afraid?" Jenny asked her.

"Afraid of what?"

"Anything. Like bears or wolves or cougars."

"I'm more afraid of humans," said Mom.

"What humans?" asked Jenny.

"None in particular," she said. "There just seems to be more to fear from humans than from any of those animals. Humans are unpredictable."

After we lost her, I tried to put together a list of the

important things Mom told us: Never make big decisions late at night. Don't touch the sides of the tent when it's raining. Never lean on a stove because you never know when it might be hot. Don't drink from a creek if you don't know what's upstream. Humans are unpredictable.

A sound outside the tent woke me. At first I thought it was the wind coming up. Then I recognized the low hum of an engine and the soft crunch of tires, moving slowly towards our camp. Mom was still out by the fire. I heard her push her lawn chair back and saw her shadow on the tent as she stood. I held my breath. It seemed to me that if I didn't let on that I was awake, I would not have to be a part of whatever happened next, or even that it would not happen.

The vehicle stopped and a door opened, then closed with a soft click.

"You nearly scared the life out of me, coming in here with your headlights off like that," said Mom quietly.

A man's low voice answered her. "You knew it would be me, didn't you? Who else knows this road in the pitch dark?"

"What, have you been following me?"

The words alarmed me, but there was a teasing tone to her voice. She wasn't scared of this man.

I heard the chairs scrape again and then the mumble of their voices wove into the gurgle of the creek. I wanted to get up and look out at them. I thought about lifting the door flap. But I was too close to sleep. I woke again later to the sound of a high wind moaning through the tops of the firs. I tucked my blankets closer. Mom's soft laughter sounded below the wind. She was still out by the fire. The man's voice murmured, deep and soft. The fire snapped. I felt cold. When I sat up, Mom was beside me, her body curled warmly between Jenny and me.

I was the first one up and out in the chilly morning. The bright blue sky promised a nice day. Sun filtered through the feathery fir branches. No high wind, only the gentle swaying of the wild rose bushes near the creek. A squirrel scurried along the ground and flew up a tree trunk. Behind the tent, I scanned the earth for tire tracks. I couldn't see any. Our car still sat on the road, the windshield winking in the sun, and I felt as if I had dreamed the night visitor.

After breakfast, Mom sat sipping her coffee from a blue enamel cup. She closed her eyes as she drank, then tilted her face a little to the sunlight streaming through the fir trees.

Jenny laid two battered tablespoons on the ground between us. "Guess what these are for?"

"Cereal?"

"We already ate. Guess again."

"We're going to make something?"

"No—we're going to look for something," Jenny corrected. "Chiwid's treasure."

"Using spoons."

"We don't have any shovels. Anyway, she wouldn't have to bury it very deep."

Mom smiled and tilted her head towards us. "Chiwid's treasure?"

"She must have some," Jenny said. "Don't you think so, Mom?"

"I suppose she would. I'm not sure she'd bury it, though."

"So no one would steal it. It makes sense. She knows the bush like nobody else. She wouldn't carry it around. That would be too dangerous."

"And heavy," I said. "What are we going to do if we find some?"

Jenny's face fell for a moment, then she brightened again. "I know. We'll *add* some money to it—just a bit. And we can write her a note saying we found your money, but we're not going to steal it. So maybe she'll start to trust people again."

"That's a nice idea, Jen," Mom said sleepily, and closed her eyes again.

"Why do you want her to trust people?"

"Let's just dig," said Jenny.

The day warmed as the sun's angle widened and lit the pink fireweed along the creek edge and the scrub aspens and tangle of salmonberry bushes growing in over the logged clearings. We dug in the springy fir-needled soil, beside unusually shaped trees and deadfall that we thought would make landmarks for Chiwid's memory. Some distance away, Mom crouched, in her baseball cap, picking berries. She had found a patch of ripe wild strawberries, late for the time of year, and she ate as she picked, humming happily.

I kept looking for an opportunity to ask Jenny if she'd heard the night visitor. But I didn't want Jenny to dig into it in her usual fearless, reckless way. Jenny could ask so many questions she'd make herself cry with the answers. I never did that. If I could picture an answer I didn't want, I wouldn't even ask.

Mom had hummed yesterday, too, I told myself. Camping with Jenny and me made her happy. But that distant soft pleasure I saw in her as she foraged in among the radiant pink feathers of fireweed and shafts of sunlight—that was something else, I knew. It was not a gift given to her by Jenny or me.

[SEVEN]

BACK AT HOME A FEW DAYS LATER, Mom bent to sip her coffee and Rita bent to sip hers, the two heads nodding in unison in the shade of the spruce tree. Then Mom leaned back the way she did when she savoured her coffee, the tang of spruce, the perfect warmth of the day. Rita turned to her and smiled.

Their conversations differed from the ones Mom had with Glenna—less actual talking, more pensive sipping, bouncing of bare crossed legs, watching of swaying grasses and patterns of summer light through the trees.

Rita liked to talk about her projects. She had built a three-compartment composter that could break down almost anything—bread, bones, paper, pasta, along with the usual potato peels and coffee grounds.

"No rodents, not a one. There's no smell if you do it right."

Mom nodded and smiled. They sipped, in unison.

"I could make one for you," Rita said.

Mom's snort caught on her mouthful of coffee and she jerked forward to spit it in the dust. They both broke into giggles and had to set their cups on the ground.

They often broke into helpless laughter that way, set off by almost nothing, and they laughed till their eyes ran with tears. I sat on the step making cigarettes with a little black machine Rita had brought. For every twenty-five cigarettes I made for her, she'd promised to pay me twenty-five cents. I liked the fresh smell of the tobacco when I opened the tin and spread a line of it along the paper in the rubber holder.

A car came slowly up the driveway, an old maroon Mercury Monterey with the back window missing. It stopped a small distance away and Agnes got out. She walked slowly towards us with her careful, elegant gait.

"Agnes." Mom smiled, wiping her eyes.

"Irene."

"Have you met Rita?"

Both women nodded. Mom went in the house to get coffee for Agnes.

"You're the one who lives without a man out Nakenitses Road," Agnes said.

"That's right."

Mom came out with a mug and handed it to Agnes.

"I have something you better come look at," Agnes told Mom and pointed with her chin towards the car. The three women walked out to the car. I understood that I was not meant to come. They bent over the back seat and Rita straightened and shook her head, but she was smiling. They spoke for a couple of minutes, but I couldn't hear what they were saying. Then Agnes lifted a cardboard box out of the back and handed it to Mom. They walked slowly back to the house, all of them now looking at me. Mom put the box down in front of me. Inside it was a little white and orange kitten curled up on an old towel.

"That one's the runt," said Agnes. "Other ones, five other ones, won't let her near the mother. She needs to be fed."

Mom asked me, "Do you want a kitten to take care of?"

"Really?"

"Feed her with an eye dropper," Agnes said. "Give her goat's milk." She brought a jar out of her pocket and handed it to me. The milk was still warm.

I named her Cinnamon, because of the orangey patches on her head and back. She lapped goat's milk from the dropper with her tiny pink tongue, then fell asleep on my chest, her little paws kneading me in her dreams. Cinnamon purred like a tractor, that's what Rita said. I liked to take her under the spruce boughs and watch her bat around spruce cones and test her claws on the tree roots. She didn't wander. She ventured out in a small circle around me, returning to me every few minutes, climbing onto my legs. She liked me to hold her on my chest, with her paws and head resting on my shoulder so that she could observe from a safe height.

"That kitten is more dog than cat," Jenny said. "The way she follows you around. That's not normal cat behaviour."

It was true that when I walked in the bush, Cinnamon hopped along behind me, sometimes stopping to sniff the ground or cackle at a bird, but always running to catch up with me again. She didn't go out unless I did. Mom had warned me about coyotes and eagles that would be attracted by Cinnamon's snowy white fur. When school started in September, I left her each morning sleeping safely on my bed. But I worried that she could get out the kitchen window that Mom left open a crack. Or that as Mom went about her day, she might leave the door ajar and Cinnamon could slip out.

"I'll be careful," Mom said each morning as she kissed me goodbye at the door.

Jenny and I walked up the driveway after school, with the early fall chill taking the summer edge off the afternoon sunshine. The yellow aspen leaves flickered like lights against the turquoise sky, like the day Dad and I had built the lean-to by the lake. A familiar ache spread out from my centre. Sometimes it felt like it slowed my whole body down—I couldn't run as fast as normal, and my feet felt leaden. It would grow if I couldn't find a way to stop it.

Jenny chattered about the oil pastel drawing of a deer she'd done in art class and how she'd tried to get the shading right for the ears. "Ears are hard," she announced, getting no response from me.

Our house appeared beyond the big spruce tree. The front door was closed; a pot with a lid on it sat on the step, a wet newspaper beside it, covered in a pile of potato peelings. Mom liked to peel potatoes on the step. I opened the door, dropped my books and went to my room where I expected to see Cinnamon stretching her legs and yawning at my arrival. She wasn't there.

"Cinnamon?" I bent and looked under the bed where she sometimes curled herself up on a triangle of bedspread that touched the floor.

"Mom!" I heard Jenny call. She came to our bedroom doorway. "Where's Mom?"

"Is she lying down?"

"No. She's not in the house. Maybe she's in the shed." Jenny headed back outside. I heard her calling.

I followed her out, calling for Cinnamon. She always greeted me when I came home; she was always here. Jenny stood by the shed and screamed "Mom!" at the top of her voice. Just then Cinnamon came bounding out of the woods past the edge of the vegetable garden. She ran right to me and I picked her up and buried my face in her fur. I realized I was crying, my tears wetting her soft fur, and she licked at my hand with her rough tongue.

Mom was right behind her, tripping through the underbrush and bursting out of the trees like someone who had been lost and has at last blundered on home.

"Mom!" Jenny shouted. "What are you doing? We didn't

know where you were—we came home from school and you were gone." She ran to Mom and threw her arms around her and now Jenny was crying, too.

"Girls, girls, relax," Mom said. "I was just out for a walk in the bush. I lost track of time. I'm sorry."

But something seemed odd about it, about her. She came in the house, picking burrs from her shirt and laughing as she drew Jenny close.

"I'm sorry about the cat, Maggie. She followed me. She was with me the whole time. Are you two hungry? I'm starving."

Her eyes shone and she was flushed and giddy, her skin mottled with red, not just on her face, but down her neck and chest, into the white skin beyond the soft V of her flannel shirt.

"But what were you doing?" Jenny persisted.

"I just needed to get out of the house for a while, so I went for a walk. Cinnamon must have slipped out when I opened the door, and I didn't notice. But after a while I saw her following me." Mom got out bowls and the chocolate syrup. "Time for our reward!" she said brightly.

"You bought ice cream?" Jenny said.

Mom pulled a small carton from the icebox. She scooped a large curl of vanilla into each bowl, then broke bits of graham cracker over the tops. She set them on the table and let us pour our own chocolate sauce.

I watched Mom as she ate her ice cream. She was absorbed, not noticing my eyes on her. She licked her spoon slowly, thoughtfully, then she got up and went to get the pot of potatoes from the step. She bent and took another pot from the icebox and carried it to the stove. Then she stretched her arms over her head, a long, deep stretch, and said, "I'm going to take a nap before supper."

I was mad at her about letting Cinnamon out, but what bothered me more was the distance that seemed to have opened up between us. It seemed as if, for now, she was not really my mother, but some beautiful woman with flushed skin going to have a nap in my mother's bedroom.

[EIGHT]

WHEN I REMEMBER the first fall without Dad, I think I can see that a change was coming. I should have been expecting the second thing, known it was building from the grey days when we came home from school and found Mom lying on top of the blankets on the bed, Cinnamon stretched innocently alongside her. But I could never have guessed where it would come from.

It was not the normal thing for Jenny to have to make supper. She tried to percolate along cheerfully, as if she didn't mind, as if she liked it, liked to experiment with things she found in old spice jars under the sink, improvise a spaghetti sauce from the jars of stewed tomatoes that neighbours had brought. When we sat down to eat, she would not allow a gloomy silence; she described the things she drew in coloured chalk on the board at school for Halloween, Thanksgiving, Remembrance Day.

"We each used a whole orange chalk on the pumpkins, right down to the nubbins. The nubbins, I tell *ya!*" Jenny's science teacher that year had a verbal tic and punctuated his sentences with "I tell ya." It made Mom laugh the first time Jenny mimicked him, so she used it often.

Jenny had real friends and sometimes spent the night at their houses. I had Mickey, who I didn't even like most of the time, and who couldn't spell at all, not even words like "don't," which she spelt "donet," or "when," which appeared variously as "wen" or "wan." This bothered me enough to make me think we could never be real friends.

I pretended to be sick some school mornings that fall and Mom pretended to believe me. These were usually the days after the nightmares I'd started to have about Cinnamon. In the dream I came home and she was gone. Her absence was thick and sharp and it was the sound of my own wailing that woke me. In the morning, I couldn't bear to leave Cinnamon knowing I would have to worry all day about whether Mom was paying proper attention. I held her in my lap in Dad's chair by the fire and smoothed her fur. Mom let me stay home and brought me a salted boiled egg and a cup of weak sugared tea. After school, Jenny squeezed herself into the chair with me and tickled me until I fell out.

—

Rita came over on a cold Saturday in early November to help Mom split the wood that Glenna's husband Ron had brought. Then the house smelled of coffee and tobacco and the light changed, like there was a spark of something warmer in the air, and Mom seemed to wake up. Rita put a Carole King 8-track on in her truck and kept the doors open while they chopped and we stacked.

They both sang along to "I Feel the Earth Move." They synchronized their movements, two axe-wielding dancers matching rhythms until someone's axe stuck and threw them off. That night, Rita stayed over. I listened to their low voices rising and falling in the kitchen. When I came out of our room for a glass of water, the conversation stopped.

"Can't sleep?" Mom said, and they waited while I filled my glass and stood drinking. Back in my room, I heard them start again.

"I feel like a teenager," Mom said.

"Do I make you feel like a teenager?" Rita asked, and they burst into laughter.

Jenny was listening, too, and smiled. We both liked Mom's mood better when Rita was around. In the morning, she was still there, teasing Mom while they made breakfast together.

"Those eggs are all cooked the same," she said.

"I know," said Mom.

"Why'd you ask me how I wanted them, then?"

"I was hopeful. But I always break the yolks."

"Next time, I'll do the eggs."

After that, Rita came more often, always bringing something—fresh eggs, deer sausages, a moose roast, a bottle of her homemade berry wine. Mom brightened, and Jenny didn't have to pretend to be happy. Rita and Mom stayed up drinking wine. I fell asleep listening to the hum of their voices, talking, talking. Late in the night, the clatter of the stove being stoked woke me and then their soft laughter and the squeak of the bedroom door was reassuring.

Jenny teased them about their pyjama parties. "You two *are* like a couple of teenagers."

We drove the three and a half hours to Rita's farm on Nakenitses Road for a few days over Christmas, with Cinnamon sleeping peacefully on the rumbling floor of the station wagon. We pretended not to notice that Dad wasn't with us. We pretended not to miss the game he played, tapping the roof on Christmas Eve, Jenny and I imagining it was reindeer hooves. We pretended not to care that the selection of the Christmas tree from the bush and digging it out and chopping it down was mostly carried out by Mom and Rita, who warmed themselves with a flask of peppermint schnapps and giggled and cursed their way through the ritual with none of the proper solemnity or democracy, no standing and considering with us in respectful silence, no fire in the snow nearby.

Christmas night I'd always felt a sadness I couldn't explain. Maybe it came from Mom and Dad who I could see tried their best to make our little family everything we needed. But there was an absence even then, of something I had never understood. I missed it because they missed it, their links to their families broken or missing. This year, without Dad, it was worse. I couldn't help resenting Rita a little for not being Dad and for trying to keep us from noticing he was gone. In my head I repeated *Dad is dead, Dad is dead.* Feeling the pain of it—properly feeling it burn and squeeze in my gut—was almost a relief.

Rita roasted one of her own ducks for Christmas dinner and, after she opened a bottle of her homemade wine, she placed a glass each in front of Jenny and me.

"Special occasion," she said. "It's not very strong."

"It's good," said Jenny, trying to hide a slight shudder as she swallowed. I liked the taste of it. After a couple more sips, Jenny said, "Why didn't you get married, Rita?"

"Jennifer!" Mom said.

"I just wondered."

"It's okay," Rita said. "I didn't think getting married would make my life better. I wanted to be independent."

"Like Chiwid?"

"Not quite like Chiwid, no. Maybe I didn't want to end up like Chiwid. You want to be careful you don't marry someone who's going to crush your spirit."

"Let's hope you can aim a little higher than just not crushing your spirit," Mom put in.

"Hear, hear!" said Rita, and they clinked glasses.

On Boxing Day, we put on snowshoes and headed out in the deep snow behind Rita's place. I led the way because I could walk along on top of the crusted snow, sometimes not breaking through for a long time. In the wide-open meadow below the mountain, sun glinting on the blue expanse of snow, I forgot that they were behind me. It was just me and some chubby little winter birds feeding on frozen berries from the scrubby branches poking through the snow. I felt detached from my body, as if it were some amazing machine that lifted my knees, one after the other. Then everything disappeared except the snow and the webbed sinew of my snowshoes, forward, forward, forward and the reassuring pounding of my heart—*not dead, not dead, not dead.*

The next day, just before we were to head home, a snowstorm blew in, plugging the road and Rita's driveway with wide drifts. I was happy to be stranded, but Jenny wanted to get back to her friends, and even Mom seemed restless. That night, as the wind peppered snow against the windows in a frenzy, and the little house shook with the storm, I heard Mom's and Rita's voices rise in the living room.

Rita said loudly, "Well I don't understand what you object to."

"It's nothing. I can't explain it, Rita. Just quit—I don't know what. I don't even know what I'm trying to say. I'm just grouchy. I want to sleep in my own bed."

"Fine. I understand that. I'm just trying to be a good friend."

"You're a great friend, okay? You always come to my rescue and you're Rita my saviour, is that what you want to hear?"

It was quiet for a minute.

"No, not really," Rita said. "I don't really want to hear that at all."

More quiet, but now the wind screamed around the eaves of the house, like a human voice, rising and falling in moans. I pictured the meadow, the snow belting it in whirlwinds and the winter birds huddled in the pines for shelter, and I wondered if Chiwid was sleeping out tonight or safe in someone's house with the fire stoked up red-hot. That was what they said about Chiwid, that she was warm outside, but when she was coaxed in by people who couldn't stand the thought of her out in forty below weather, she always felt cold. She'd been responsible for nearly burning down the cabins of a few people when she over-stoked their stoves, trying to get warm.

"Listen to that wind," Rita said. "I'll try and get the tractor out tomorrow to clear the driveway."

In spring, Mom announced she had got a summer job baking for a fly-in fishing camp. We would be based at the camp owners' beautiful log cabin on Dultso Lake about two hours west on Highway 20, just the three of us. Float planes would arrive every other day to take the baking into camp. The owners had agreed to let Mom start after the school year ended. Mom wasn't much of a baker, but they told her they had their regular recipes she could follow. Rita knew the owners, who were mostly concerned about getting someone they could trust to look after their house while they were away at the camp. In the past, their teenage daughter had done it, but she had moved to Vancouver.

Jenny calls Dultso Lake the best place we ever lived. I call it the last place we ever lived. I find it hard to call nights playing another family's Scrabble game with Cinnamon sleeping warmly on someone else's blanket our "best." For the first time, we lived in a house with a TV. A giant antenna extended up the side of the cabin and we could get shows from the U.S., like *The Partridge Family*. The TV was run, like all the other electric appliances in the house, by a generator that hummed through the day. At night, when Mom shut it off, the quiet flooded back into the house like the rightful owner.

Beside the TV was a shelf stacked with Yahtzee, Monopoly, Life, checkers. There was a hi-fi in a dark wood cabinet with a sliding door that enclosed someone else's records: Elvis, the Beatles, the Bells, Conway Twitty. Jenny played Sonny and Cher's "I Got You Babe" so many times that summer that even now I can't hear the song without expecting the crackles and static of that album. On quiet afternoons, while Mom's bread was baking and Jenny sat out on the dock reading, I leafed through these records, wondering about the family who had picked them out.

I developed an intense dislike for the album *Conway Twitty*. The cover pictured a grinning Conway Twitty in a red shirt with a smoothed-back hairdo. His songs had titles like "I'll Have Another Cup of Coffee" (then I'll go) and "Guess My Eyes Were Bigger than My Heart." I think for me this album came to personify everything about this stupid, fortunate family with this oversized house by the lake, equipped with everything their hearts desired. This was not a family who had their wounded or dead dragged out into the public eye at the Duchess Creek nursing station. The worst things that had happened to them could be made into maudlin songs that you could sing along with. Or so I believed that summer, with a hatred burning in the pit of my stomach that puzzled even me. Sometimes I took out the Twitty album just to stare at it and enjoy hating the fortunate family.

Most days, I went walking in the bush around the lake, sometimes only coming home in time for supper. Cinnamon came with me, hopping along in her curious way over fallen logs and tree roots. When I stopped, she stopped, finding a patch of sunlight to sit in, her paws neatly together as she watched me. Sun lit the longer hairs on her fur in a halo around her. Sometimes the two of us nestled against the warm side of a rock and slept.

One day when we were out walking, a high wind came up, sifting through the treetops and making the big trees sway and creak eerily. I was headed for the crescent of sandy beach I'd found on the west side of the lake. If it started to rain, I could build a shelter there for Cinnamon and me. I turned to let her catch up, but she wasn't there. A sudden scuffle of leaves and branches came from about thirty feet away and then a short yowl. I ran back to see the flash of her white fur streaking through the woods, some small animal chasing her.

"Cinnamon!" I called sharply. What good was that going to do? I followed the scuffling until I couldn't hear it anymore and I had to stop and listen. Nothing but the rush of wind like a waterfall through the spruce and the trees swaying.

"Cinn-a-mon!" I called in the singsong voice she would recognize. I walked and called, then stopped and listened. I couldn't hear anything but the wind.

What an idiot I was to let her get so far behind me. What was I thinking?

I think about two hours passed before I started to cry. I didn't know what to do. She could have gone in any direction. Dad used to tell me that if you were lost, you shouldn't let yourself cry. Or if you had to, you should sit down on a rock and cry until you were done, then wipe your eyes and nose and take ten deep breaths until you were calm again. Crying could lead to panic and you didn't want to panic. I sat down on a log and called her name a few more times, then I wiped my nose on my T-shirt and decided that the best thing to do would be to go back to where I'd seen her last and call her. If she still didn't come, I would go home and get Mom and Jenny to help me look. There was still a lot of light left before night fell.

When I thought that I might not find her, I sobbed until I was mad at myself. I wiped my eyes again and took the ten deep breaths, then stood up. The creaking trees sounded like plaintive meows, and so did the little peeps of birds sneaking through below the moan of the wind once in a while.

Back at the spot I'd seen her last, I busied myself by building a small teepee shelter, big enough only for a cat. I didn't really think she would use it, but I needed to mark the spot with something and I needed to keep busy as I waited. I found sticks to use for poles and I set them into place, stopping every few minutes to call her again. When it was done, I called once more, then walked home.

Jenny was standing on the deck, looking out. "Maggie, where have you been?" she yelled. "Mom's been worried about you. Maggie? What's wrong?"

"I lost Cinnamon," I burst out, and Jenny came running and put her arms around me.

"Don't worry," she said. "We'll find her." She patted my back. "We'll find her, Maggie. She'll come home. That cat loves you like crazy. She'll come home."

They had already eaten supper, so while I picked at the potato salad and ham Jenny put out for me, Mom scurried around collecting things to take with us on the search. "We'll take a flashlight because it gets dark earlier in the bush. Jenny, get that box of catfood. We can shake it when we call her.

We'll need jackets; it's getting chilly already." Mom put her hand on the back of my neck. "You know, I wouldn't be surprised if she comes back before we're even ready to go."

But she didn't. As we headed back into the woods, I felt so sick with worry I thought I would throw up.

"That little cat knows where home is," Mom said, glancing sideways at me.

But I wasn't so sure. If she did, why would she always follow me so closely? Maybe being taken away from her mother so early meant that she didn't have all the proper cat instincts.

That evening, as we made circles out from the teepee and back again, crossing paths with each other, our three voices singsonging through the woods, Jenny rattling the box of cat food as she called, I believed that I was protected by their love and this would not be my second bad thing. As it got dark, I sank down on a log and stared into the dense woods, sure that any minute now I would see her hopping through the woods toward me. After a while Mom came and took my arm and helped me up. "I bet she'll come home tonight. She could be there right now, for all we know." But she wasn't.

I don't think I slept. I think it was the first time in my life that I stayed awake all night, listening for scratching at the door, drifting and then starting awake again to listen to the house groan and the wind hum through the TV antenna. As soon as light showed through the skylight, I got up, grabbed an apple and one of the sweet buns Mom had set on the counter, and left the house. The morning was still and cold, a grey light washing the sky. A heavy dew lay on the trees and grass. Little creatures skittered into the underbrush as I made my way back to the teepee. I sat on a log. I was conscious of being cold and shoved my hands into my pockets. My voice sounded out of place as I called her. I listened. Then I thought I heard a tiny meow. I stood up and called again. I heard it again, a tiny, tinny meow. I walked maybe fifty feet into the woods, following the sound. It was louder now. "Cinn-a-mon!"

And there it was again, very close. I looked up. Way up, high in a tree, she perched on a branch, looking down at me and crying. "On my god, Cinnamon, you crazy nut." I laughed at her, ecstatically, crazily relieved.

The tree she had got up was a tall skinny spruce with no lower branches, no footholds until about twenty feet up the trunk. I didn't think I could possibly get up there. I tried a few times, clutching with my arms and trying to get a toehold on the bark, but it was futile. Another spruce, only a few feet away, had plenty of sturdy limbs. I hoisted myself into it and hauled myself up, calling softly, "Don't worry, Cinnamon. I'll get you out of there. Good kitty."

But at about twenty feet, I couldn't climb any higher. The branches were too small, and even if they could have held me, the trunk was now too far from the one Cinnamon was in. I considered going home to get Mom. But I just couldn't stand the thought of leaving her there, so I stayed in the tree. "Mom will come looking for me," I told her. "Don't worry. She knows where to find me and she'll get you down."

After about an hour, the sun started to come up in the distance and I felt a bit warmer. A little while later I heard the screen door slam and then I heard, very faintly, Mom calling "Ma-ggie!" I knew that we would not have long to wait. I heard the screen door slam again. It was either Mom going back in or Jenny coming out. I stood up on a thick branch so I could see them coming.

Maybe ten minutes later I saw a flash of colour through the trees. "I told ya, I told ya!" I sang to Cinnamon. "Mom! Jenny! I'm way up here."

We told and retold the story of rescuing Cinnamon like a legend, to ourselves or whoever came to visit. Mom had wrapped the tree trunk with her jacket and used it like a sling to shimmy up the bare trunk, finding footholds on the slightest swellings and scars. When she reached the branches, she climbed quickly to where Cinnamon stood eagerly, rubbing her back against the tree. I've heard that mothers can perform incredible feats of strength when their children are in danger—lift a car off a leg or fight a cougar. My mother's feat that morning, climbing the unclimbable tree, descending with the scared cat clinging to her shoulder, proved that she would do anything for me.

[NINE]

WHEN THE END OF AUGUST CAME, we had to leave the well-equipped house in Dultso Lake, the records and games and the foreign smell of someone else's life. I wasn't sad to go, but Jenny grew anxious as the time approached.

"Where are we going to go?" she asked at least three times a day, sometimes asking me, sometimes Mom.

"First we're going to camp," Mom said. "We haven't really had a holiday this summer. We'll find a nice spot and settle in for a couple of weeks."

"I don't want to camp," Jenny said. "It'll be too cold. I want to go home."

"Well," Mom said, then smiled tightly. She didn't say what we all knew—that we had no home anymore. She had given up the house in Duchess Creek because she didn't want to pay the rent on it for the summer, and we had left our most important possessions in a shed at Rita's. Anyhow, there was no work for her in Duchess Creek, and she needed work.

"Will I be able to go back to my old school?" Jenny wanted to know.

"We'll see," Mom said.

"'We'll see' means no," Jenny muttered.

In a way I suppose I blamed Jenny for what happened next. All through the bright cooling days of an Indian summer, our gypsy life—sleeping out, fishing for trout in the river, frying them crackling in a cast iron pan over the fire, even learning to shoot with Dad's 30.30 and, once, helping to bring hay off a field for pay—was soured by Jenny's constant questions about school. Mom grew tired of trying to reassure her, and the lightness went out of our adventure. We drove the dusty back roads in silence, each of us occupied with our own worries.

Once September came and school had started, Jenny became sullen and stayed in the station wagon all day with Cinnamon, reading and rereading old Archie comics, chewing her nails to ragged nubs and staring out the window while Mom and I fished or made camp. About the second week in September, Mom drove down the Nakenitses Road to Rita's, and Rita came out on the porch and hugged each of us tightly and made a fuss over how much Cinnamon had grown.

There was a school at Nakenitses Lake, but Jenny didn't want to go to it. "I want to go to my own school," Jenny demanded. "Why should I start school here and be the stupid new girl if we aren't even going to stay? Then I'll just have to do it over again somewhere else."

I didn't want to go to school at all, and at first Mom, distracted and irritable, let it go. She left us with Rita some days and went off in the car, returning late. I watched for the station wagon headlights swinging into the driveway and sweeping across the living-room wall. Rita didn't like it when Mom was gone, I could tell. She grew testy and tried to play the parent with us, which she hadn't done before. "Don't you think you should clean that litter box?" or "You better turn on the lamp or you'll ruin your eyes." One evening after Mom had been gone all day, I was doing the dishes and broke a glass trying to get the milk ring out of the bottom. I cut myself, only a little, but blood seeped into the hot water. It looked like a lot and Rita, who was drying, snapped, "Oh for Christ's sake. Now what?"

"It's nothing," I said. "It's just a cut." I put the two pieces of the glass in the garbage, feeling my face flush with shame. It was all I could do to stand there at the sink.

"I'll finish them up," said Jenny, coming up beside me. I felt tears well up in gratitude. I dried my hands and went to the bathroom to get a strip of toilet paper. I sat on the couch with my hand wrapped and stared out the window, trying not to cry. The dishes clattered in the awkward silence.

"It's only a glass, guys," Rita finally said. "We'll live, right? Will we all live?" She looked over at me and I nodded, trying to smile.

—

That night we were in bed when Mom got back. I don't know what time it was, but I'd had long enough to imagine the various horrible accidents that could have befallen her. She came into the room and kissed Jenny and me on our foreheads. "Sleep tight, my sweets," she said, and relief coursed through me.

I had drifted to sleep when Mom and Rita's voices woke me.

"I think you should send them to school," Rita said. "At least Jennifer. She's thirteen—she's at that age when she just wants to belong. You're a conformist at thirteen."

"When I was her age my mother had already died and I was only three years away from being pregnant with her."

"What does that have to do with anything?"

Silence.

"Have you been drinking?" Rita asked.

"'Have you been drinking?' What are you, my mother?"

"Well, it seems like you could use a mother."

"Ha. I've been managing just fine for many, many years. If anyone is going to remember what it was like to be thirteen, it's me."

"I'm just giving you my opinion as your friend."

"Rita, I'm tired."

"Here's an idea—come home earlier. It's not like I don't worry."

"I appreciate what you do for us, I really do."

"I'm afraid you don't get it, Irene."

Jenny and I started school in Nakenitses Lake the next Monday. I was in grade six and in a room together with the grade four and five kids, and Jenny was in grade eight and in with the sevens and nines. Because the fall weather had turned warm, the teacher had us outside collecting leaves for a project. After school I wandered far along a creek and out to the lake, looking for more leaves. At Rita's, I used the iron to press yellow aspen leaves, red maple, the heart-shaped cottonwood and paper birch between two sheets of wax paper. I labelled them with name and habitat. I got the project back on Friday, A+.

Mom wasn't there when I got home. I waited on the porch, the leaf project in my lap, until Rita called me in and wordlessly placed bowls of canned spaghetti on the table. Jenny read at the table as we ate, and Rita didn't tell her not to.

I kept the leaf project beside my bed all through the night, woke up to touch it, check the colour of the light coming in the window and listen.

When Mom drove up on Saturday afternoon, I was sitting on the porch waiting. But when she kissed me lightly, I was too overcome with relief to show her my project.

"Did you miss me?" she said on her way in, as if being gone all night was nothing.

Jenny came out a minute later and the two of us sat and listened to the argument going on inside.

"What am I, your babysitter?" Rita shouted.

"You're my friend." Mom's voice, calmer, but still insistent.

"And what does that mean to you?"

"What does it mean to *you?*" Now her volume rose, too. "You've got some rigid formula of debits and credits and every time you do something for me I feel as if you're waiting to see if I fill in the matching thing on the ledger. I'm always just a little in the red with you."

"A little?"

"See. This is pointless." Mom came outside, letting the screen door slam behind her. The three of us sat there gloomily. Through the trees, the afternoon light shadowed the mountains. We had nowhere to go—the porch, the car, that was it, the safe zones. I picked up Cinnamon and went and sat in the car. Its smells and warmth cocooned me in familiarity. I might sleep in it if Mom would let me. That way I wouldn't have to worry about her slipping out of my sight.

Sometime in the middle of the night the car door jerked open and a blast of cold air rushed in. Mom began throwing in blankets and pillows. Jenny climbed in on top of them, groggy with sleep, her eyes barely open. The two of us sat in a stupor as Mom made several agitated trips in and out of the house, piling armloads of our possessions into the back of the station wagon. She slammed the hatch and got into the driver's seat, all without a word to us. Then she started the car, revved the engine for a minute, and drove out onto

Nakenitses Road, ribboning out in front of us in the moonlight. I don't know how long it was—maybe twenty minutes, half an hour—before Jenny spoke. "Why was Rita crying?"

"Never mind, honey." Her tone said that was the end of it.

Rita crying was such a bizarre and improbable thing that I couldn't even imagine what it would look like. A long time later I asked Jenny about it. She told me Rita had sat in a kitchen chair with her face in her hands and cried like her heart was broken.

We drove all night. I woke up once when the car stopped and saw Mom outside, leaning against the car smoking a cigarette. The northern lights sent fingers of green light creeping, retreating, shooting up into the night sky. Cinnamon sighed and stretched in the nest of blankets, then settled herself again. Mom climbed back in and put her hands on the wheel. For a moment I felt intensely happy. Everything I had was in this car and safe.

[TEN]

THE EDWARDS' PLACE in Williams Lake smelled of old hamburger grease with an undertone of mothballs. This was not the scent of a happy house. I could sniff some tragedy—large or small, I didn't know—hanging in the close air. I wondered what it was. It may have had to do with the husband, Ted, who sat in the kitchen in his wheelchair, using a bent spoon to dunk his teabag in a stained white mug. He smiled crookedly at us as we came in.

I disliked Mrs. Edwards instantly, with her straw blonde hair and her runny eye. She was not like my mother or Rita, women who took charge, did what needed to be done, enjoyed their competence. Mrs. Edwards seemed helpless, trapped, a woman who wrung her hands and wept and moaned—I could see that right away. I could tell by the dingy house, lit by fixtures dimmed with drifts of insect bodies inside the glass globes, the TV on in the corner, dusty drapes drawn against the brilliance of a fall morning.

Our mother's need to find a viable solution to whatever problem plagued her must have been strong, because she blinded herself to what was obvious even to an eleven year-old: Mrs. Edwards was not a happy woman and she would be no use to two unhappy girls.

Our mother took us into a bedroom with two twin beds covered in matching blue bedspreads with a synthetic sheen to them. I expected a puff of dust to rise up when I sat on one. Later, when I had had a lot of time to reflect on every object in the house, every plastic, pretend-crocheted doily and scented, fake flower–decorated toilet roll cover, I thought that even the bedspreads spoke of Mrs. Edwards' unhappiness and helplessness. Only a person who had no idea how to be comfortable and happy in the world would pick such a slippery, staticky, uncomfortable fabric to adorn a guest's bed.

"You're going to billet for a while with the Edwards," Mom told us, as Jenny and I sat side by side on one of the beds, frightened by the look on her face.

"What does billet mean?" Jenny asked.

"You're going to stay here," Mom said. "The Edwards are old friends of your dad's. They're good people. They'll take care of you while I go cook in the logging camps."

"I don't want to stay here," Jenny said.

"Neither do I," I said. "We can come with you. We won't be any trouble. I know how to take care of myself."

"I know you do," Mom said. "But they don't allow kids. Those are the rules. We need money."

"Why can't you get a job here in town? Why can't you be a secretary or something? Why couldn't we go back to Duchess Creek? Glenna could get you a job in the nurses' station."

"Stop it right now," Mom said. "This is the best I can do. Let's just hope it won't be for long."

"How long?" I asked.

"Let's hope not too long."

"How long?" Jenny said. Her voice cracked and she started to cry.

"Stop it," Mom said sharply. "There's nothing I can do. The Edwards are good people. You'll be able to go to school here."

Good people. Never trust someone described as a "good" person. I know now that "good" means that they won't murder you, throw you out into the snow or let you starve. But also that there are obvious shortcomings and you're going to find out what they are pretty damn quick. Those were the kind of people our mother left us with.

Jenny pulled her knees up under her chin and cried softly into the circle of her arms. She was like an island on the slippery bedspread. I knew she would be of no more help to me in persuading our mother to collapse with regret, then drive us to the nearest campground where Mom would boil up some coffee, lean back in her lawn chair, gazing up, then Jenny and I would ask her for spoons to dig for Chiwid's treasure by the river.

—

Mom led me outside to the car. I remember the feeling of my small hand in hers. She was still my protector that day. If I held on to her hand, I didn't think she would let me go. I didn't think she would be able to. But at the car she shook free of me, and there was nothing I could do.

"Maggie," she said. "I know Jenny's the older one, but I'm going to rely on you. You were right when you said you know how to take care of yourself. I don't have to worry about you."

She must have meant it as a compliment, a way to get me to look at myself as something other than a helpless child. But when she said it, smiling at me softly, her face open like a wish, it felt more like a recognition of a weakness I had, a thing I'd always have to live with, like a harelip.

"Okay," I said because I couldn't say anything else. Mom began to unpack the car. I picked up Cinnamon from the back seat and carried her into the hamburger-smelling house. Mom followed with our pillows and suitcases.

"What's that?" Mrs. Edwards said.

"What?" Mom said.

"Is that a cat?"

I slipped quickly into the bedroom and dropped Cinnamon to the floor, as if I could hide her.

"No, no," Mrs. Edwards said. "We can't have cats. I'm very allergic."

"Beatrice, please," Mom said. She pulled the bedroom door closed and I heard their voices going back and forth.

Jenny raised her head to look at me. Behind her on the wall above the bed hung an embroidered picture of two hands clasped together, praying. I picked up Cinnamon and she curled two soft white paws over my shoulder and clung to me like a baby. I buried my nose in her blanket-scented fur. She began to purr, deep contented trills. Cinnamon could be happy anywhere, as long as she was with me.

When Mom came into the room, I could tell by the look on her face that she had lost.

"I'm sorry, Maggie," she said. "I promise I'll take good care of her."

That was the second time I saw Mom cry. Tears filled her eyes and ran down her cheeks leaving tracks across her brown freckles. Some brief understanding of her situation flickered in my brain, just for a moment, and I wanted to say something to make her feel better, maybe tell her that Cinnamon wasn't a city cat anyway, but a lump had risen up from my heart and was choking me, and I couldn't say it.

Neither Jenny nor I said a word about this being our second thing. To acknowledge it openly would be to acknowledge that the third thing was still to come.

I had once seen a house demolished, a little shack of a house in Duchess Creek where an old man had lived until he died. The shack was razed to be replaced by a bigger, solid log house, the kind that wants to look rustic even though it's brand new. Jenny and I had watched from the road as the backhoe bit into the roof and pulled down the walls like they were cardboard. Faded flowered curtains, still on the rod, clung to the tines of the backhoe as it came up for another round, then the curtains and rod were folded into the dust of the ruins and disappeared. With my unpacked suitcase on the bed in front of me, I felt like that house, a tumult of dust and disorder, nothing where it should be, nothing left standing.

[ELEVEN]

I CAN'T SAY THAT MOM was wrong about my being able to look after myself. I soon recognized Bea Edwards for the ticking time bomb that she was. Only three weeks into our stay, I learned that what could set her off was unpredictable. It was my job to set the table each night. Sometimes Ted didn't come home until after supper, when one of his drinking buddies dropped him off and pushed him up the plywood ramp to the door. He could do it himself, unless he'd had a few.

One night I thought I might save time by finding out if he'd be home. "Should I set a place for Ted?" I asked Bea, as I took down the plates.

"How should I know?" she snapped.

But this was nothing. This was just normal Bea impatience. It was later, when we were washing up the supper dishes and I tucked Ted's clean, unused plate in with our three dirty ones that Bea exploded. Her soapy hands shot up from the hot dishwater and tore the steaming eyeglasses from her face. She hurled the glasses across the kitchen, where they skittered against the refrigerator grill, and she screamed, "Do I have so little to do around here? Do I? Do I?" Her pale eyes popped wetly in the midst of the red blur that was her face. "Now I'm washing clean dishes! I'm washing dishes that haven't even been used! Is that how you do things at your house? Here!" She began clumsily scooping clean plates and saucers and bowls and cups from the cupboards and piling them haphazardly beside the sink. She didn't stop until she had cleared every last dish from every shelf.

I stood back, my hands knotted tightly in front of me. I watched as her face swelled, grew redder and redder, the veins throbbing at her temples. She might literally explode, I thought. But instead she went limp as a wet dishrag and with a choked sob hissed, "Wash them." She left the kitchen, the door swinging in her wake. And so I did.

One day not too long after Bea's explosion, I was wandering around town after school, killing time until Jenny was done volleyball practice. Jenny liked the novelty of living in a town. She'd bought herself a paisley wallet at Stedman's and tucked the money Mom had given her into it. After school, when she wasn't playing volleyball, she went to the Tastee-Freez with her friends. She had an easy charm that I didn't and acted as the buffer between Bea and me. Up ahead, the doors of the Maple Leaf Hotel swung open and Ted rolled out into the sun. Ted had a way of wheeling his chair that I wouldn't have expected from a man who couldn't walk. There was a vigour to it, the way his hands gripped the wheels, pushed off strongly. He was not feeble, Ted, and it seemed like he wanted anyone who saw him to know it. He had broad shoulders, a straight back and large, lean hands. He had silver-grey hair, lots of it for a man his age, I thought, although I didn't really know how old he was. He went to the barber once a week for a trim. Ted wore the same kind of flannel shirts and blue jeans as my dad had worn, so that made me like him a little.

He stopped when he saw me and waited till I caught up to him.

"Hello, Maggie."

I thought I might do a good deed, not for Ted, but for Bea, by delivering him home for supper. Or maybe the good deed was really for myself.

"How was school?" Ted asked.

"Fine," I said. He set off again, wheeling along the road with me beside him.

"How do you like Williams Lake?"

"It's fine," I said.

He laughed. "You like the bush better, don't you? You're like your dad."

It pleased me so much to be told that I was like my dad that for a minute, I just walked along smiling.

"If you push me, I can show you a good place," Ted said. The Edwards' place wasn't far from the hotel, but we wheeled right past their street. "We can't go over the railroad tracks in this thing, so we have to take the long way. You're not in a hurry, are you?"

I thought of Bea. "No," I said.

At the end of Oliver Street I helped push him along to the highway. A small fear took hold of me. What if I lost control of the chair? What if he went wheeling down the highway towards Vancouver? But Ted said, "Here we go! Hang a right. You got a licence to drive this thing, Maggie?" I laughed and felt a lightness rise in me, the giddiness of adventure.

I pushed Ted with difficulty down a narrow trail bumpy with tree roots and fir needles. Scent rose up as we crunched over them. No wind, but a warmed air, a different air, gently wrapped me. Something invisible inhabited the long shadows and winked from the silver spiderwebs running from wild rose to birch. The knot of worry that had been twisting my gut since Mom left us loosened. My shoulders relaxed.

"Pretty place, isn't it?" Ted said. "You keep heading up the river that way, you'll get to the Fraser." We could not get very far with the chair. So I parked him and sat down, leaning against a tree.

He took out his tobacco and began tamping it into the bowl of his pipe. I must have been looking at Ted in a funny way, because he said, "I can tell you how I ended up in this chair. Most people are curious and I don't mind." A crow began to squawk and fuss on a high branch above us and the birch leaves trembled. A swallow hovered and dove at the crow and Ted and I laughed. He lit a match, drew the flame into the pipe and a cloud of sweet-scented smoke curled into the air.

"I was working with an outfit north of here, logging a steep hillside. We lived in tents, rough and ready. It was a gyppo show. That's what they call a small outfit. That can be okay if guys know what they're doing. If they're careful and they get along. But from the get-go, I never liked the way the hook tender did things. He was the boss, but he was strung tighter than a fiddle and he wasn't happy unless everybody was going in three different directions at once. I was planning to quit as soon as I could.

"That day I had a bad feeling. It was hot, stinking hot. We woke up to heat and it stoked up to a furnace as the morning went on, sun blazing down on the hillside. Everyone was tetchy, but that joker of a hook tender poked and screamed, jumped on one foot. I sometimes wondered if he was all there.

"Three of us choker setters were on the crew that day, me, old Jim, and a greenhorn we called Dewy, because he had this soft white face he washed with special soap every morning. We were down in a ravine, attaching the choker and climbing back up in that inferno to get clear. It was exhausting. We decided to take turns, give each other a rest. It's Dewy's turn and he's walking down a steep log. His cork boots got caught up on the bits of loose bark and he lost his gription. Tumbled head over heels and winds up upside down, on his head, out cold. Jim and me climbed down to him and pulled him out, gave him a drink of water and he went back to work. That's what you did.

"The day before, some men were standing on a stump watching the logs being yarded. No one saw the haulback catch on the roots of a big old stump. The stump broke loose and came thundering down the mountain, heading straight for these guys standing there, mouths open. It hit the ground about fifteen feet in front of them and flew up and over their heads. Barely cleared them. We teased them about the shave they got that day. But those things can happen, even in the best-run show."

Ted held another match to his pipe and the ripe cherry smell floated on the air. "At lunch I sat on a stump. I was soaked with sweat, not a dry spot on me—even my socks were sopping. The bugs were out, I was itching from the dust and bark that stuck to me. I thought about walking off the job, right then and there. That's how sure I was that something was going to go wrong. It was Friday anyway and I was going home for the weekend, and I'd already decided I wasn't coming back. This old-timer, Jim, he'd been a faller, was mostly deaf now. All morning he grumbled about this being the worst job he'd ever been on and hadn't he paid his dues? This fella was comical, Jim. He had no front teeth. He had dentures but he didn't wear them on the job. I suppose he thought he'd break them or swallow them while he was working or something. He was skinny, too, but still muscled like a racehorse. He knocked over his coffee at lunch. That was the last straw for him. He let out a blue streak of curses from his toothless old mouth. I said to him, 'Jimbo, why don't you and me just bunch it and head on home?'"

"So did you?" I asked.

Ted looked off through the lace of leaves and sunlight and was silent for so long I thought I'd asked the wrong thing.

Finally he said, "No. No we didn't leave. We did what you do, which is to finish the job. It's funny, when I think about it now, how sometimes the good lessons you learned can sink you.

"We were close to done for the day. I kept thinking about the ice-cold beer I was going to drink when we got to town. Jim was at the top of the ravine, Dewy was down below, and I was standing clear. The whistle blew and all of a sudden I heard a snap, like a giant guitar string busting. There was a shout, some curse I won't repeat, and guys diving left and right. I saw Jim's head coming up like an old hound dog sniffing the air. I shouted 'Jim!' at the top of my lungs and he looked at me and I saw the change in his eyes as he understood and he made a move, digging in as if to run, then the cable came whipping through the air and carried him right off the hill."

"Oh no!" I said. "Did he die?"

"Oh yes, he died all right." Ted's pipe had gone out and he sucked deeply on it, twice, then held it in his big hand on his lap. The sun had sunk behind the hills and the air felt chilly now, the light gone flat and lonely among the trees. But I hadn't yet heard how Ted ended up in the wheelchair.

"Poor old Jim deserved better," he said. "We wrapped him up to bring him home. But then, when we got back to camp, what with all the confusion, we had to wait for our cheques. I couldn't stand it. I wanted to go. Finally I made up an excuse, I got paid in cash and I got out of there as fast I could. I got a lift to town where my truck was parked and I had a cold beer and supper. Then I felt, well Maggie, I'm ashamed to say it, but I felt glad it wasn't me. I was just glad to be alive. Really glad. And I wanted to go home.

"I headed out. It was getting dark, but that time of year it never does get entirely dark. And then the moon came up and the road ran out ahead of me shining like a river. Gosh I was happy. What a beautiful night. Then I thought I heard that snapping sound again, of the line right there in my truck. I thought that was strange. I shook my head and I opened the window to get some fresh air. Bugs flew at my windshield and I saw them coming at my headlights like a gentle rain. Then I heard it again, that crazy whipping snickety-snack. And there in front of me in the headlights I saw someone running along the road. Right in the middle. So I slowed a bit and this runner came alongside my open window and yelled something. I saw his face and it was Jim with that big toothless mouth. 'What?' I yelled back and then I heard him, clear as a bell, 'Wake up!'

"I opened my eyes. Right in front of me was the grill of a truck, no headlights on. In the split second it took for me to figure out that it was parked on the side of the road, I jammed on the brakes, then I slammed right into it.

"Old Jim saved my life, yelling at me just like I'd yelled at him on the hillside. The truck I hit was loaded with a big load of logs, and the driver had pulled off to have a nap. The cops said the tracks showed I had been driving on the shoulder for nearly a mile. The hood of my truck accordioned under his and then the two trucks went slowly over, the weight of the logs carrying us. My truck ended up in the air, clamped onto his grill. I don't remember any of that. I was in a coma for seven days and when I woke up, I was in a hospital bed in Williams Lake and I'd never have to work as a logger again." Ted laughed quietly. "That's it. That's the story."

I pushed Ted's wheelchair through the chilly dusk back along the trail, across the highway and up the Edwards' street, even when Ted could have rolled it himself. Bea and Jenny were clearing away the supper dishes when we came in bringing a drift of fall air into the steamed house. Jenny looked up in a combination of surprise and relief. Then she arranged her mouth into a tight-lipped line and tried hard not to smile. Bea said nothing, didn't meet our eyes, just disappeared into the kitchen. Ted hung up his coat and wheeled over to the table where his bare plate sat staring up between fork and knife.

"I'll get your food," said Jenny. I should have helped, but I didn't want to go in there. I went to the bathroom and washed my hands. Then I took my place at the table and began to eat. Jenny sat and watched, smiling a little now.

I waited for the slams and crashes of Bea's rage to reverberate off the kitchen walls and come ringing through the house. But I heard only the rush of water filling the sink, the sucking of the dish detergent bottle and the clink of silverware against glass.

Jenny passed me an envelope across the table. "This came today." Jenny & Maggie was written in Mom's handwriting in pencil on the envelope. I took out the letter, a single thick sheet torn from a sketchbook.

Dear Girls,

I hope you like Williams Lake and are having fun living in a town for a change. I've sent some money to the Edwards to cover your expenses, so if you need anything, just ask Mrs. Edwards. You can buy yourselves a treat now and then, too. Don't go crazy, though! All is well here. Bye for now.

Love Mom

There was nothing in the letter, nothing about when she was coming back, or where she was, or where Cinnamon was. My eyes filled with tears but I kept eating. I wouldn't cry in front of Ted. I thought of him instead, out on the lonely road with old Jim running alongside him.

"I think I'm going to try and get a job," Jenny said. "I saw a sign at Frank's. I could be a waitress or a cook. Couldn't I?"

"Sure you could," Ted said.

"I'd have to arrange it around volleyball practices, though.

The Duchess Creek team is coming to our school to play us. Cool, eh?"

I heard her, but I was out on that road, with the night insects flitting around in the headlights of a truck lifted right off the ground.

[TWELVE]

If I walked to the end of Yorston Street, where the Edwards' house was, I could see the lake, and the smoky blue hills beyond it. I sat out there sometimes and waited for the moon to come up. I thought that wherever Mom was, she'd be looking at the same moon.

A path wound from the end of the street down to the stampede grounds. I always cut through there on my way to school, though it took me longer. Mornings, leaving the Edwards' house, the fresh air was a balm, the nowhere between house and school a sanctuary of dirt, weeds and wind. I took my time. Escape ran through my mind like a melody. I picked up snatches without really noticing. Kicking a clod of dried manure, I thought horses would be perfect for packing gear through this country, covering some distance. I never thought of a destination, except back. I could picture her smiling when she saw us, trying not to, trying to hide how proud she would be that we had done it, we had found her.

When I tried to fit Cinnamon into the picture of Mom working in a logging camp, the uneasiness I carried constantly billowed up in my body and I thought I might vomit or my legs give way. A cat in a logging camp wouldn't last long. She would be dragged off by a coyote or, with her white fur, picked from the night by an owl or a hawk.

At school, Mrs. Wallace, the teacher of the split grade six and seven class, had decided that I was an exemplary student, and she had taken to reading out my descriptive paragraphs to the rest of the class and singling me out for special jobs like writing on the chalkboard. It must not have occurred to her that this would make my classmates even more suspicious than they already were of the new girl who carried her books in a paper bag and whose running shoes were stained with mud and grass.

The other student she often singled out was a Carrier boy named Vern George. He was in the seventh grade. Vern kept his head down. He had white North Star running shoes with blue stripes, but one of his laces was a piece of twine. This intrigued me. Mrs. Wallace liked to ask him, "Vern, are we keeping you awake?" but no one laughed, the way they did when she said the same thing to Marv Dressler, the class clown. Vern smiled mildly at her. When she changed the seating arrangement so that my desk was beside his, I saw that he kept a book tucked inside his textbook. His head was down because he was reading, not frightened like I thought.

One day I was sitting on the school steps after the dismissal bell, carving a small branch with Dad's knife. I was waiting for Jenny, because we were planning to walk to Stedman's together. I had pared off the bark and was trying to carve my initials into the smooth, peeled wood when Vern came out, carrying an armful of library books. I looked up at him and then turned back to my stick.

"What are you doing?" he said.

I jumped.

He laughed, something I had never seen him do. "I scared you."

"No you didn't."

"Can I see?"

I handed him the stick. "I just started it."

He turned it over in his hands. "Cool." And he handed it back and walked down the steps and off the schoolyard. I went back to carving the stick, but lifted my eyes every now and then to watch as he disappeared at the end of the street, his arm tucked around the library books.

When Jenny came we went to Stedman's, where she bought navy knee socks and I bought grey wool work socks, then I left her at her new job at Frank's Chicken and Pizza.

At the Edwards' house, I let myself in and was surprised to find that Bea wasn't home, though the TV was on, *The Flintstones* theme song drifting from the living room. In the two months or so that we'd been here, I had never seen Bea leave the house, though she must have gone out to get groceries while we were at school. The door to her bedroom was ajar. In there was a dainty roll-top desk she called a "secretary." When Ted asked her where some paper was, her answer was almost always, "In the secretary." It was where she sat to pay bills, and if Mom had written a letter to the Edwards, that was where it would be. Maybe she had explained herself more to them.

I wondered if I had time to look through Bea's desk before she came back. Their bedroom was at the back of the house so I couldn't watch for her coming out the window, but I thought I would hear her come up the steps. I got a glass of milk and a cookie, took a bite then put it on the coffee table in front of the TV. If I heard her coming, I'd scoot out to the couch and she'd never know.

The Edwards' bedroom smelled of Yardley lavender powder and the menthol liniment Ted used. The bed had been made, the nubby white spread pulled tight and tucked under the pillows neatly. Why go to the trouble when you're only going to get back in it later? The desk was closed and my eye fell on the little keyhole. I hoped she hadn't locked it. But no, Bea Edwards had no secrets worth locking up. I stopped to listen, but I heard only Fred Flintstone's "Yabba dabba do!" and Barney's chortle. There were some bills in one compartment. I leafed through them quickly. In another, there were a few envelopes and on one of them, the Edwards' address in Mom's handwriting. But the letter inside was even briefer than the one to us: "Here's the amount we agreed on. Thanks for helping us out. Irene." I checked the front of the envelope. No return address, but over the postage stamp there was a red post office stamp that said Kleena Kleene. I put the envelope back, closed the desk and went to the couch to watch the rest of *The Flintstones*.

Out the window, I saw it was snowing, just a few light flakes straggling down, and there was Bea, coming up the sidewalk wearing her short, black fur-topped boots and a yellow woollen tam with a pompom on it. I felt a tinge of pity for her and the bland life she led.

By the time Jenny got home, there was enough snow to soak her canvas running shoes. A sharp wind had begun to sweep across town and snow eddied around the yellow porchlight. Jenny burst through the front door, gasping. "My feet are icicles!" She kicked off her shoes and stood in her knee socks, shivering over the heat register.

"Maybe school will be cancelled tomorrow," I said.

"We can always hope."

Bea called from the kitchen, "It'll be gone by morning."

"Three feet of snow on the ground in two hours and she thinks it'll be gone by morning," Jenny said to Ted.

"There's not three feet of snow," Bea called.

"Come and see for yourself." Jenny pulled the curtain wide as Bea came out of the kitchen, and she huffed in surprise to find the front steps buried. Jenny poked her in the side with her finger. "Told you," she said.

Bea actually laughed. "That's not three feet, that's drifted, that's all."

But the wind whinnied and flung snow against the window screens all night and by morning the streets of Williams Lake were plugged, the snow was still falling, and no one was going anywhere.

I tried to read one of Jenny's Nancy Drew books, *The Mystery of the 99 Steps*, but I kept drifting into sleep. I wanted to be outside.

Jenny sat with five bottles of nail polish lined up beside her on her bedspread. She started with frosty brown, carefully painted each fingernail, then blew them dry and surveyed them. "It matches my hair, don't you think?" She was happy as long as I made some kind of noise of agreement. She reached for the nail polish remover and dipped a Q-tip into the bottle.

"Jenny, you're asphyxiating me," I said.

"I didn't ask you to sit in here with me."

I left the book on the bed and went to the basement. There was a spot between the dryer and the furnace where a heating duct ended in a vent that could be opened. I opened it and sat on an old scrap of carpet with a blanket around my shoulders. Warm air blasted down on me. The small window above the dryer was drifted over and I listened as the wind whistled through the cracks and the snow shifted, piling into a peak against the glass.

I wondered if the shelter Dad and I built could still be standing. In extreme weather, Dad said, it's best to hole up and wait it out. People can die of fear, Dad told me. Once, when he was working up north, a man he knew drove his truck off a remote road in a snowstorm and got bogged down in several feet of snow in a wide ditch. There was no way he could budge and the weather was so bad, he knew he couldn't expect anyone to come along to help. Huddled in the cab of the truck, sheltered from the wind by the ditch and snow, he should have been safe. The man told Dad later that he started to worry that he was going to starve. He had visions of hot turkey dinners, gravy, warm apple pie. After about three hours in the truck, cold, but not freezing, he left the shelter of the cab and set out walking in an irrational search for food. He lost all his toes and fingers, his face was scarred by frostbite, and he nearly died.

"The last thing you need to worry about is starving," Dad had said. "It's not fun to be hungry, but it'll take a long time before you have to worry about dying from it. Shelter first, then water, fire and food."

The snowstorm raged and Beatrice's anxiety festered and bubbled in the confines of the house. She went from room to room picking things up and muttering, sometimes about the fact that Mom's monthly payment was late. I pictured her day while we were away at school and wondered how she filled it. I could only see her in a dim cavern of smelly vacuum cleaner, dirty blue carpet, freezer-burned meat, mugs of Nescafé coffee, a stack of *National Geographics*.

It used to be, when we were storm-stayed, Mom dropped her normal routine and we played games of rummy, drank sugary tea and roasted pieces of meat at the open door of the woodstove. We lit the lantern early in the afternoon; it was us against the elements and I loved the sound of the wind battering the house.

Beatrice had started in at breakfast, saying to Ted, "The bills aren't going to wait. I hope she didn't forget to send it."

Ted said, "She's not going to forget. Quit fretting about it." And he winked at me.

"Bea," Jenny said, catching the wink. "Always buzzing about something." Bea gave her a sharp look, but a smile played around her lips. I kept shovelling my corn flakes in, thinking it was amazing the things Jenny could get away with.

I came up from the basement around one o'clock, the time the mail usually arrived. I was putting my boots and jacket on near the door when Bea pushed past me, opened the door and reached her hand out into the cold, fishing in the mailbox.

"It didn't come again today," she announced.

"Of course it didn't come today. No mail came today," I said. But I couldn't manage the same light, teasing tone as Jenny had.

Bea turned on me. "Don't get smart with me, Margaret Dillon. If you think I do this for the good of my health, you've got another think coming."

Jenny had looked up from her reading. I could see her measuring how much magic her charm could work. She looked at me, then back at Bea and said, "Oh, Bea. Be honest. You'd keep us for free just for the pleasure of our company."

"One of you, I would," Bea said, and stalked away from the door.

Jenny's eyes locked on mine with an expression that was a combination of warning and apology. She had tried; I should too. I couldn't. What mechanism did Jenny use to sit there pleasantly like that? It was missing in me. I put my mittens on and left the house.

I wore a pair of snow boots that I had found in the basement a few days earlier. They were army green with thick felt liners. I'd tried them on down there by the furnace. They were too big, but I could wear two pairs of woollen socks inside them.

"Can I borrow these?" I'd asked Ted, dropping them on the living-room floor in front of him.

"Borrow them? You can have them. They're no good to me anymore."

I clumped along down the middle of the street, through the deep, powdery snow, pleased at how warm my feet were. A neighbour was out on his snowmobile, sending up a spray of snow in his wake, right in the middle of town. The storm shut down the normal order of things. If someone had to be rushed to the hospital or someone else was out of bread, no one could do anything about it.

I had stuffed my pockets with cookies, matches, a short stub of candle, my jackknife and a wad of toilet paper. I didn't bring water because I had nothing to carry it in. Dad had told me that out in the bush, people often lose their common sense. In fear, they follow stupid advice they heard somewhere, like rubbing snow on frostbitten skin or sucking the poison out of a snakebite. Across the deserted highway, with the wind snatching my breath from me, I walked face first into the storm. I thought that Dad would understand I wasn't leaving shelter, but looking for it.

I crossed the tracks and followed the river north. My hands were cold at first, but as I swung my arms, they warmed up so that they were almost hot. My face flushed warm against the biting air and snowflakes melted as they touched my skin. In the fresh snow, my footsteps went deep and I had to lift my legs high to step again. There was a smell to the snow that I loved, dry and metallic, like the taste of a smooth grey rock.

In the open grassy areas, I was pummelled by the wind. At a tall stand of cottonwoods I headed off the trail and into the bush. The trees had snow stuck to one side of their trunks. The forest was deep white, soft and quiet, except for the sound of my own sharp breathing and my pants brushing together as I walked. A few yards in, I stopped. I stood still, held my breath and listened. Nothing. No wind, no birds, no traffic noise. The snow still fell and I watched the flakes coming down, sometimes in clumps, and I thought I could hear them making a tiny muffled tinkling.

Farther along, I saw some tracks that had been lightly covered in snow. There was a fallen tree leaned against a huge fir stump and I climbed up and sat on the stump. I wasn't cold at all; if I had food, I could walk for days. People do it, people who know the bush. I could do it, too, if I learned to trap.

I climbed down and began to walk again, confidently. The brush beneath the snow had thickened and I struggled to lift my heavy boots through it. A sense of doubt crept over me and all at once I didn't know which way to go. I looked up at the sky, but everything was white, no sign of where the sun was. I thought I should retrace my steps while I could still see them. The wind was gusting stronger and already the snow was smoothing over the tracks I'd made. Just about the moment that thought hit me, I realized my hands were cold because I hadn't been moving very fast. I turned and picked my way along what I thought was my trail, but the pattern began to dissolve in front of me. Dips and indentations that looked like a trail stopped, and then nothing looked like a trail, and there was just the quiet expanse of white, dipping and rising over deadfall.

I stopped and whirred my arms around like helicopter blades, then shook out my hands to get rid of the numbness. I knew I hadn't come too far off the river trail and if I kept calm, I should be able to find my way back. The wind had been coming from behind me, so I headed into it. I tried to walk more quickly to keep warm, stumbling over hidden deadfall and brush.

Then the wind shifted and seemed to be coming from all directions and the trees looked thicker and the terrain unfamiliar, deadfall everywhere crisscrossing at knee level, almost impassable. I stopped again and listened, and this time, below the sound of the wind hissing, I heard a crunching, like an animal digging. I turned slowly in the direction of the sound and as I did, a head popped up from behind a mound of snow.

"Hey!" I called, at the same moment he saw me.

Vern George was kneeling in the packed snow at the entrance to a cave he was digging out with his mittened hands.

"Hi," I said.

"Hi," he answered. He kept digging and I watched him for a minute.

"That's a good cave," I said. I struggled over to him, and bent down to get a look inside.

"I built a better one last year," he said, without looking up. "Better snow."

"This snow is dry," I said.

He didn't answer.

"Do you know how far the trail is?" I asked.

Vern stood up and brushed the snow off his knees. "Are you lost?" He smiled and the sweetness of it startled me again.

"Not really. Maybe a bit. I've only been in this woods a few times, and there was no snow then."

"A bit lost." He smiled again and so did I, in spite of myself. "Well, it's a ways," he said.

I beat my arms against my sides, trying to pump blood into my hands. "Which way? My hands are freezing."

"It's twenty below," he said, watching my face for a reaction. I kept my eyes on his. "We better make a fire."

"I've got matches."

"If you collect some wood, I'll make a pit."

I went off, flailing my arms against the cold and broke dead branches and dry fir boughs from standing trees. When I came back with a big armload of wood, Vern had dug a nice firepit in the snow, a few feet in front of the entrance to his cave. I broke up some little twigs and made a teepee. Vern held a lit match to it and we fed it the fir boughs, then bigger pieces, till the fire was roaring and I could take my mitts off and hold my hands close to the flames.

Vern stood by the fire and, slipping off one boot at a time, held his feet to the heat.

"Where do you live?" he asked.

"In town," I said. "Where do you live?"

"With my uncle, at the trailer park up the road."

"Where are your parents?"

He shrugged and I thought it was a shrug that meant he wouldn't say, not that he didn't know.

"Me and my sister billet at these people's house in town. My mom works in logging camps."

"She does?"

"As a cook," I added, feeling like a liar. "Do you know where Kleena Kleene is?"

"Yeah, it's on the way to Bella Coola. Is that where she works?"

I shrugged.

"Where's your dad?"

"He died last year."

"I can dry your mitts," Vern said, picking up a long, forked stick out of what was left of the woodpile. I handed them over and he put one on each fork and held it above the flames. In a few minutes, steam rose from them.

"I'm going to try the cave," he said. He poked the branch with my mitts into the ground so that they hung near the fire. I watched him crawl in, feet first.

"How is it?" I asked.

"It's great," he grinned. "Warm. You can come in if you want. There's room."

I edged in. There wasn't much room, but we weren't touching the walls.

"If we had to spend the night, we'd have to close the entrance in better," Vern said.

"And maybe make the walls thicker," I said. "In case it gets even colder."

"We'd need to find something to melt snow in for water. We could make fir needle tea."

"We'd want to find some food," I said. "If we had to stay a few days."

"If our plane went down, way back in the wilderness. No towns around for hundreds of miles."

"Then we'd have to build something more permanent. We wouldn't be able to walk out till spring. We could use pieces of the plane for things. Like a stove."

The stick holding my mittens shifted and they bent a little too close to the fire.

"I have to get my mitts," I told Vern and I crawled out. He followed me.

"Want me to take you back now?" he said.

"Sure."

We dumped snow on the fire and Vern marked his cave with a long branch. When we got back to town, it was almost dark.

"Bye," I said.

"Bye," he answered.

When I got home my face was stiff with cold and my thighs were stinging between where my jacket ended and my boots began.

"Holy moly, it's a Mag-sicle!" Jenny called as I came in the door. "Twenty-five below and she's out for a stroll."

Bea hurried to the door and helped me take my boots off. "You could freeze to death out there, you really could," she said. "I'll bring you some tea." I knelt by the heat register, thawing my limbs. Bea's kindness was as unpredictable as her rage. I accepted it, always wary.

"Where'd you hike to?" Ted asked.

"Up the river, the way you showed me."

"Come and play a game of Canasta with me. I'm about ready to go out of my gourd with boredom here."

We sat at the table and Ted shuffled the cards. Bea brought the teapot and cups.

"Your dad liked to hike around the bush, too," Ted said. "He'd go out in any weather. I met him back before he knew your mother. I was working as a faller with an outfit around Bella Coola and he came on as a bucker. Right away I could tell he was a good one. You see a lot of sunshine loggers come and go. They come in, big plans, big talkers, work harder than they need to right off the hop, something to prove, and then they peter out. A little bad weather, they're grumbling and whining. But your dad was steady. Hard-working, quiet, nothing showy. He had a feeling for the bush. You could see the ease he had there."

Ted beat me twice, then he sat back in his chair and fell asleep.

That night as Jenny and I lay in bed in the dark with the wind still humming outside, I said, "Do you think Mom is really a cook in logging camps?"

Jenny didn't say anything for a minute. "I don't know."

"She never liked to cook. And it's winter. Do they even have logging camps in winter?"

Jenny didn't answer and I turned towards the wall and pulled my blankets up.

A little while later I heard Jenny crying, trying to stifle her sobs in her pillow.

[THIRTEEN]

THREE DAYS LATER, after streets had been ploughed, sidewalks cleared, cars jump-started and windows scraped, I arrived home from school and found an envelope on the dresser addressed to us in Mom's hand. I held it to the light, smelled it, picking up a faint musty odour. Maybe this would be the letter telling us when she would come to get us and where we would go. Jenny hoped Mom would rent us a house in Williams Lake, or even an apartment in the building near Safeway. I wanted to go somewhere else, far from here. I couldn't wait for Jenny to get back from work, so I opened the letter. A twenty-dollar bill fell out. I held the letter to my nose, too. Nothing familiar.

Dear girls,

The $20 is for Maggie's birthday. I can't believe you're 12! I hope you'll buy something practical like new jeans. You needed them in the summer. You would like it here. The other night when the moon was full, a whole pack of wolves sat on a hill above the lake and sang all night long. One night I even saw a wolf down at the lake. He was crossing the ice and so was I. Jenny, I'll send you some $$ before Christmas. I hope you like Williams Lake. Be good!

Love Mom

You need practice to be able to handle disappointment, and I didn't have enough of it yet. I lay down on my bed and tried to breathe past the crushing heaviness on my chest. For some reason, I thought of Vern, pictured his lean brown hand as he held the lit match to our teepee of sticks. A flicker of comfort flared deep in my chest and was gone again.

It took about fifteen minutes for the disappointment to brew into anger.

"Do you have any scraps of denim?" I asked Bea. She was lying on the couch with her glasses resting precariously on her forehead. An open *National Geographic* lay across her chest. I didn't care if she was sleeping. Today I didn't fear her wrath.

She opened her eyes. "Denim? What for?"

"I need it to patch my jeans."

"I think I have some." She pushed herself upright with a groan. I would never get old the way she was, I thought. "Would you like embroidery thread?"

Bea found the denim and a sewing case with twelve colours of bright embroidery thread, still in their paper wrappers.

"This shows you how to do different stitches," she said, handing me an old book.

From the denim, I cut out oval patches for the knees of my jeans and over the next few days, I stitched my own design: a campfire of orange and yellow flames, brown logs and white stars of snowflakes falling above it. Bea came by once in a while to watch over my shoulder, even saying once, "You picked that up pretty quickly." As I stitched, my anger flared and sputtered and flared again, and finally formed into a kind of plan. If she wouldn't come back to us, then we had to go and find her.

This time, I found the outside envelope from Mom's letter by accident. It was lying in the kitchen garbage can and it caught my eye as I threw some orange peels in. I smoothed it and looked closely. Again there was the cancelled stamp from Kleena Kleene, but nothing else.

The first day I wore my jeans with the new patches to school, I went and sat on the swing next to Vern at recess.

"You going anywhere for Christmas?" he asked.

"No. You?"

"Maybe. I might go see my mom."

"Cool. Where does she live?"

"Nistsun Lake. Know where that is?"

I nodded. We swung in lazy half circles, our feet on the frozen ground.

"What's that on your knee?" he asked, leaning over. He didn't say anything, just tapped my knee twice with his finger and, as the bell rang, headed back to school.

After school I had two things to do. I walked over to the bank and opened an account. My first deposit was twenty dollars. Next, I went to the Esso station on the highway. Inside, there was a man on his knees arranging quarts of oil on a shelf.

"Are you the manager?" I asked.

"Who's asking?"

"Me. I'm looking for a job. I can pump gas and work the cash register and I know how to check oil and top up radiators."

"Hand me that box, will you?" He gestured to a box on the counter and I lifted it down for him.

He took a jackknife from his shirt pocket and slit open the top. "Can I trust you?"

"I billet in town here and I'm very responsible," I said.

"How old are you?"

"I'm thirteen," I lied.

He pushed himself to his feet. He had a round paunch under his Esso shirt. He stuck out his hand. "I'm Bob," he said and we shook. "I could use some help over Christmas. How about I try you out? I'll give you two weeks to show me what you can do."

"Two weeks is great!" I nodded. "I can start today if you want."

Bob looked around the store. It smelled of motor oil and chocolate bars. "Don't you have to let someone know where you are?"

"I can phone."

Just then the gas bell rang. Bob looked out at the pumps where a long Chrysler had just pulled up.

"Okay," he said. "You can start with this guy. He'll only get a couple dollars of gas but he'll want his oil checked, windshields washed, front and rear, and he might even ask you to check the air in his tires."

Vern's uncle worked for the highways and stopped at the gas station about twice a week. The first time I met him, I was filling up his tank and peered over the edge of his truck into the back. He had some bags of sand, a large folded-up tarp, rope, axes in a bucket, a shovel, a spare tire and a large wooden box locked with a latch and padlock.

"You're Maggie, aren't you?" he said, as he climbed out of the cab. Two long braids hung down the front of his plaid jacket, tapering to neat, skinny ends.

"Yes."

"I'm Leslie. Uncle Leslie, Vern's uncle. He's told me about you."

I smiled and hung up the nozzle and tightened the gas cap.

"Want me to check your oil?"

"Good idea," he said. "He says you come from Duchess Creek."

I nodded.

"Come up to the trailer sometime for dinner. I'm a good cook."

"Okay," I said. I checked the dipstick. "You're down about half a quart."

Now that I was earning my own money, I started buying some of my own food. I used the excuse that I didn't want to inconvenience Bea when I got home from work after suppertime. I stopped at Safeway and picked up canned stew, instant mashed potatoes, tins of devilled ham, and oranges. As I put the food in my basket, I liked to imagine that I was outfitting for a wilderness trip. I would need some packets of instant oatmeal and some sugar and tea. But I wouldn't buy those just yet because Bea would ask questions.

At the checkout one day someone behind me said, "Real potatoes are just about as fast." It was Uncle Leslie. He had a cart full: a big bag of flour, oats, potatoes, onions, fresh carrots, tomatoes.

"You were going to come for supper. I guess I've got to give you a day. How about tomorrow?"

"Okay," I said.

"Come with Vern after school. Make sure you ask Mrs. Edwards first."

The next day it was snowing as Vern and I walked up the hill to the trailer park. Big flakes floated in the air, caught on the wind, and seemed not to land at all.

"Uncle Leslie thinks you must be homesick," Vern said. "He's making deer stew."

"Really?" I said, so eagerly I felt embarrassed. I tried to reclaim a casual tone. "Yeah, we used to have deer stew a lot."

"Ever go hunting?"

"Not really. Not with a gun, I mean. You?"

"Yeah. But I don't really like it. I mean I like everything but the killing part. And that's supposed to be the point, right?"

The trailer was a neat white one with a bay window on one end. There was a cedar porch with two wooden loungers on it, dusted in snow.

"Come on in," said Uncle Leslie when Vern opened the door. "Leave your boots there and I'll give you a pair of moccasins to wear. The floor gets a bit cold."

The trailer smelled of stew and a hint of wood smoke. A stack of wood was piled beside a black woodstove.

"Will these fit?" Uncle Leslie held a moccasin next to my foot. "Looks about right."

I put them on. "Perfect," I said. "Thank you."

The only trailers I'd been in were the kind you pulled behind a car. This one seemed bigger than the Edwards' house.

Uncle Leslie made three mugs of hot chocolate from some packets and water from a kettle that was steaming on the little woodstove. Then he washed the spoon, dried it and put it away. I caught a glimpse of the inside of his cupboard, neatly loaded with food, boxes on one shelf, cans on another, jars of canned fruit and salmon on another. A pair of oven mitts hung on a rack by the stove, along with a ladle, spatula, slotted spoon, long fork and different-sized frying pans in a row. The knives were ranged in a block of wood on the counter, from large to small, and beside that were big jars of flour, rice, sugar, tea and coffee, all neatly labelled. On a dishtowel spread on the counter, various sizes of jars and lids, washed and with their labels removed, sat drying. On the window ledge above the sink were four potted plants. I recognized one as parsley. My eyes went to the drawers alongside the fridge. I was tempted to look inside them. The neatness, all the order and organization, was as appealing here as it was claustrophobic and repulsive at the Edwards's.

Uncle Leslie sat with us as we drank our hot chocolate. He got up once to stoke the stove.

"I got this deer we're about to eat right around Duchess Creek in the fall," he said.

I nodded and we sipped.

"Well, no rest for the wicked." He stood and carried his dirty cup to the sink.

Vern and I played cards as the smell of baking buns filled the trailer. A pungent scent of deer stew wafted up each time Uncle Leslie opened the lid of the pot. I glanced over at him, clad in an apron, with his braids tucked inside his shirt. He whistled and rattled pots and pans busily. Something sweet floated below the savoury smells.

When supper was almost ready, he called Vern to set the table.

"I'll help," I said.

"Okay, because it's a lot of work," Vern said, smiling.

Uncle Leslie set down the pot of stew, a steaming dish of spinach, roasted potatoes, a basket of fresh buns and a saucer of butter.

"Uncle Leslie thinks you eat too much junk," Vern said.

"Girls your age need iron," Uncle Leslie said. "Now take spinach, for instance. There's lots of iron in that."

"My mom used to make stinging nettle," I said.

"Oh yeah, that's even better. Takes a bit of work to get it, though."

"I used my Dad's work gloves."

"Then you need to boil it twice to get the sting out."

"Mrs. Edwards won't eat any of that kind of thing. 'Weeds,' she says. 'They could be poisonous.'"

Uncle Leslie laughed at my imitation of her voice.

"Sure," said Vern. "You'll wind up dead and then who's going to take out the garbage?"

When we were done the stew, Leslie put bowls of apple crumble and vanilla ice cream down in front of us. "I wonder what you two sound like when you imitate me," he said.

[FOURTEEN]

When the money from Mom stopped coming, we didn't know for three months. For some reason Bea had decided to keep it to herself. I can't decide now what motivated her, if she had gotten used to having us there, or if the money had become less important now that Jenny and I both had jobs. Maybe it was compassion, who knows. Stranger things have happened.

The last letter had come just before Jenny's fourteenth birthday in May. Mom wrote that she hadn't been feeling well. She didn't say where she was or what she was doing. The envelope, which I had taken from the mailbox myself, was addressed in someone else's handwriting—small, tight writing that I took to belong to a man. I couldn't make out the cancellation over the stamp, but it didn't look like it said Kleena Kleene.

I can't say it worried us that Mom wasn't feeling well. It barely registered. We took it as a thing you say as a little tidbit of news in a letter that tries to be intimate, but is really hiding something. Namely, that she wasn't coming back yet, but wouldn't say why.

Jenny pocketed the twenty dollars Mom sent. For her birthday party, she and her friends Tracy and Lila went to see *The Poseidon Adventure* at the Starlight Drive-in with Tracy's brother.

Ted and I were playing Canasta at the table when they came home, wound up, playing a game where they would only speak lines from the movie.

"Hard left!" Jenny said and steered Lila into our bedroom.

"You're going the wrong way, dammit!" Tracy said.

"That's our only chance!"

"Sail yourselves into the kitchen and have some cake," Bea called.

"She's right. That's the way out!"

They gave Ted and me a blow-by-blow of the plot as they ate the cake at the table, then they disappeared into our bedroom to drink orange pop. Later, when Jenny was giggling uncontrollably as I got ready for bed, I learned they had spiked the pop with lemon gin that Tracy's brother had given them.

By summer, Bea had things to worry about other than money. One night about an hour or so after suppertime, I arrived home from the gas station. A couple of neighbour boys squealed and hopped in and out of the sprinkler sweeping across the dry patch of sunlit lawn in front of their house. The sprinkler cast a rainbow in the air, and behind it, a man sat on the step smoking and watching the boys. He lifted his hand to wave at me and I lifted mine in return. It was a hot evening and Bea had the screen door open and a fan going in the living room, the stale hamburger grease smell floating out into the street. I didn't want to go into the hot house. I would have some supper, then go for a hike down to the river before dark.

"You're finally home!" Bea said as soon as I stepped inside.

The clean plates were still on the table.

"I was at work," I said. "I'm not late."

"Did I say you were late?" She advanced towards me, waving her dishtowel wildly. I stepped backwards; I was familiar with the winding-up Bea. She would begin shrieking any minute, and she did. "Go find Ted! I can't think what in God's name he thinks he's doing. It's not like I don't have supper on the table at the same time every night. If anyone notices, I try to provide a routine around here. Like you give a damn. You show up whenever you damn well please . . ."

Bea didn't need to tell me where to look. I walked towards the Maple Leaf Hotel, where Ted spent his days in the cave-like dimness of the smelly, windowless pub. I passed Francie's Famous Bakery, which always radiated the smell of fresh bread and reminded me of the summer in the log house at Dultso Lake. And I passed the three drunk men who hung out on the sidewalk in front of the liquor store and called me sweetheart when they asked for money.

I was still half a block from the pub when I saw him, slumped in his wheelchair by the side of the road. I assumed he was drunk, although he rarely showed any visible signs of drunkenness. Once in a while he fell asleep in the pub and the owner, Mr. MacNeil, phoned the house for me to come and get him.

"Ted!" I called.

He didn't respond. When I got close, I saw he was running with sweat. A drop of it was poised on the end of his nose, ready to fall. His eyes were only half-open.

"Ted!" I said and shook his shoulder. He winced. The drop of sweat landed on his shirt front.

"Mag," he whispered. "Better take me home."

Ted had stomach cancer.

"I told him what it would lead to," I heard Bea say to her sister on the phone. "You don't pour that much alcohol into your system without some kind of consequence." Then she started to cry, tried to poke her Kleenex up under her glasses, had to take them off. "They have him on morphine—for the pain." She said it pitifully, lingering on the word "morphine."

But Bea rose to her trouble; it enlivened her. She shredded apple and made it into puree for Ted. She boiled up beef bones, added a hash of cabbage and carrots and carried it to his hospital room in a Thermos. "They give him broth made from powder," she said disdainfully. "How is that supposed to make you healthy?"

She brought him fresh pyjamas and a stack of *National Geographics*, left them with him for a few days, then exchanged them for new ones. There was no evidence that Ted read them. He mostly kept the tiny TV a few inches from his face, and dozed in and out with the ebb and flow of morphine. But Ted reading them was not the point; Bea needed to be the model bereft wife. For her efforts, she received tender pats on the arm from the nurses at the hospital, as well as sympathetic noises from the grocery store clerk and her sister's late night phone calls. Her life finally had purpose.

I believed that my worry was a jinx. I had never saved anyone with it. Quite the opposite, it seemed that, one by one, those I cared about were slipping under the spell of my worry and being carried away. And so I was determined not to worry about Ted.

I went to see him after school. He was awake and playing solitaire on the table pulled up to his chest.

"Mag!" he said. "Sit down. I've got sweet bugger-all to do here."

"Want to play Canasta?"

"Get the other deck out of the drawer."

Ted shuffled the cards and began dealing. He looked different in the hospital bed, smaller, and older. The light blue gown tied loosely around his neck emphasized his bony collarbone, the pale blue veins of his neck and the almost translucent skin of the hollow at his throat. He had lost about thirty pounds, according to Bea's phone reports, and he was in constant pain. But today he was awake, at least.

We played, cards snapping quietly on the table. Ted shifted his position gingerly every few minutes and I saw his face twist with pain. He tried to hide it.

After a while, he said, "I can tell you what I know about your dad if you like."

I nodded.

"I met Patrick in about 1957, I think it was. He told me he came to the U.S. from Northern Ireland when he was twenty. There was some bad feeling between his father and him. His father was a drinker, I understand, and he could get pretty mean when he tied one on. Didn't work much. Sounds like they were hand to mouth, most of the time. When Patrick got old enough, he joined the RUC. Do you know what that is?"

"Dad said he was a policeman once."

"That's right. The Royal Ulster Constabulary. A kind of police force and border patrol combined. The pay was good, but there were very few Catholics. Patrick's dad was livid when he found out. They were Catholic, of course." Ted paused and laid down two more eights to make his first Canasta. "I got lucky there," he said.

"My mother's family is Irish, too," he went on. "We've got long memories, the Irish do, and we know how to hold a grudge like nobody else. I don't know where exactly your dad lived, but his father thought joining the RUC was a cop-out. Said they'd never accept Patrick, being Catholic. Patrick could do a funny send-up of him, with his Irish accent. 'You're after turning soup-taker, me own son. Never thought I'd live to see the day. Colluding with the filthy prods.' Well, I can't do it justice.

"But the thing is, Patrick said, his father was right. The little songs at first, then the taunts. One of his partners started each shift by saluting: 'For God and Ulster.' One day Patrick found something nasty scrawled on his locker. He wouldn't tell anyone about it, and for damn sure not his father. So he took his next paycheque and bought a ticket to the United States. Left without saying goodbye to anyone. He couldn't bear to tell his mother. I imagine he felt bad about that to the day he died. I suppose your mother would know that story. After he'd met your mother, he told me they had that in common: they were both orphans."

Ted had started a meld of queens, so I threw down a three of clubs to block him from taking the discard pile. I knew Dad had come from Ireland; he had a lilt in his voice that his friends teased him about. But he rarely talked about it.

"Living in such a sensible place as this, it's hard to imagine the bitterness back there. Families turning against their own. And that was in the good times. Now, well, your dad didn't live to see Bloody Sunday. What am I going to discard here?

What's going to do the least damage?" He threw down a nine of hearts and I took the pile.

He picked up Dad's story again. "In New York, he met up with a guy going to Oregon. Patrick went along. That's where he learned to log."

Ted exhaled a long slow sigh and I thought he was about to tell me something I wouldn't want to hear. My stomach contracted in readiness. But he reached for the buzzer to call the nurse instead and then sat back against his pillow and closed his eyes. He let his cards fall on the table, face up; I pushed back my chair and went for the door just as the nurse was coming in.

Ted whispered he was sorry and I sat with him for half an hour, as he sank into the relief of the morphine. Then I put the decks away in the drawer and slipped out.

[FIFTEEN]

THAT FALL, AS TED LAY dying in the hospital with tubes poking out of him, Vern and I built a tree fort in the bush. Vern found scrap lumber around the trailer court and I brought hammers, nails and a saw from the Edwards' basement. We built a platform between three aspens. Each time we went there and sat back in the lemony light of the fragrant trees surveying our work, we thought of something new to add: a wall to lean against, a window, a rope ladder, then a real ladder. We didn't need a roof because the leaves of the aspens formed a golden canopy that flapped around us like tiny flags in the breeze. In the sun, the leaves flipped and tossed patterns of light on the rough floor of our fort. Even in the slushy fall rain, we were protected; the wet flakes pattered a rising and falling song against the leaves. Eventually, if we stayed long enough, we would get wet, but it was worth it to be inside that sound.

"If you were blind," said Vern, "I bet you could learn the names of trees just by listening to how they sound in the wind."

An eagle hovered, then landed on a fir snag near our fort. He was a regular. Vern and I had watched him a few times.

"My grandma says that if you call someone's name when an eagle is near, that person will hear you, wherever they are."

"Ted!" I called.

Vern joined me. "Ted! Ted! Ted!"

The eagle lifted his giant wings and rose with a rush of air. We watched as he cruised towards the hill where the hospital was. Vern and I grinned at each other.

When the leaves had all gone from our fort, we hammered planks into place for a partial roof to keep the wind off. We still went after school when I didn't have to work, and put our backs to the wall where we could catch the last of the sun.

"How's Ted?" Vern asked one Friday.

"Hanging on. Or so says Beatrice." I drawled her name. I had no real idea how Ted was. He was doped up now most of the time I visited, which Bea said was because they'd upped his dose of morphine.

"Do you know how to braid?"

"Sure. I braid Jenny's hair sometimes."

"I want to braid my hair."

"It's almost long enough. We can practise with some twigs." I pulled out my pocket knife. "We need three skinny twigs."

"What about practising on you?"

I met Vern's eyes. He was smiling. "My hair isn't long enough," I said, smiling back.

He slipped down the rope ladder that we still used even though we'd built the sturdy wooden one, and found three small green shoots. He scrambled back up into the fort.

"Okay, it's really easy." I set the twigs on the boards in front of me. "You cross this one over the middle one. Then this one over that one. Then you just keep going." My fingers moved down the twigs till they were braided into a coarse braid.

"We need something smaller."

We untied the shoelaces from both of Vern's runners and one of one mine and I showed Vern how to make a nice, even braid. I untied it and he practised with the shoelaces till he had the method down.

"This is a cinch," he said. "But can you do it in my hair?"

"Barely," I said. "Your hair really needs to get a little longer."

Vern fished in his jeans pocket and pulled out a fine, black comb. He handed it to me. I positioned him in front of me and set the comb gently into his hair. Ravens cawed raucously from the woods and burst out of the trees in a fury of black wings, fighting over something.

I lifted the comb and started at his forehead, working gently.

"Your hair is thick."

"Yeah."

As I smoothed Vern's hair, the warmth of his back heated my legs where he rested against me. A shampoo scent wafted from him.

"Stop moving," I said, and held his shoulder. It was warm and solid.

"Ever think about going to see your mom?"

"My mom? I think about it," I said. "I don't know where she is right now."

"I thought she was cooking in a logging camp near Kleena Kleene."

"I don't think she's there anymore. She'll write to us soon and tell us where she is."

"I think I'll go see my mom," Vern said. "I'm free to go whenever I want."

I divided his smoothed hair into three and began braiding, pulling it close to keep it tight.

"Is it working?" he asked.

I laughed. "It'll be short, but it'll be a braid."

We heard a high whistle above us and Vern pointed to the eagle, cruising in on a wide circle. It landed on top of the fir snag and looked out over the trees as if it were deliberately ignoring us. Vern twisted around to meet my eyes and he was smiling.

"Hey, quit moving. I'm not done," I said.

"That's a good sign, you know," he said. "I think it means it's good that I'm braiding my hair in the Indian way."

"Give me your shoelace," I said.

"My shoelace?"

"I need to tie it."

He handed it over and I tied his braid.

"Cool." He swung his head and touched the braid gently. "I hope it stays in."

"Braid it when your hair's wet. That's what Jenny does."

We watched the eagle lift off and ride a thermal high above the trees. I thought that this eagle could also be a sign for me, but I didn't mention it to Vern. Maybe it was a sign that Ted was getting better. Or maybe my mother had heard me say her name. Maybe she had been cutting onions in some makeshift shack of a kitchen, and her eyes had begun to run with tears. Maybe at that moment the knife had stopped, resting against the cutting board, and she had looked up, listening for my voice. But then I remembered that "Mom" was not her real name. If I called to her, I would have to call her Irene.

"I'm going to hitch to my mom's place tonight," Vern said suddenly. "Do you want to come?"

"Tonight? Bea won't let me go, I know that."

"So don't ask her. I'm not telling Uncle Leslie. I'll just go."

"I don't know," I said. I was worried about leaving Ted, but I didn't want to be worried. I was not supposed to be worrying. "Not the best hitchhiking time of year."

"True. Well, I might go," he said. "I'll have to see."

On Monday, Vern was at school. He hadn't hitched anywhere after all. But having the plan was important, I knew that. My birthday was a few days away. I had hoped a letter might come from Mom, but nothing did and even Bea let that pass without comment. Jenny baked a chocolate cake and drew a big "13" on it in yellow icing. She studded the cake with thirteen yellow candles. I blew out the candles in the kitchen with the lights off and then Bea flicked on the fluorescent light above the sink, put her hands on her hips and sighed, "Well!"

"Open your present," Jenny said, clapping.

Unwrapping it, I felt a wave of nausea; this moment was not right, could not be right without Mom and we all knew it.

"Moccasins," I said. "Thanks." They were fur-trimmed slippers, with a shimmery flower beaded on each one. I held them to my nose and smelled the smoky tanned hide.

"Do you like them? Vern's uncle got them for us from a lady on the reserve," Jenny said.

"They're great," I said. And I meant it, but I couldn't keep that disappointed sound out of my voice.

"Cake!" said Jenny. "Who wants ice cream?"

Two days later I was at the gas station, my parka hood laced tight around my face against the cold wind. I filled Mrs. Gustafson's truck, peering over the edge of the box as I usually did—two bags of sand, spare tire, a length of chain. I saw Jenny hurrying across the highway towards me with her nylon-stockinged legs and white runners, her coat tossed on unbuttoned over her Frank's Chicken and Pizza uniform.

Her face was red with the cold. "Ted's dead," she said and I couldn't believe that we both smirked at the rhyme. "No, but he is, Mag, he died about an hour ago. Bea wants us to come home."

I tightened the gas cap on Mrs. Gustafson's truck. Jenny and I looked at each other for what seemed like a long time. "I'll come home after work," I finally said.

"You sure?"

I nodded.

"Okay, then. I'm going to go home now." She wrapped her coat tighter around herself and turned to walk away. She hesitated. "You . . . you know. Be careful or whatever."

"What?"

"I don't know." She looked around the gas station. "Don't light any matches or anything." Then she ran off, the wind gusting so hard, it made a part in the back of her thick, dark red curls as she leaned against it.

I took the twenty Mrs. Gustafson handed me, rang it into the cash register and brought her back the change. Standing on the pump island with the wind whipping at me, I watched the wheels of her truck as she drove away.

After the funeral, Jenny said, "That was our third thing. And it's not that bad. I mean, I'm sorry he's dead but I'm not that sorry. I didn't know him enough to be that sorry. Well, you did I guess, so it's worse for you. But my point is, our third thing is an easy one. And now we're free and clear."

She waited for me to say something. We were in our room taking off our good clothes. Beatrice had bought us both black skirts and sweaters and leotards. They had not been washed yet, and the new smell mingled with the sweat that flowed from being corralled in a church hall, surrounded by strangers who seemed to think we wanted their sympathy.

"We should look for her," Jenny said.

"She's the mother. She should look for us." I said it without thinking, but later I thought I must have been saving it up for a long time for it to have come out like that.

Jenny said, "For a girl, you're sure an asshole."

[SIXTEEN]

THAT SPRING, AS THE meltwater trilled from the eaves and the smell of wet, bare earth rose on the night air, I sat doing my social studies homework on the bed. Bea was in the kitchen, on the phone with her sister.

"It's not the money now," I heard her say. "I've got enough from Ted's pension. But we haven't heard a thing for months. It's like she's dropped off the face of the earth."

A silence.

"I don't know anyone who knows her. It was Patrick that Ted knew. I'm not a mother, but . . . ." Her voice dropped to a murmur, which was followed by another long silence.

The meltwater ran from the eaves, making a prolonged note. My blue pencil crayon scratched a low accompaniment as I coloured Hudson Bay on my map of Canada. Eventually all the snow would melt, and the note would change then die out.

Bea's voice rose. "It may be that. Anything could have happened, I suppose." Dropped again, too low to hear. Then: "It's not like that up here. Not if you don't want to be found."

Bea could talk for hours. She'd circle around and around and alight on fruitless little thoughts, like the bee of Jenny's nickname. I turned on the radio Jenny had bought for herself. Elton John was singing "Crocodile Rock" and I turned it up. A couple of minutes later I heard the clump, clump of each of Jenny's shoes as she kicked them off at the front door. She opened the bedroom door and brought the fresh spring air in with her. And something else. The skunky scent of pot smoke.

She tossed her books on her bed, then threw back her head and launched into the la-la-la-la-las.

"Where were you?" I demanded.

A quick knock on the door and Bea came in. She would do that, knock, but not give us time to answer before she barged in.

"Where were you?" Bea's tone was more playful than mine.

"I was out with Brian. We went to Rudy Johnson Bridge and watched the ice floating by on the river." She was glowing, her cheeks a fiery red.

"Crazy," said Bea, wiping her weepy eye. "Watching ice melt. Not exactly my idea of a great date."

"I didn't say we were watching it melt," Jenny laughed. "I'm freezing, though. I want a hot bath."

"Oh my! Freezing for love," said Bea and let her eyelashes flutter and rolled her eyes heavenward. "I'll run it for you."

I was surprised she didn't comment on the scent in the room. Could she really not have noticed it?

"I hope you're not forgetting about your homework," I said after Bea had gone. "It's nine thirty."

"What are you, my mother now?"

I hated the sound of my own voice, the tight, needy worry. But Brian was a liability to me, to my plan. If I had thought about it then as I do now, I would have realized that Jenny being happy was a liability. I could not have her behave as if our lives were normal, as if we weren't the people adults felt sorry for and for whom voices dropped to cluck and murmur over. I didn't want their sympathy, but I needed Jenny to be aware of herself as an object of pity. Self-pity is supposed to come naturally to fifteen-year-olds. But it didn't to Jenny. Jenny was sunny; she was sweet; she was happy.

Vern and I were out on the highway, heading west. The moon was a pale wafer, brightening by degrees in the dusky sky. Before us, the road opened up, spun out to the horizon, a flat, dun ribbon cut through dry brown fields. Spring in the Chilcotin and everything was still brown, waiting. It might rain. It might rain tonight. A bank of clouds was piling up, purple on grey on navy blue.

We walked, Vern with a small duffel bag slung on his shoulder like a hobo. I had nothing—only my soft blue and black flannel jacket, pockets stuffed with Kleenex, Dad's pearl-handled jackknife, four Fig Newtons and some wooden matches. Frog song filled the air, rising and falling in waves. All along the road, their chorus rose up, then dropped as they heard our footsteps crunching in the gravel. As we passed they took it up again, trilling high and urgent and joyful.

I didn't care that only two cars had passed us in an hour. I didn't care that as the first one drew closer, we hesitated over who should stick their arm out or if we both should and whether the thumb really needed to be crooked into a hook like we were trying to catch a car instead of signal it. We both broke down laughing and I nearly peed myself and had to run for the cover of some bushes. The next one, a pickup loaded down with hay, slowed before we'd even recovered from the first. The driver, wedged in tight with three other passengers in the cab, lifted his hands from the wheel in apology and drove on.

A giddiness had risen in my chest, like the frog song. I was happy. Happy that my running shoes were crunching along this wide-open road beside Vern, happy that my jacket was warm, that dew was settling on the fields and a pungent smell of spring perfumed the dusk.

My shoulder bumped Vern's. "Sorry," I said.

"Watch where you're going, will ya!" he said. "Do you want to get me killed? Look at this traffic screaming by! It's a death race out here."

Just then a pair of headlights bobbed over a rise and we broke down laughing again.

"No, come on Maggie, get serious," said Vern. He dug out his flashlight, straightened and watched the approaching vehicle. "We need a ride or we'll never get to Nistsun tonight." I fell in behind him and we both stuck out our arms, then he turned to assess my hitchhiking form. He nodded approval, faced the approaching lights again. At the same moment, both our thumbs popped up.

The car sped towards us, kicking up gravel. "Do they see us?" I asked. Vern shook his flashlight; the light kept cutting out. Only a murky wash of daylight remained. I edged over to the grass, afraid of being creamed. The car swerved violently to the side of the road and slid to a stop just past us. Led Zeppelin's "Rock and Roll" blared from the open windows. As the dust settled, a pale-faced boy with a shaggy blonde haircut draped himself out the passenger-side window. He dangled his arms against the dirty door panel. "Hey, you guys need a ride, man?"

"Yeah," said Vern, stepping forward.

"Where you going?"

"Nistsun Lake."

"Nistsun?" The pale boy exploded into giggles. "Shit. You got a ways to go."

The driver leaned over and called, "We're going as far as Duchess Creek." Vern and I bent to look at him. He took a long swig from a mickey of rye, sat back and wiped his mouth. "I think," he added. They both broke up giggling again. The mention of Duchess Creek made my heart leap. But I wasn't going anywhere with those guys.

"You can clear a space in the back there," the driver said when he caught his breath. The car was a black Mustang fastback, the backseat littered with 8-track cassettes, balled-up clothes and blankets and crumpled chip bags.

Vern looked at me.

"I think I'd rather walk," I said, and I didn't whisper it.

That set the pale one off again. His laughter turned to coughing and choking and he slapped the dashboard. The driver hesitated, unsure if he should be insulted or not, then started laughing himself. He had a high-pitched girlish giggle and Vern and I couldn't help laughing, too.

"She's honest!" howled the pale one. "You gotta give her that! She's honest!"

"You sure?" asked the driver, putting it into gear. "It's a long walk . . ."

Vern waved them off.

"You sure? Last chance!" the pale one shouted out the window as they fishtailed off down the road.

Vern put the flashlight under his chin. It lit up his face. "Margaret, Margaret," he said, in a pretty good imitation of Beatrice. "You're such a rude girl. That was a minty-cool car, too."

We heard a low rumbling and thought another car was approaching. But it died down a bit, then grew louder and closer.

"Thunder!" we both said at the same time. I looked up and the white face of the moon was half-hidden by boiling clouds.

"We're gonna get wet," Vern sang quietly.

Thunder split the air with a terrifying crack. A quick

white flash lit up Vern and me and the ribbon of road. He grabbed my arm.

"Come on. Let's walk faster," he said.

I laughed. "What's that going to help?"

"The faster we walk, the less drops can hit us."

"That's not true. If anything, it's just the opposite."

"Let's just hurry," he said.

"You're scared!"

The thunder rumbled again, then exploded right overhead, shaking the ground. Vern screamed and started running down the road. I was laughing so hard I could barely keep up. His scream trailed behind him and as big drops of rain began to fall, he flailed his arms theatrically.

"Whose idea was this anyway?" I shouted.

"Who was too good to take our one and only ride?" Vern shouted back.

"A little rain isn't going to kill us."

"Maybe not. But I'm worried about getting hit by lightning." Vern was loping along the road sideways now, in big scissor strides. "If we were in that car, we wouldn't have to worry. Rubber tires."

"We wouldn't have to worry because we'd be in the ditch! Nice and low."

I caught up to Vern and we slowed to a walk. The rain bucketing down chilled us through. Beyond the roadside all we could see was thick, murky blackness. We had no idea how far we were from any kind of shelter. If we could find a fir tree, with low drooping branches, it would be dry enough under there. And we could put some boughs on the ground to sit on, in case the rain ran in. But we'd have to worry about the lightning. I couldn't see getting a fire going in this downpour. Right now a gas station or a restaurant sounded a lot more appealing. Vern and I walked closer and closer together till we were bumping elbows and apologizing repeatedly.

The thunder was moving away from us when I heard another rumbling.

"I think this time it's a car," I said.

Sure enough, we could see the points of light, far away and blurred through the rain.

"They won't see us," Vern said, but he flicked his flashlight on anyway and pointed it in that direction. It cut out, he shook it, it came back on, flickering wanly. The car came towards us slowly. Round headlights. High. A truck. It drove along cautiously. The flashlight cut out again and when Vern shook it, it wouldn't come back on.

"Great," he said.

"It's a truck," I said out loud. We waved our arms as it came closer.

"Ford," said Vern. "That's Uncle Leslie's truck."

"Oh." As it pulled up beside us, I asked him, "Are you in trouble?"

Vern laughed.

Uncle Leslie leaned over and rolled down the steaming passenger window. "Well, if it isn't two drowned rats."

I looked at Vern. I was secretly overjoyed to see Uncle Leslie. Vern pulled open the door.

"Want to sit in the middle?" he asked me.

"Sure, okay," I said, trying to keep the enthusiasm out of my voice.

"I better turn some heat on, eh?" said Uncle Leslie. "You two are about as wet as you can get. I'm going to have to wring my truck out tomorrow."

Vern slammed the door and we were inside. The heat was blowing and the radio played "Heartaches by the Number." A big shiver overtook me.

Uncle Leslie shook his head, back and forth, as he made a wide U-turn on the road.

"Anytime you want to go to Nistsun Lake, I'll take you. But not tonight." Then he said to me, "Beatrice called. Well, first your sister did, then Bea got on the line. She's not too happy with you." He laughed. "That there is what you call an understatement."

I nodded, but didn't say anything. I just wanted to ride along in the truck, the wipers slicing the rain across the windshield, fiddle on the radio moaning in time.

We drove east, the rain still coming down hard, back to Williams Lake.

Uncle Leslie pulled up in front of his trailer. A yellow bug light burned outside. He said to me, "I have a little piece of advice for you. Gained over years of experience. Phone home and tell Bea you're safe and you're going to camp out on the couch here tonight. I'll take you home in the morning. She'll still be mad tomorrow, but not like she is tonight."

He held his hand on the key in the ignition and looked at me.

"Thanks," I said and smiled. He switched off the truck and killed the lights.

"Okay, let's go find some towels."

I dripped a puddle on the kitchen linoleum as I made the phone call. Jenny answered.

"Mag, you're dead," she said simply.

"Don't exaggerate," I said.

"No, Bea, I told you! Put that butcher knife away! What did you say, Maggie?"

"Jenny, tell her I'm going to stay at Vern's. His uncle will bring me home in the morning."

"You don't want to talk to her?" Jenny asked sweetly.

"No."

"Well, she doesn't want to talk to you either. She's too busy sharpening her axe." I heard Bea say something in the background. I couldn't help smiling. I knew this was Jenny's way of telling me it was okay.

"You're crazy," I told her. That was my way of thanking her.

It was dim in the trailer, just a warm orange glow cast from the coloured globes of a pole lamp by the couch. I found a rag under the sink and wiped up the puddle I had made. Uncle Leslie handed me a fluffy yellow towel, a pair of Vern's jeans, a soft flannel shirt and wool socks.

"You can use the bathroom," he said.

In the bathroom, I stripped off my clothes and rubbed my chilled body with the towel. I could feel the welcome heat returning, more intense the way it is after you've been wet and cold. I rubbed my hair and put on the warm, dry clothes. In the living room, Vern sat wringing out his skinny, wet braid. Uncle Leslie brought us hot chocolate studded with mini marshmallows. We all gazed through the window of the woodstove at the crackling fire inside. I suppose that our night had been ruined, our adventure scuttled, and maybe Vern was angry, but he didn't look it. He blew on his hot chocolate and took a sip. I thought that I would have to keep it secret that this had been the perfect end to a perfect day and I hadn't felt so happy in a long, long time.

Uncle Leslie spoke calmly. "It's hard not to have your mother with you. That's the way it is with some families. Lots of different reasons. It's not easy for you. A father gone, that's different. We learn to live with that. But your mother, that's a kind of ache that won't go away. I know how that is."

He sipped his hot chocolate. "You have to be strong for yourself. Talk to her in your mind. Tell her how you feel. Don't think it's because of something you did. It never is."

Vern and I both watched the fire and sipped our hot chocolate. The silence was not awkward. After a while, Uncle Leslie said, "Get many rides?"

"The only one who stopped, Maggie turned down."

"Why was that?"

"The guy was drunk," I said. "I wasn't getting in that car."

"Good for you! Good for you!"

"She said, 'I'd rather walk.' So polite, right to his face." Vern tossed his head back and laughed.

"You'll go far, Maggie," Uncle Leslie said, draining the last of his hot chocolate and getting up. I wasn't sure what he meant, but his words stayed with me and I would summon them sometimes, later, when I felt the need of them.

We did go to visit Vern's mother, Jolene. It was in May, about a month after our hitchhiking fiasco. Vern invited me to go along, one night when I was at his place for supper and we were doing dishes afterward.

"We're going to Nistsun Lake next weekend," he said. "Do you want to come?"

"To see your mom?"

"You'd like her. She's nice."

"I'll have to trade shifts with someone."

"And make sure Beatrice says it's okay," Uncle Leslie said, coming into the kitchen.

We headed out on a sunny Saturday morning. At Duchess Creek Uncle Leslie said, "Your old stomping grounds, eh Maggie? We'll stop and get some cold drinks here."

"Maggie Dillon," Uncle Leslie said to the man behind the counter as he handed me my Orange Crush. "She used to live in Duchess Creek."

"That right?" said the man. "Me and my wife just bought the place. We lived in Quesnel before this."

We got back in the truck and we drove right by the driveway of our old house. The yard looked overgrown and deserted.

"Do you know where Kleena Kleene is?" I asked.

"It's about two hours up the road. But there isn't much to it. I'll point it out to you."

Later, when Uncle Leslie slowed and said, "That's Kleena Kleene," all I saw was an old log house close to the road with a post office sign on the wall. There were no more houses, just rail fence stretching all along the gravel road, beyond that the forest, then mountains. I wanted to say something to Uncle Leslie, but I was embarrassed. How could I not know where my own mother was? It seemed to me that the adults we knew kept quiet because they understood something that Jenny and I didn't want to admit—that Mom didn't want to be found.

When we got to Vern's mother's house on the reserve, she opened the door and pulled Vern to her.

"Hey," she said, rocking him back and forth in her arms. She looked at Uncle Leslie and me over Vern's shoulder and smiled, but I could see her eyes tearing up. "You've got a braid," she said, touching it gently. "You're getting so big. You're as big as me already."

Actually, he was bigger. Jolene was a small, delicate woman and young, younger than my mother. Everything about her was slim and compact, like a doll. As she hugged Vern, I noticed her slender fingers and her perfect fingernails, painted a rosy pink. When she released him, I saw her face—small, heart-shaped with skin as smooth as cream. Her black hair was cut in a pixie style and her eyebrows were perfectly arched and thin. She wore frosted pink lipstick to match her nails and a pink and white gingham blouse, tied at the waist above slim white jeans.

Jenny would have loved the look of Jolene. Even her feet. Dainty little bare feet in open-toe pink slippers. I was in my navy blue and black flannel jacket, patched Lee jeans and dirty runners.

Jolene ushered us in. I started to take off my runners.

"Oh, no! Don't worry about that," she said. "Your feet'll be black. This place gets like Grand Central Station."

Vern and I sat on the couch as Jolene poured coffee for Uncle Leslie. A man came out from one of the bedrooms. He was a big white man, over six feet and muscular, wearing a tight black muscle shirt with faded print on the front that read Jim's Towing above a picture of a cartoon woman wearing a bikini.

"Lester!" he boomed.

"Jim," Uncle Leslie acknowledged. I could tell right away he didn't like the man.

"Coffee?" Jim scoffed. "It's four o'clock in the goddamn afternoon. Way past Miller time."

"Watch your language," Jolene said pertly and gestured towards Vern and me.

"What'd I say? Christ! I gotta watch my language in my own house now?"

Jolene carried a tray over and set it in front of Vern and me—on it were pickles and buns with salted meat in them. Vern's leg bounced in impatience. Then his cousins came in and crowded around the couch.

"Come and see my car," one of them said.

We all tramped across the reserve to the edge of the bush where a car sat on several stout logs. Three girls joined us, one about my age and the other two younger. Sharman, the owner, pulled off a canvas tarp. The Beaumont was sleek and gold. It had no tires and no roof, so it gave the illusion of a boat, waiting for the water to rise. Sharman climbed in behind the wheel. "You two get in the front," he said to Vern and me. Everyone else climbed in the back or perched on the hood.

"It's going to be cool when it's done. Look at the upholstery. It's like factory," Sharman said.

"Cool," said Vern. "Where'd you get it?"

"Guy over at Redstone."

We relaxed into the car, the afternoon sun heating us. I leaned my head back against the seat and closed my eyes. A dog barked and some kids shouted and voices murmured in the car. I wondered why Vern didn't live here. He'd never told me the reason. His mother seemed nice and she lived in a house with two or three bedrooms.

A boy named Lawrence, Sharman's younger brother, said, "We have to come back tonight when it's dark and see if we can see the ghost."

"What ghost?" said Vern.

"Don't you know about the ghost?" said Lawrence. "Man, you've been away too long."

"Tell him about the ghost," said Sharman, and some of the other kids said, "Yeah, tell the story."

"I don't like that story," said the littlest one and one of the girls said, "Don't worry, Normie. I won't let it get you."

"My uncle told me about this story," Lawrence began. "It happened before I was born. Not too long before, though. Lots of people on the reserve still remember. There was these two brothers. One was real handsome—tall, slim, muscular. He wore a white silk scarf tied at his neck and a cowboy hat. Had cheekbones like a woman. He was a charmer, could tell jokes that'd make anybody forget the bad stuff they were worried about. All the women loved him. His name was Louis.

"His brother, Henry, was pretty much the opposite, kind of a porky fella, but good hearted and real quiet, real shy. He played guitar like some kind of Spanish angel. People say when Henry played, the animals all stopped what they were doing, moose held their heads up listening, owls stopped hooting and eagles lost the field mice they were hunting and everything just stood still. Which is all well and good but he couldn't do much else. He wasn't no hunter and he wasn't no cowboy either. And of course Louis was both. And a logger. Louis excelled at any kind of physical work you could throw his way. He was the best rider, never broke a bone, and he was a crack shot. He could bag a deer with a .22, just perfect aim and pow, down. Louis was the kind of guy that women wanted for a husband."

"I don't like the next part," little Normie said.

"Shhh."

"Sit still. Quit rocking the car!"

"Now, Louis had a girlfriend," Lawrence resumed. "The prettiest girl this side of Williams Lake, and probably all the other sides, too. I never saw her, but I heard she had lo-ng hair as black as a raven's wing, right to her ass." Everyone laughed. "And her eyes sparkled like summer stars and she had a step as light as a fawn. Her name was Etoile, which, in case you don't know, means star in French. They say her mother was a Métis from the Prairies and she gave her that pretty name the moment she saw her sparkling eyes. Etoile and Louis weren't exactly married but they lived together like husband and wife in Louis's little cabin in the bush. It was just over there. If you walk in about half a mile, you can find the stone foundation in the grass. The stones have been blackened by fire, but that comes later."

"No! Don't tell that part!" wailed Normie.

"That comes later, Normie. You can plug your ears."

"Tell me when it's coming, okay?"

"Shh!"

"Louis left Etoile alone for long stretches when he went off to work. He loved her, there's no doubt about that. But he couldn't stay put for long. He liked to be off, being praised for climbing the tallest spar-tree, or rounding up the most wild horses, or guiding tourists on the best bear hunt. That was Louis. So Etoile stayed alone and sometimes when Henry had nowhere else to go, he visited with her and he played that angelic Spanish guitar. That didn't bother Louis any. He was glad Etoile had the company.

"One winter when the snow was deeper than this car, deeper than the roof of that house over there, and Louis was out looking for horses to bring back to someone's ranch, Henry put on some snowshoes and strapped on his guitar and hiked out to see how Etoile was getting on. That was hard going, seeing's how he was kind of porky, as I said. But he worried about her, maybe the way Louis should have. They say Henry had to dig down in the snow to get to Etoile's door. She was okay in there. She'd bagged herself a deer and she had a good stew going on the stove, though her woodpile was getting low.

"Some people say that Etoile fell in love with Henry, plain and simple, even though he was kinda porky and couldn't hunt worth a damn. Some say that that night while he played his guitar, the northern lights came down and touched that little cabin and enchanted the two of them. That cabin wasn't very big. They ate the deer stew and Henry played by the fire and the wind raged outside and jack pines in the woods split like thunder in that cold winter night. You can imagine what else happened," said Lawrence, and everyone laughed again.

"The next day, Louis came through that deep snow on a half-wild cayuse and dug down through the snow to get to the door, a little worried since he hadn't been home in over three weeks. Henry and Etoile didn't hear a thing. They were still sleeping off their night and when Louis pushed in the door he found them in bed, in each other's arms.

"Nobody knows exactly what was said and who said it. But Etoile gathered up her things and got on the half-wild cayuse and rode away and nobody ever saw either her or the horse again. As for the brothers, Louis opened up the first bottle in the case of whisky he'd brought home and they drank that. By the time they reached the bottom of that bottle, Louis was laughing a little. And halfway through the second bottle, he said, 'What the hell!' But by the third both Louis and Henry were in tears and they cried and cried that they'd lost the best girl this side of Williams Lake.

"They slept a couple of days, didn't eat at all. And they began to drink again. Everything outside was as still as death, the storm over, the snow settling heavy in the woods. Something evil crept into that cabin. When Henry passed out, Louis eyed him and fingered his hunting knife and thought about how he'd do it, how he'd pierce that fat flesh and find a vein to open. Then he shook himself and took another drink and when he passed out, Henry woke up and watched his brother and hated every slick thing about him, every curve of his muscles, every long black eyelash, each strong-boned finger. He eyed Louis's rifle and thought about where he'd bury him. That night, blind drunk, hate as thick as greenwood smoke filling up the cabin, the brothers made a pact."

"Plug your ears, Normie," said the girl beside him.

"Oh, no!" Normie cried and slapped his hands over his ears.

"They made a suicide pact. Each one would aim their rifle at the other's neck and when they counted to ten, they'd shoot the other dead. They could barely stand up. They stood only about five feet apart, swaying and leaning. They took aim and started to count. At four, Henry said, 'Wait, wait, I got my safety on.' So they started over.

"They got to three and Louis said, 'Wait. Are we shooting <u>at</u> ten, or just after?'

" 'What's the difference?' Henry said.

"'Big difference,' said Louis. 'One of us is dead, the other one's still standing there holding his gun like a dick.'

"'Okay, we shoot at ten. Right at ten. Say it, then POW.'

"'Say it, *then* pow?'

"'Yeah, say ten, then shoot.'

"'Ten then pow."

"'Ten then pow. Right. Got it?'

"They started counting again. This time there were no mistakes, except at the last second, Louis lost his nerve and knocked the barrel of his brother's gun away. His own went off. He shot Henry dead. Henry's bullet hit Louis in the left shin. Louis passed out. In the morning, he woke up and found his brother still dead. He put him in the bed and covered him up, then he set that cabin on fire, burned it to the ground."

Everyone in the Beaumont was quiet. "Holy shit," I said. "Is this a true story?"

"Can I unplug my ears?" Normie sang out. The girl took his hands and lifted them away from his head.

"It's true," said Sharman, and everyone nodded.

"Louis took off deep into the bush and lived as a hermit for a while. Then one winter someone came across a camp he'd made and found him hanging from a tree, frozen solid. But he haunts the bush out here. You can hear moaning and whisky bottles rattling and smell the fire sometimes. And when the northern lights are out, you can hear music, that Spanish angel music that Henry played on his guitar."

"I know what happened to the girl," the oldest girl spoke. "My aunt was married to her cousin. She said Etoile hitch-hiked all the way down the coast to Mexico. She ended up in a town as far south as you can go and still be in Mexico. A family of Germans took pity on her and took her in. Their daughter had just died in childbirth and so they gave the baby to Etoile to raise. Eventually, she became just like a mother to that child."

Twilight had fallen and the air had turned cold. "I'm hungry," said Vern.

"Come back later tonight," said Lawrence. "We might hear the ghost."

For supper Jolene had made roast beef and scalloped pota-toes and peas. She put the food on the table using dishcloths to keep from burning her hands. I watched her, and when she caught me staring, she smiled at me. Jolene talked, mostly to Uncle Leslie, about people they knew. Then she turned to Vern. "So how did you two, a boy and a girl, become friends?"

"You really gotta ask?" said Jim, leering. "I mean I can put two and two together and get four, even if you can't. A teenage boy, a pretty girl . . ."

I flushed red and hated Jim.

"It's not like that," Vern said sharply. "We're friends for the same reasons any two people are friends."

"Oh, well," Jim began.

"Leslie says you come from Duchess Creek," Jolene said to me, before Jim could say more.

I nodded.

"I have friends in Duchess Creek." Jolene began to tell a story of some people and the dog they had that had to be put down.

"They don't want to hear that," said Jim.

"Yes we do," said Vern.

"Can't you shut up?" Jolene said to Jim. "This is my son and my house. Why don't you go get drunk somewhere else?"

"Oh, so now it's your house."

"I'm going to have to get going soon," said Uncle Leslie. "It's getting dark."

"You going to turn into a pumpkin?" Jolene went to the kitchen and got a beer out of the fridge, then sat at the table sipping it, her plate of food untouched. While we ate the chocolate cake she'd made for dessert, she opened another beer and smoked two cigarettes, pressing the butts into her cold scalloped potatoes.

After supper we sat outside and more people gathered. Vern and I threw a Frisbee for the dog.

"Where are those kids sleeping tonight?" Uncle Leslie asked Jolene.

"Vern can be a gentleman and give Maggie his room," Jolene said. "He can sleep on the couch."

"No," Uncle Leslie said, and I could see he was mad. "He won't get any sleep there and you know it."

Jolene looked angry, too. "Well, we can set up the cot in my room."

"Put the cot in with Vern," Uncle Leslie said. "Is that okay with you, Maggie?"

"Yeah, it's fine," I said quickly.

"They're fourteen," Jolene began.

"It's okay," Vern interrupted. "We can put the cot in there. It's no big deal."

"There's a man who knows what he wants," said Jim.

"Shut the fuck up," said Uncle Leslie. It was the first time I'd ever heard him swear.

"All right," Jolene said and she closed her eyes and took a long drink of her beer.

"Hey," Vern said, taking me by the arm. "Let's go see the ghost."

We walked with Sharman and Lawrence and little Normie back to the edge of the bush.

"Jim's a fucking asshole," Sharman said. "I wouldn't let anybody treat my mother that way."

Vern looked at the ground and didn't say anything.

"Don't go any closer," Lawrence said. "This is close enough. Now we just have to wait."

A light breeze was blowing and we watched the trees as the evening turned deeper blue.

"He's a freeloader, too," Sharman continued. "Mr. Big White Guy. Smashed up his tow truck on a drunk one night and now he lives off a little Indian woman's welfare cheques in her house on the reserve. If you were bigger I guess you'd paste him, eh?"

"Yeah," said Vern. Then, "But she likes him. I don't get why she likes him."

"Shh. Hear that?" Lawrence cocked his head.

Something was rustling, moving through the trees. Not far away, an owl hooted.

"Means a death is coming soon," Lawrence whispered.

We stood perfectly still and listened.

"Look!" Lawrence whispered suddenly. Through the trees we could see something white moving.

"Let's go back," Normie said.

"Shh, you'll scare him off."

The white disappeared and we sat and waited till the night dew made the ground damp.

When we got back, Uncle Leslie had gone. Vern's mother was sitting on the kitchen counter holding two halves of a broken plate. Her face was loose, her features like a blurred photograph. Jim had been saying something, but stopped when we came in and said instead, "You can take it or leave it, but I see the big picture."

"The big picture," Jolene mocked, then she burst out laughing. "Come and see your old mother, son!"

"You're not old," Vern said.

"You're such a good boy. You know just the right things to say."

I said goodnight and slipped away to Vern's room just as Jolene said, "You'll always be my son. You know I love you, my son. Leslie thinks he knows better because he's my big brother but you belong with your mother."

"Boys don't want to hear that," Jim said.

"It's okay whatever she says," said Vern.

Jim laughed hard at that. I could still hear him when I closed the door. The room was crowded with boxes of clothes, an ironing board, a drying rack, shelves of fabric and an old sewing machine. The blankets had been turned back on the bed. Moonlight flooded the room and I sat on the bed watching it cast silver light on the homemade quilt. Who made this quilt? Who took the time to cut these floral pieces and set them in this pattern, four narrow strips surrounding a square? The back was soft flannel. I held it to my nose. Some dim memory fought its way to the surface, something from when I was little and my mother gave me her mother's quilt for my bed in Duchess Creek.

I climbed between the sheets with my flannel shirt still on and lay there, listening to the din in the kitchen. A few minutes later, Vern came in.

He undressed and got into the cot in the dark. We could hear the voices rising in the kitchen, then harsh bursts of laughter.

"Do you like my mom?" Vern asked through the darkness.

"She's pretty. And she's nice."

"I'm going to paste that jerk, Jim. She'd be way nicer if he wasn't around. Uncle Leslie can't stand him."

We heard a thud in the kitchen and shouts. Outside a band of coyotes took up barking at the moon.

"Do you believe about the ghost?" Vern asked.

"Do you?"

"Maybe. But there's more than just that kind of ghost. Spirits. Good ones. You might not see them, but they're there."

"Like angels?"

"Same thing," Vern said. "We've all got one on each shoulder."

"Really?"

"Sure. Maybe an animal spirit or maybe an old one who died a long time ago."

More thudding came from the kitchen and the voices grew louder, shouting. There was no more laughter. My heart was racing.

"Do you hear that?" Vern asked.

"Yeah."

"No, not the yelling. Listen. Outside. Drums."

As soon as he said it, I heard the drumming, like a heartbeat carried on the spring night. I shivered. I could feel the beat in my chest slow to match it. From the kitchen came the smashing of glass. Vern put on his pants in the moonlight and went out.

I listened, but the only thing I could follow was the drums. After a few minutes he came back and got into bed.

"She sometimes throws things when she gets mad," he said. Then he giggled. "My mom's small but she can throw a scare into that asshole when she gets going."

In the morning there was no broken glass anywhere and Jolene made us bacon and eggs and toast with homemade blackberry jam for breakfast.

[SEVENTEEN]

MONTHS PASSED AND still no word came from Mom. I was ashamed of her silence, what it meant. Jenny and I walked down to the lake, and swam with all the other kids and their families. When Lila and Tracy showed up, they all smeared themselves with Hawaiian Tropic coconut oil and smoked menthol cigarettes, practising their elegant exhales. I munched Freezies. We said nothing about her.

The stampede came to town. Teepees and tents and trailers moved in and all day dust billowed, bands played, and the announcer's voice drummed up the crowd, rising and falling over the loudspeakers. I could smell the pungent odour of horses and cattle manure coming in the bedroom window. At night music and shouts sailed out over the town from Squaw Hall, the open-air dance hall on the stampede grounds. At the end of the street where the Edwards' house was, I sat in the grass and looked down at the lights strung above the hall and heard the crash of beer bottles being thrown over the walls. One night when a band called the Saddle-ites was playing, Jenny and her friends decided to go dancing. They were all underage but no one asked questions.

Later, they snuck back in the house shaken but giddy.

"I can't believe that guy grabbed my ass," Tracy kept saying. "Next time I'm gonna get juiced before we go in there."

"No way José," said Lila. "You won't catch me going back there. Sickos grabbing your tits. I was ready to paste somebody."

"It was mental, Mag," Jenny said. "People fighting and throwing beer bottles, broken glass and beer all over the dance floor. And the band just kept playing."

I hiked the river valley with Vern, past the hoodoos and cliffs, then Vern went west to Nistsun for a while and I stayed, pumping gas for tourists on the highway. I went to rummage sales on the weekend and bought an old canvas tent that I set up in the backyard. Jenny and her friends hot-knifed hash in Beatrice's kitchen late at night with the windows open, crickets chirping and the summer breeze carrying away the smell. They giggled and made elaborate, salty snacks, BLTs and tuna melts, and I came into the kitchen at one in the morning, drawn by the aroma while Bea slept.

How could Mom not come? How could she not send word? I sometimes thought of Vern's mother and her sewing room. Once, Jolene was that mother who dreamed up patterns out of colourful bits of cloth and bent over her sewing machine to make quilts for the people she loved. Who was she now? Girlfriend to an asshole whom she almost seemed to hate. Maybe our mother had become someone known only as Irene, a pretty redhead with muscled thighs and work-strong hands.

Beatrice was worse than useless. She no longer threw her glasses across the room in frustration; Ted's death had freed her and she seemed almost happy. But she continued to fry sausages and boil potatoes, check the mailbox, refrain from comment—loudly. Comment was called for now, but now she failed to make it. I blamed her for not doing something to find our mother. I hated her for her silence. I could see she was embarrassed for us. I hated her for that. All around us piled up this impenetrable silence about the thing most important of all.

Sometimes I wanted to accost some stranger and demand, "Where is my mother?" Or a teacher or a policeman. "Do you know where my mother is? Can you help me find her?" Why did I stay silent?

When Vern came back, I told him I had a plan to find my mother. I made him swear not to tell anyone, not even Uncle Leslie.

We were on our backs in the tree fort, watching the aspen leaves flapping back to front like hands waving against the turquoise of the sky.

"When will you leave?" he asked.

"I have to convince Jenny first."

I was waiting for the right moment to tell her. I found it a week later when she finally broke up with Brian. I don't know why it took her so long—the guy was dumber than a bag of hammers. But Jenny had a soft spot for sad sacks and Brian was that in spades. Nothing he did turned out right: he drank too much, his father was mean, he smashed up his car, he lost his job (several times), there was talk that he had even fathered a child by a girl down near Lillooet and she was demanding money from him. Jenny rose to that kind of tragic story; she wanted to be his saviour. He did thoughtless things. He left her stranded at parties while he took off drunk in somebody else's car. He flirted with other girls. Still, Jenny had some notion of loyalty that couldn't be fazed by such minor transgressions.

But one cooking-hot Saturday night I was sitting outside on the front step when Jenny came marching up the sidewalk, strands of sweaty hair plastered to her face and neck, the bottoms of her white jeans and her runners coated in dust, and her face flushed bright red.

"What's up?" I said.

She looked at me. I knew this look. Her eyes were on fire. I could see the anger sparking off her.

"I can't speak right now," she said, and she went inside. Sometime later I found her on her bed, a pillow held tight in her arms as she stared up at the ceiling. She was listening to Supertramp on her record player. *Crime of the Century* was Jenny's favourite album. Usually she listened repeatedly to "Dreamer," but tonight it was "Bloody Well Right."

When the song finished, she put it on again. I stretched out on my own bed and listened with her.

After a while she spoke. "You know, when people are drunk they do stupid things. I don't like it, but I can understand it. Brian's done a lot of stupid things. But he crossed the evil line tonight."

I waited a bit. "What did he do?"

"Oh, Maggie, you don't even want to know. It'll bother you even more than it does me, knowing how you feel about cats."

"Cats?"

"I know. I don't even like cats all that much, but there's no excuse for what he did. Just being cruel for no reason."

"Don't tell me," I said.

"I won't. But I begged him not to do it, all of them, but him especially, I begged him. And right then I realized that he doesn't care what I think. He really doesn't. He's just a selfish, stupid, conceited idiot. A great big evil asshole."

I had to let her think she was the first to notice his true nature, so I bit my tongue. But I saw my opening.

"We should leave here. We need to look for Mom," I said.

"She's the mother. That's what you said. She should look for us."

"I know I said that, but maybe I was wrong. We can't just stay here and wait forever. I have a plan."

"You have a plan?" Jenny said. "And in this plan, what do I have to do?"

"You drive," I said.

"One slight problem. You know I don't have my driver's licence, right?"

"You can get your beginner's now. By your next birthday, we'll be legal."

"There's the small matter of a car."

"I'll get the car. That'll be my job. I've already got most of the camping equipment we'll need."

"Hell of a plan."

"Shut up. I don't see you coming up with anything better."

Jenny's face clouded and her lip began to quiver. I felt bad so I said, "How about we go on a test run? Next weekend."

"With whose car?"

"Not with a car. We'll hitch. We'll just head out. Like Chiwid. Hit the Freedom Road."

Jenny smiled. "Sometimes I like you."

We left after work late one afternoon. I met Jenny at Frank's Chicken and Pizza. She was dressed in her wide-legged white Wranglers and a peach top that laced at the front.

"For Christ's sake, Jenny. Nobody hitchhikes looking like that."

"I wanted to look presentable," she said.

"Take this," I said, and helped her heft her pack onto her back.

"Are you kidding, Maggie? This thing weighs a ton."

We got our first ride quickly, from Jenny's friend Ron.

"I'm not really going anywhere," he said. "But I'll take you out of town." When his Ted Nugent 8-track looped around to start over again, he said, "How about here?"

We walked as the sun went down. Cars swerved carefully around us when they saw our outstretched arms, and kept on going. The evening was mild, good for walking, but our gear was heavy.

"I've got to rest," Jenny said, and she dropped her pack and sleeping bag to the ground. She sat down on top of it. I put my pack down beside her and sat, too. We leaned back-to-back against each other and listened to insects trill from the roadsides.

Each time we saw a car approaching, Jenny jumped up and stood with her thumb out.

The car that finally slowed was a newer white Pinto. A middle-aged, ordinary-looking man with short hair and a sea-green leisure suit was driving. He smiled and said we were in luck—he could take us as far as we wanted; he was going all the way to Vancouver. It looked like a good ride to me. We threw our gear in the back and Jenny scurried in beside it.

That meant I had the front. But when I went to get in, the man's hand was there, palm up, where I was supposed to sit. My left foot was already in the car. For a moment I was confused, but only for a moment, because when our eyes met, I saw the grin, the steady stare, and I knew.

"Jenny," I said evenly. "Get out of the car."

"What?" she began, but I had already reached over her and yanked my pack out onto the gravel. She tumbled out after it, dragging her backpack. I slammed the door so hard the little Pinto shook before it buzzed off down the highway.

"You fucking scumbag!" I screamed after him as he pulled away.

"Maggie!" Jenny stared at me like I'd lost my mind.

My legs gave way and I sat down on my pack again. My hands were shaking, so I squeezed them between my knees.

Jenny just stared at me, opening her mouth to speak, then stopping, till she finally said, "*Why* did you do that?"

The look on her face was so ridiculous that I started to laugh. "I'll tell you why I did that!" I said. "I didn't like his stinking looks!"

After I'd told her what had happened, she said, "Oh Maggie. This was a bad idea. We're girls. Hitchhiking is dangerous for girls. I mean, I know you act like a boy, but—newsflash—you're a girl. Sorry. You did get your period, remember?" She put her arm around my shoulders and pulled me to her. "Maggie-girl, let's just sleep here somewhere." And for once I was happy to let her act like my big sister.

Down a little grass track below the highway we found a trail that in our pale flashlight beam seemed to head into a field and peter off to nowhere. We spread out our tent in the long dry grass beside it, laid our sleeping bags on top and pulled the corners of the tent up so they covered our feet.

Across the meadow, we could see the orange-lit windows of a cabin. Once in a while we heard traffic slide past on the highway above us. We'd positioned our heads beside a mound of earth for a little wind protection and put the packs on either side of us.

"Remember Mom used to say you should never sleep on a path because ghosts will walk over you and keep you awake all night?" Jenny said.

"We aren't on a path."

"Well, we're very close to one. What if there were three ghosts walking side by side? Or what if a phantom wagon came through here?"

I closed my eyes on the stars and settled deeper into the sleeping bag on the hard ground. A truck geared down on the road. I thought about Chiwid, digging a bed in the earth, settling in, letting the snow drift over her so that she seemed part of the land. I was so tired, but every time I started to slip into sleep, I felt the pressure of feet trying to get by—soft moccasins, the bony hooves of deer, stiff leather boots and paws.

I woke to find it had turned cold and that a heavy dew had settled over everything, including our sleeping bags. I tried to pull the tent further over us, but it was wet, too. My feet were cold and my nose was like ice. I drifted back into sleep, woke to check the sky for signs of morning. When dark finally began to turn milky silver I saw a grey mist hanging over the field. I closed my eyes and when I opened them next, a ragged coyote stepped calmly out of the mist. He sat on the path and watched me. Then he ambled off, disappearing into grey.

As soon as the sun burned through the fog, it was too hot to sleep. I kicked off my sleeping bag, covered my face with my hands to keep the sun off and tried to fall asleep again. But I could hear ranchers out starting engines and rattling around. I sat up. My eyelids felt like sandpaper. Below us, a truck slowly wound its way through the pasture. It might be coming this way. I shook Jenny's shoulder and she yawned and stretched.

"I had such nice dreams," she said.

Breakfast was bread, cheese sliced thin with my jackknife and an apple each, washed down with swigs of already-stale water from a plastic canteen.

Jenny balanced her diary on one knee and scribbled in it as she ate. "Want to hear my poem?" she asked as I was rewrapping the cheese.

"All right."

She cleared her throat. "Here we are on the freedom road, and there's not a cloud in the sky. We're carrying a heavy load, but we're going to fly."

"Huh. Not bad. It even kind of rhymes."

"Kind of? It does rhyme. That's why I changed 'road to freedom' to 'freedom road.' I couldn't think of a word to rhyme with freedom."

Jenny closed her diary and tucked it back into her pack.

"Not the greatest camping spot," she said.

"This was just a practice run. Next time we'll find something better."

"Like a campground?" she said. "I'd at least like to swim."

A cowboy from Quesnel gave us a ride back to Williams Lake, the sun burning in through the windshield. Nestled in the hills, I saw a deserted log cabin chinked with white plaster between the squared, weathered grey logs. There were deserted cabins like that all over the Chilcotin. They were solid, cured by the sun and wind. I didn't see why we couldn't move into one, fix up the roof, put glass in the windows and live off the land, me, Jenny, Mom and Cinnamon.

[EIGHTEEN]

"I WONDER IF I COULD live like Chiwid does."

Vern didn't say anything.

"You know Chiwid, right?" I asked.

"Yeah, I do." I could tell he was thinking. "You couldn't do it," he said. "I just mean, I couldn't do it either. People say she's left her body. She's a spirit now. What happened to her, it was too much. She survived but she's free of her body. Do you get it?"

"I think so."

"She's a spirit walking around in a human body. But she doesn't really need the body. That's how she survives. Out in the winter, twenty below, and no fire. Some people say she's an animal spirit. My aunty heard this screaming one night. They were camped near Eagle Lake and they heard this crazy howling in the hills above camp, kind of like a cougar, but scarier. They all got their guns ready. Aunty said the next day they went up there and they found Chiwid and her little camp. Chiwid was smiling. She's always like that."

We stretched out on the sun-warm boards. Aspen leaves like plump green hearts shivered in the summer breeze. I closed my eyes and could still see the dappled pattern of sun and leaf and blood against my eyelids. Beside me, Vern's skin had a familiar, clean smell—soap and sun. I breathed it in. I opened my eyes. He'd crossed his warm brown arms over his white T-shirt. A small indentation at the top of his ribs dipped and rose with his breathing.

"So you're going to leave," he said.

"That's the plan."

He took my hand and held it to his chest and his heart padded against my palm as if I could catch his heartbeat.

"Mom was good at finding lost things," I said. "Funny, eh? Jenny lost her Barbie doll once when we were out camping. She was only wearing her bathing suit."

"Jenny?"

"No, Barbie."

"So she was worried she might catch her death?"

"She really was. She was just young. I don't remember how old, maybe eight or nine. Mom said, 'Start at the beginning. Retrace your steps. Tell me everything you did with her.' And while Mom closed her eyes and listened, Jenny went through it step by step. 'I got her out of the tent after breakfast. She climbed a mountain and rescued Stick Man, who broke his leg because his horse got spooked by a bear and bucked him off. Then we had lunch. Then she married Stick Man. She went swimming in the creek, then she was sunbathing.'"

"Barbie?" Vern said.

"Yeah. And Mom said, 'That's where you'll find her' and sure enough, there she was, sunbathing in the mud by the creek. Under the stars."

"So you're going to retrace your steps," said Vern.

"That's the plan."

It didn't take long for Jenny to meet another boy. His name was John. This one was different from the others. I liked him, and that made me nervous. He played three instruments, drums, piano and saxophone, not only in the school band, but also in the country and cover bands that played at weddings and community dances. Jenny said he stayed up all night composing his own songs. He had unsettling blue eyes and a gaze like an X-ray. When he looked at me, I squirmed.

Also, Jenny had started to worry about what would happen to Bea without us. I sensed my plan unravelling. As she was getting ready to go out with John one evening, Jenny said, "You should get out yourself more, Bea. Why don't you ever go to the Elks Hall?" She blew delicately on her freshly painted nails.

"What would I go to the Elks Hall for?" Bea said.

"I don't know. Dancing? Maybe for fun? Do you even know that word, Bea? Fun is not washing dishes, not doing laundry, not even watching TV—well, except for *Get Smart*."

Bea laughed and waved Jenny away with one hand and wiped her weepy eye with the other. "I don't like drinking and those smoky places bother my eyes. And dancing with some smelly drunk is not fun to me."

Jenny smiled, her nail polish wand poised for the second coat. "Okay. I can see that. But what is fun to you? You're not so old. You've still got lots of time. Who wants to waste away in this little house in Nowheres-ville, B.C.?"

"Shh, Jenny!" Bea said, as if her boring life was a well-kept secret and someone listening might be offended.

"So what is your idea of fun?"

"Oh, I don't know."

"See, it's been so long since you've had any, you forget what it is."

"Well," she said hesitantly, "I do like to bowl."

Jenny threw her hands up dramatically. "You like to bowl? You like to bowl?" Jenny looked at me, where I sat silently, impatiently, leafing through a *National Geographic*. "Bea likes to bowl. For heaven's sakes, Bea—that's so simple. You can bowl right here in Williams Lake. I thought you were going to say you liked going to art galleries or something and we'd have to ship you off to Paris or New York."

Bea took off her glasses and rubbed her eye harder, laughing.

"What else is fun to you?"

"Oh, I don't know. I thought once I'd like to go on a cruise."

"That can be done," Jenny said. "Do you have any money?"

"That's not a polite question. But since you ask, I have enough to get by. But who would I go with?"

"You don't need to go with anybody. That's why you go on a cruise—to meet eligible men."

"It's no fun going alone," Bea said.

"You live alone. I'd say going on a cruise alone is a heck of a lot more fun than being here alone."

"I don't live alone." Bea looked at Jenny strangely.

I shot Jenny a murderous stare, silently pleading, shut-up, shut-up, shut-up.

Jenny looked at me with stupid alarmed bird eyes, her mouth clamped shut. "I meant, you're alone, like not with a husband or anything."

Bea nodded at that and it was okay again. "I would like to swim in the Caribbean Sea. I've seen photographs of that white sand and turquoise water. They say it's like bath water. I read about that in the *National Geographic*. Have you seen that, Margaret?"

I looked up, startled, because she never included me in their conversations.

"Yeah. I think so."

"That would be something. You can put on those scuba diving outfits and get right down under the water."

It was more enthusiasm than she'd shown for anything, ever, around us.

"They've got fish, all kinds of colours, really different from what's around here." Bea waved her arm in the general direction of the kitchen.

Through the heat of August, Jenny and John went for long walks down to Scout Island and around the lake. He wore no shirt. His jeans hung loosely around his hip bones and his chest was lean and tanned. When it cooled off in the evening, he put on his flannel shirt with the sleeves rolled up and the buttons undone. I suppose I had a crush on him. One night he sat on the front step with me while Jenny was inside getting dressed.

"Hear those crickets?" he asked. "When I'm old, I'll dream about that sound every winter. I'll want just one more summer, so I can hear them again. Winter makes you old. I want to live in a place where I can walk around all year with no shirt on, feeling the wind on my skin."

Talk of wind on his skin made me shiver. He was sitting so close, I could feel the heat from his body.

"Would you like that?"

"Pardon?"

"Where would you live where you could be what you really are?"

"I don't know."

"I mean, there must be a place where Maggie Dillon would be so comfortable in her skin she wouldn't care what anybody else said or what clothes she wore."

"There would be crickets," I blurted.

He laughed. "I like that. I want crickets, too. I wonder if there are crickets in Mexico."

Jenny came out. When she looked at John her face softened. He smiled. There was something between them that made me jealous. It made me think that as long as John was in Williams Lake, I would not get Jenny to leave.

WATER

[NINETEEN]

BY SEPTEMBER, JOHN was gone. He'd taken his saxophone and the clothes on his back. That was the story around town. I heard it from Bob in the gas station when John's parents had pulled away after stopping to fill their tank. People said it with a touch of wonder and admiration.

He didn't tell Jenny he was leaving, but he mailed her a thick letter. I wanted so badly to read it, but after she'd read it through, she took it out to the backyard and set it on fire. I watched her.

"He asked me to burn it," she told me. She didn't cry and at first she seemed proud that she'd been the one he singled out. He entrusted her with the secret of where he'd gone and why. School had started again and she rose to the sacrifice her loyalty required. But after school, she started closing herself in the bedroom with the window open, smoking cigarette after cigarette.

Bea could smell the smoke, of course, but she didn't say anything. She wouldn't risk upsetting Jenny, who could do nothing wrong in her eyes, or so I thought.

Some days, Jenny asked me to phone Frank's Chicken and Pizza to tell them she wouldn't be able to come to work. They were tolerant with her—everybody liked Jenny—but I worried she would lose her job.

One night, I heard Bea call, "Who used all the hot water?" I had my homework spread out on the dining-room table, and she came to the doorway of the kitchen and glowered at me.

"It wasn't me," I said.

Half an hour later, Jenny emerged from the bathroom, steaming and red like a boiled tomato. She slammed the bedroom door behind her. She was in a mood. These moods had become frequent.

I heard a strange thumping sound. I put down my pen and went to the door to listen. What was she doing in there? I opened the door a crack. Jenny was in a T-shirt and underwear, doing jumping jacks. Her breasts bounced with each jump.

"Close the door," she said.

I did. The sound continued.

I went back to my homework. I pictured John stripping off her T-shirt. I pictured him pulling her against his bare chest. He said, "Maggie Dillon, where would you live where you could walk around all year with no shirt on?"

I couldn't concentrate on my homework. The jumping had stopped.

"Jenny?" I said, opening the door carefully.

She was on the bed with a black look on her face, holding a bottle of cod liver oil. "Have you ever tasted this stuff?"

"Why are you drinking cod liver oil?"

"You don't drink it. You are so dense sometimes, Maggie. Other times, you're quite bright. But I can't believe you haven't figured it out yet. We do share a room."

"It's about John, isn't it?" Suddenly I knew. "You're going to run away to be with him, aren't you?"

"Have you been watching soap operas with Bea? I'm not 'running away' with John, as you put it. Or any other way you want to say it. Don't worry, I'm stuck here. Really stuck. Fuck it," she said to the cod liver oil, and she reached for her smokes and lit one up.

"Don't you care if Bea finds out?"

"Finds out what? That I'm pregnant?"

"What? Jenny, what? Jenny, no."

She laughed. She laughed until she cried. Then she threw up in our little tin garbage pail.

[TWENTY]

"ARE YOU GOING to tell him?"

"Who?"

"John."

"No."

"I think he'd want to know."

"What would you know about it, Maggie? You are so naive, you don't even know how naive you are. Anyway, what would I do, write to him at P.O. Box Wherever the Hell You Are?"

Jenny didn't intend to tell Bea, either. I don't know what her plan was, but it didn't include throwing herself on Bea's mercy. That was my idea.

I was convinced Bea would do anything for Jenny. I told Jenny how it would go.

"She'll need to sit down. She'll collapse on the couch. She'll be kind of shocked at first. Her mouth might hang open and she'll stare at you like a raccoon in a flashlight beam. She'll take off her glasses and rub her weepy eye. She might even start to cry and say how disappointed she is in you. Like, oh, Jenny how could you let this happen? And what about your future and how will you finish school. But then she'll pull herself together. She'll say something like, 'What's done is done. There's no use crying over spilt milk. The cat's out of the bag. The roosters have come home to roost. The ship has sailed.'"

By this time Jenny was laughing. I think I had already persuaded her.

"Bea's lonely, Jenny. Who has she got but us? This'll give her something to do."

She was about two and a half months along when she told Bea. It was a rainy night in October. Jenny had come home from work, had a hot bath and put on her pyjamas. Bea had made hot chocolate, so it seemed like she was open to mercy.

Jenny came into the bedroom. "Will you tell her with me?"

"Me? Why do you want me there?"

"You're my sister. You're all I have." She teared up so I couldn't say no, even though I thought it was a bad idea.

Bea had a look of fear in her face when Jenny and I both sat down on the couch. It was rare for me to sit in the living room. Jenny said, "Could we turn the TV off? I have something I need to tell you."

Bea's face went pale right away. I don't know what she was expecting. "All right," she said, and got up and did it.

Jenny had rehearsed a little speech. She had tried it out on me and I thought it was pretty good. She started, "You've been really good to us, Maggie and me. And I hope, well, I hope . . ."

She was floundering. Bea just gaped at her, a frown creasing her forehead.

Jenny was supposed to say something about hoping we hadn't been too much trouble and that she'd made a bad mistake and then ask for forgiveness. But it came out differently. "You're going to be surprised," she said. "It looks like I'm pregnant." Her tone seemed almost gleeful.

Bea did look shocked. Her mouth did kind of fall open. "It looks like?" she said. "Are you or not?"

"I am," said Jenny. She started to cry.

"Oh don't turn on the water works with me," Bea said, deadly calm. "If you think that's going to work with me you've got another think coming. Who is it? Is it that John? I knew there was something fishy with him. I had a bad feeling when he took off like that."

"He doesn't know anything about it," Jenny said.

"I will not have this house turned into the talk of the town. Everybody thinking we're just running wild over here, that I'm keeping a pair of sluts, no men to look after them. I want you out of my house."

It was my turn for my mouth to fall open. She ran on. "I've lived in this town for sixteen years. We're respectable people. Poor Ted will be turning over in his grave."

"Shut up!" I shouted. I stood up. I wanted to slap her.

"No, you shut up. This is my house and you'll do what I say. I can see I've been far too lax. I felt sorry for you. And all the while *this* has been going on behind my back. I must be the laughingstock. I want her out of my house."

Poor Jenny started to sob and ran to her room.

I shouted, "This is 1974, you cow!"

"Don't say another word," Bea said, calm again. "Don't say another word to me. You go to your room, I don't want to see either of your faces. Go!" She screamed the last word so hard the house shook.

Except for Jenny's heartbroken sobs, the house fell quiet. My mouth had gone dry, but I wouldn't leave our room to get water. I wasn't scared so much as shaken. I couldn't believe my instincts had been so wrong.

After a while, I heard Bea on the phone. She would be calling her sister.

I could not think of a single thing to say. Jenny got up, went to her dresser drawer and took out the letters from Mom. As she read through each one, she sobbed even harder.

"I shouldn't have called her a cow," I finally said.

"What?"

"I called Bea a cow. I shouldn't have done that."

Bea swung the door wide.

"I found a place she can go," she said to me, as if Jenny wasn't there. "She can stay there until she has the baby. They'll arrange the adoption."

Jenny kept her head down and said nothing.

"Where is it?" I asked.

"It's in Vancouver. It's a home for unwed mothers. Run by the nuns. Maybe they'll knock some sense into her head."

"What about school?" I said.

"What about it? She should have thought about that before she went running around. Now she's made her bed."

"Do I have any choice?" Jenny finally said.

"No," said Bea and left the room.

Jenny and I stayed awake most of the night. I couldn't stand to see her so broken, but we had little to say to each other. Outside, the rain fell steadily. Winter coming on. We couldn't escape to the woods or the tree fort. There was nowhere to go. My mind kept going to Chiwid. She was out there dug in under a tree, trying to stay dry.

Bea bought a ticket for Jenny the next day. The day after that, she would get on the bus to Vancouver. I went to Stedman's and bought her a travel toothbrush and soap holder and a box of stationery, printed in pink gingham and scented like strawberries.

"I'll write to you every day," Jenny said, as she climbed on the bus. I watched her go. I had managed to keep myself from asking her the question that had been hounding me for three days: what's going to happen to me?

[TWENTY-ONE]

Dear Maggie,

Here I am in Our Lady of Perpetual Help Home. Lots of pregnant girls here (obviously). I'm the only one who isn't showing, which makes me wonder what I'm doing here. All they talk about is "relinquishing" or "keeping" and their due dates, and if they're carrying high or low, whatever the hell that means, but it's supposed to tell you if you have a boy or girl, but who fricking cares since almost everyone is "relinquishing" anyway, which means putting it up for adoption, though some are still "undecided." Kind of like the dating game, bachelor number one, bachelor number two or bachelor number three. Except sadder.

If you ask me they're pretty obsessed about the whole thing. Some girls are even knitting stuff, like little hats and blankets. Remember when we used to play house with our Barbies? It's kind of like that, except no Barbies. I just want to get it over with.

But in case you're worried about me, there are no bars on the windows or anything and the food is pretty good. I have a nice room, too, all to myself. There's a bed (obviously), a dresser, a bedside table with a ceramic ballerina lamp on it, and a desk in front of the window that looks out onto the back lawn and gardens. It's pretty decent, even in the rain. It hasn't stopped raining since I got here, which was exactly twenty-five and a half hours ago. I know that because I didn't really sleep last night and I could hear the rain all night long, that and a sound like wind, which I figured out today is actually traffic. This house is in a nice neighbourhood, though. I was surprised when the nun who picked me up at the bus depot drove up to this big old house surrounded by trees. It's like a mansion, actually. You might like it. But don't go getting any ideas. If I have to get a freaky, disgusting stomach like these other girls, that's my punishment.

Oh yeah, you might ask yourself why I have a desk in my room. Homework. Yes, they have classes here. The nuns teach them. I met the English teacher today. She's a nun, but really young and she doesn't wear a habit. She's a writer. Her name is Sister Anne. She said we'll be doing lots of creative writing in class. So I plan to work on my poems.

Also, I guess the idea of Our Lady of Perpetual Help is that you've made this mistake but you're supposed to learn from it and learn to make better decisions and improve yourself. Which is where typing comes in. Maggie, if you want to learn a skill, which you do if you don't want to be a DRAIN ON

THE SYSTEM, you can't go wrong with typing. Apparently, if you can type, you'll always have a MARKETABLE SKILL. Do you think Mom could type? I don't think so, but I doubt there's a big demand for it around Williams Lake anyway. I could be wrong, though, since I am only an unfortunate girl who made a BAD DECISION.

Try not to worry, Maggie. I don't know what the point is of telling you that, but actually I'm okay here and it's better than staying with the double-crossing Beatrice Edwards. Actually, it's probably worse for you right now. Did you apologize for calling her a cow yet? Tell her, "I'm sorry that you're a cow." Please don't run away or anything stupid like that. I need to know you're in the same place I left you.

Love XXOO Jenny

P.S. We are allowed to make phone calls out, but only collect calls.

Bea didn't speak to me for several days, and I kept away from her. I went to school, went to work and wore a path from my bedroom to the bathroom and back. I kept my door closed and Bea kept the TV up loud, as if I wasn't there.

The snow had started. I tried to think of where else I could go. There were people Mom and Dad used to know who lived in tents all winter long, usually while they were building their cabins. They had special stoves and fitted the stovepipe through a canvas opening in the tent. They kept a hole open in the ice to get water. But if you couldn't keep in a wood supply, you'd freeze. I remember spending a few days in the fall with one family so Mom and Dad could help them with the wood. The two kids ran around wearing only shirts, no jackets. Mom said they were used to it and they weren't cold.

At the gas station, Bob was more cheerful than usual. When Vern came in, Bob said, "Hey Chief! How's it hanging?" which bugged me. "Chief" was the same thing he called the man who came in selling salmon and smelling of alcohol. Outside, I asked Vern if it bothered him. He said, "Maggie, if I got my shorts in a knot every time some dickhead called me Chief or Tonto, I'd have really knotty shorts."

When Vern had gone, Bob looked up and said, "How's life treating you, Maggie?"

"Fine," I said.

One day he asked, "How's that sister of yours? I haven't seen her around lately. I hear she's not at Frank's anymore. Frank said that's a big loss. The customers really liked her."

I thought about making some excuse. Bob was a gossip. In fact I think some of the customers preferred that I pump their gas because if Bob got going, they could be there half an hour. But something made me not give a shit. I was tired, and besides that, I just wanted to tell somebody.

"Jenny's in Vancouver," I said.

He gave an exaggerated recoil and so I knew that he already knew. News got around that town. I had only told

Vern, but of course she'd taken the bus, people had seen her, and they could put two and two together.

But Bob wanted me to tell it. "What's she doing there?"

"She's in a home for unwed mothers. Beatrice sent her there."

Bob shook his head, looking at the floor. I suppose he hadn't expected me to tell him the truth.

"I'll tell you what I think. Can I tell you what I think, Maggie? I mean, I know it's none of my business, but if you want the opinion of someone who's been around the block a few times, I'll give it to you."

I smiled.

"You want it?"

"Yes," I said. He was my boss. What else could I say?

"My thinking is, where the hell is that woman's head at? Beatrice Edwards, I mean. This is 1974."

"That's exactly what I said."

"This isn't the dark ages we're living in. We're not some backwater town here. Where does she get off sending that poor girl to Vancouver? Her friends are here. And just so you know, Frank feels the same way."

I smiled at him.

"Ah, shit. You can't keep a secret in this town," he said.

Dear Maggie,

Today I made an ashtray. We do crafts here. I'll keep it so when we get our own house, we'll at least have an ashtray. Most of the girls smoke. They're allowed, which is weird, don't you think, considering all the other things we're not allowed to do, including "loitering" in the front yard. We are allowed to sit out in the backyard if it's nice, which as far as I can tell is never.

I have a social worker. She asked me all kinds of questions about our family and wrote the answers on a clipboard and wouldn't look at me for some reason, and seemed pretty bored. (She looked at her watch twice.) But then she suddenly put the clip board aside and gave me this "poor you" kind of look which really bugged me—she has these glasses with big thick frames and she's got a huge, wide mouth, she looks like some kind of bug—and then she said, "Well, in some ways it's easier for you. Your choice is clear. You don't need to spend a lot of time worrying about your options because clearly you have no support and no means of keeping a child."

Which may be true, but still.

"You don't seem too upset," she said and sat there looking at me with her stupid bug eyes. I shrugged, which I assume was the wrong thing to do. I think she wanted me to cry. She had a box of Kleenex sitting in the middle of the table. Which also seemed wrong. Sort of like "Everyone cries, you're not so special, so get it over with." I think they could at least have the courtesy to put the Kleenex away and then take it out if you do cry, because you feel like some kind of cold fish if you don't cry.

I have too much time to think, don't you think? Though they do try to fill up our idle hands with "activities." Typing, for example. One girl here can type 80 words per minute, that's 80 wpm, like a speed limit. She'll be able to go anywhere, apparently. She wants to be a legal secretary. Who wants to be a legal secretary? Well, this girl does and she'll win some award for Most Improved Typist, aka MIT. Which I, too, could aspire to! Sister Anne says in this very dry voice that typing is useful for writing papers in university, too. She says I should try to learn it, since I want to be a writer. I might type you a letter, except it probably won't be done until I'm ready to pop.

Miss Bug Eyes wants to know who the father is. I said I didn't know. Her pen stopped in mid-air. She was waiting to write something down. I figure there must be an "unknown" box to check off. She did not like my answer. I said I had a couple of different boyfriends and I didn't know their last names. She knew I was lying.

She said, "The father's family is your only chance."

"Chance of what?" I said.

"Of keeping the baby."

"I'm relinquishing," I said. She kept her big lips pursed tight and wrote it down on her clipboard.

I don't want them to go looking for him. If anyone comes around, promise me you won't say anything. I have a good reason, but it's nobody's business.

Hi again,

It's Wednesday. Last night I talked to a girl who I'll call Ginger, because that's her name, ha ha. She's called Ginger because she has red hair. So she said she'd call me Ginger #2.

I told her I didn't like the bodily function sound of it, so she came up with Ginger-B, which I like. She has a bit of an English accent. She lived in England until she was ten, then her parents divorced and she came here with her mom. They were living with her aunt and uncle. The uncle was a real creepo and was always giving her the hairy eyeball. Her mom knew it, but never did anything, because she didn't want to upset her sister. Creeps come in many different types, right? But he was a special type of creep.

They had these parties all the time, even on school nights. The music was so loud the floorboards under her bed vibrated. The uncle had some fabulous stereo system he was awfully proud of. That's how she put it. Awfully proud. I love the way she talks. She says trousers instead of pants. Funny eh?

Sometimes a record would skip for an hour. She says you haven't lived till you've heard "Break on Through to the Other Side" skipping for a whole hour. "You ever listen to people getting drunk?" she asked me. "It could be quite interesting if it wasn't so goddamn pathetic. First they're all jolly and oh, the larks and the raucous laughter over who the hell knows what, but everything, apparently, is very, very funny when you drink, until it isn't. Then comes the snarking and the shouting and the personal attacks. Then things start to crash around. There are eerie moments of silence. You wonder if someone has cut someone else's throat and is suddenly aghast and sober. Once, my uncle took after his best mate with a hatchet. I saw it with my own eyes; the sound of splintering wood got me out of bed finally.

Sometimes I put tissue in my ears, but that's almost worse, not knowing what's coming." She said her house in England was in a quiet village and the only thing that ever disturbed her sleep was the peacocks shrieking. Her dad was nice too, and she missed him. Makes you wonder what happened.

Anyhow, one night Ginger snuck out of the uncle's house and broke into a shed on the school grounds. She brought a blanket and slept in there for a week, until one morning the janitor found her. The principal called the uncle's house and she got in a shitload of trouble. The uncle said, "If you're so high and mighty that you can't sleep in my house, then you can bloody well find somewhere else to live." Her mom told the principal that Ginger had been acting up since the divorce and it was nothing serious. Then she actually put her hands together like she was begging her and said, Please dear, don't rock the boat.

About a week later there was another party. Do you know the Cream song, "White Room"? She said she can't hear it now without being sick. I mean really vomiting. It was playing when her uncle pushed her door open. He had to push hard enough to break the lock. He grabbed her by the throat, lifted her out of bed and threw her across the room. Ginger said she can't figure out how no one heard. He picked her up and threw her again and again. She hit the dresser and the window and door. She remembers slamming into the wall between songs. She said someone had to have heard it, but no one came.

Another song started. "The album was *Wheels of Fire,* if you're interested," she said. "Kind of a bluesy feel to it. Before I left his house, I took a candle and melted patches in the vinyl. Then I put it back in the sleeve. Should give him a nice surprise next time he listens to it." He raped her for the length of time it took to play the whole album. "Slapping and punching, that's what gets him off. You don't even want to know the details." I think I really don't. She said nothing was so disgusting as the smell of him. "I've tried to name it, I don't know why," she said. "Beer breath and fish that's gone off. But then there's something that's only itself, as rank and rotten as he is."

I didn't want to believe her, but I could tell she wasn't lying. Some girls here do lie, which you can also tell, but I don't blame them. Everybody has their reasons. I think maybe if I was Ginger, I would lie. She says everybody's afraid of her uncle, but she's not anymore. He's a pathetic lowlife pig, she said, and then we chanted it, pathetic lowlife pig, pathetic lowlife pig.

She doesn't know where her mom is right now, if she's still living there or if she's found another place. And she doesn't know where her mom was the whole time that night, which obviously really bothers her.

But here's the weirdo part. She wants to keep the baby. She said she once had a kitten and her mom wouldn't let her keep it in the house because it scratched the furniture, and she had to put the kitten outside and it got sick and died. I don't know what that has to do with anything, but she says no one is going to take the baby away from her. She's not a stupid girl at all—she's really intelligent—but I don't see how she plans to take care of it.

Also, she hasn't told the social worker or the nuns about the uncle. She says they suspect something, partly because she came in here looking like she'd been run over. But she doesn't want to tell because she thinks they might take the baby away if they know. And, she said she can just picture her uncle waiting for the axe to fall. "He'll never know when I might strike and ruin his pitiful excuse for a life. It seems like a kind of justice."

Well, sorry for the el-depressing story, but I wanted you to know that even though I make the nuns sound strict, they're actually more like angels. They call Mother Mary "Our Lady" and they say, "Our Lady was once a mother in trouble, too." Kind of beautiful when you think about it.

What kind of person spends her days feeding pregnant girls chicken for supper and putting pretty little soaps in the bathroom and ceramic ballerina lamps in the bedroom to make a lonely girl feel better? I would never say anything too snarky about that kind of person. It's not their fault I ended up here.

Love xxxooo Jenny

Bea must have heard the talk around town. She had begun to speak to me, with a ridiculous courtesy that she had never used before.

"I'm making tea. Would you like a cup?" was the first thing she said. I was so startled I turned her down before I even thought about it, then realized I did want some. I made myself wait about an hour, then went and made my own cup. I wanted her to think that nothing she did could rattle me.

"Your dinner's still warm in the oven," she said another night when I got home from the gas station and was brushing snow from my gasoline-scented jacket. She had asked me to leave my jacket at the back door by the basement, so it didn't stink up the front closet, and that night she took it from me and carried it out there herself, as if it was something she always did, and as if keeping my dinner warm in the oven was our usual routine. It was spaghetti, an exotic food to Bea and usually when we'd had it, it was Jenny who had made it. Bea had even made meatballs and, as I ate in silence at the table while Bea watched *Mary Tyler Moore,* I knew that she had spent a portion of her day mixing up the ground beef and egg and breadcrumbs.

When a letter from Jenny came, she left it at the end of my bed. One afternoon, I found my clothes from the dryer all neatly folded, too, along with another strawberry-scented envelope from Jenny.

Dear Maggie,

Today Ginger and I put on wedding rings and went out walking. Believe it or not, there is a box of fake wedding rings in the TV room, and when you go out, you slip one on, kind of like a charm to protect your dignity. I chose a tasteful gold band, but Ginger went for a glass rock the size of a pea, nestled between two red rubies. There is also a closet full of maternity clothes. I'm not that desperate yet, but you should see my boobs. I know, Mom would say that's crude. It's what twelve year-old boys say, etc, etc. So tits then, I mean breasts, whatever you want to call them! The girls here trade bras all the time, because their tits are always changing size, and I now have a hot pink C-cup. In the peach top I got for my birthday, I actually have cleavage. And with my white Wranglers (I can't do up the zipper, so I safety pin it and hide it under my shirt) I look killer diller, if I do say so myself. But I wore a raincoat to hide my *shapely* figure when I went out, since the nuns get on our case if we dress "provocatively." Ginger is showing but she manages to look killer even pregnant. She wore black leotards and a tartan dress that is actually a blouse but is long enough on her—barely. Did you know that when you're pregnant you feel very—shall we say?—amorous. Or at least I do. Don't tell anyone, because I'm probably a sicko to say so.

The sun came out while we were walking down Granville Street and everything shone. The streets and sidewalks started to steam. There are stores here that have flowers and vegetables out on tables on the sidewalks. This might be a nice place to live if the sun came out a little more often and if I hadn't made a BAD DECISION.

Ginger and I stopped at one store to look at the flowers. A man came out—Italian, I think. In his elegant accent he said, "Did you two lovely girls bring this sunshine?" Then he said, "It must be my lucky day, two beautiful redheads at my store at the same time. You wait here, I have something for you." He went inside and came back with two big bouquets of flowers. "I usually keep these for my wife, but today they're for you."

So now I have a vase of flowers in my room. There are some white roses and something yellow that smells fantastic. This room is painted soft pink with white trim. I actually like it. There's a green homemade quilt on the bed and the little bedside lamp with a ceramic ballerina for the base. I think I told you.

The rest of the house is nice, but a little dark, with a lot of polished wood and blue carpets and then there's the rain. I'm trying to be optimistic, but to tell you the truth, when you go out, the light is grey, the pavement's grey, the buildings are grey, the pigeons, even, are grey—it's kind of a downer. I wash out my socks and underwear and hang them to dry on the radiator, but they're still damp the next morning. There is a leak in the English classroom ceiling and during the whole class we hear the drip-drop-drip-drop into a pan on the floor. Sister Anne says this must be symbolic, though she's not sure of what, and that the person who comes up with the most convincing symbol gets bonus marks. I say it's the passage of time. It sounds like a clock, and there we sit, waiting.

The most depressing thing, though, is all these girls sitting around playing cards, listening to Tony Orlando and Dawn, discussing due dates and eating snacks, which they buy with their "pocket money." The nuns have all these funny expressions. "Pocket money" can be earned by doing chores—folding sheets, polishing floors, cutting vegetables for dinner. The girls buy cheezies, pretzels and hickory sticks, my personal favourite. I think I'm addicted. I wander down to the laundry room to fold sheets, but I'm really thinking of hickory sticks.

Some of the girls are waiting for their boyfriends to show up, marry them, and carry them off to a four-bedroom house in the suburbs where their days will be spent blissfully Ajaxing the bathtub. Speaking of symbolism, "Tie a Yellow Ribbon Round the Ole Oak Tree," which I've now heard about fifty million times, no guff—listen to the lyrics, except it's the girls who are in prison. That's not exactly true. Sometimes this place feels like a hideout.

I'm always chilled from the rain. Luckily there is a bathtub down the hall. I soak in there every night after supper. I'm probably going to get fat. I know what you're thinking. Don't even say it.

Sister Anne had us writing poems today. We had to start with the words "something changed." Everybody was teasing her: "Subtle, Sister." I was surprised, though, by what came out. Sister read it over my shoulder when it was done and gave me a little thumbs up. She was actually kind of choked up, I could see it. Well, I shouldn't get your hopes up too much. It's just a poem. (which doesn't have to rhyme, by the way)

Something changed
When night after night
I tried to sleep
But waited
Maybe I would hear your car door slam
Maybe your footsteps in the hall
Maybe you would wake me up
Singing Sweet Caroline

Like you did when we were little
And thunderstorms were the scariest thing
Something changed
When night after night
You didn't come.

I realized something the other day. I used to cry when I thought about Mom. I kind of even liked it, the crying I mean. I always had this idea that Mom could see me, and she would feel bad for breaking my heart and she would come. Now I can't even cry, which is probably for the best, because if I did, I don't know what would happen. I'm starting to show, which makes it feel more real. I guess this is my real third thing.

Dear Maggie,

I now have a psychiatrist, as well as a social worker. I went to see Miss Bug Eyes today and a man was sitting there with her. Bug Eyes said, "Jennifer, I'm concerned." Apparently she's concerned that I don't seem to understand the serious situation I'm in (translation: I haven't bawled in her office and used up her Kleenexes). So she brought in the big guns, as Ted used to say. Dr. Ruskins.

Before I go any further I have to tell you about Robert. That's right, Robert Ruskins is his name. Cute, eh? And I'm supposed to call him Robert, not Dr. Ruskins. Speaking of cute . . . He has this soft blonde curly hair and killer green eyes, like a cat, and a voice like the guy in the band America, the one who sings "A Horse with No Name." I asked him if he's American, but he's not, he's from Ontario. I guess that explains the accent. How do I know his hair is soft, you ask? I don't, but I can imagine.

Once Bug Eyes had left the room, he told me he wasn't interested in judging me. He doesn't believe in God, doesn't even believe in marriage and thinks "sex is a normal healthy part of an adult life." Ha! I couldn't help telling him that everyone blames the boy. That's what I said. I just blurted it out, then I wasn't sure I really wanted to continue the thought. He said, "You mean you had sex willingly. You wanted to." He said it like a statement, not a question.

"Yes," I said.

"And you're feeling guilty about that."

I said, "I guess I am, now that you mention it." And he laughed. Nice laugh. I continued, "Some of the girls here have been attacked or raped. One girl even told me that she didn't actually have sex at all."

Swear to God, Maggie, this is true. She claims she's still a virgin. I think she thinks the sperm just sort of crawled up her leg.

The doctor, I mean *Robert,* smiled at me and said, "You're a perfectly normal, healthy young woman and healthy young women like sex just like healthy young men do. People will say all sorts of things to alleviate their guilt. Only some of it is true. As good as these dear Sisters are here, they serve their mercy with a heavy helping of guilt."

I liked the way he said that. He could be a writer. That line could be from a Bob Dylan song: *They serve their mercy with a heavy helping, a heavy, heavy helping . . . of guilt.*

Anyways, he kept saying "sex" as if it was no big deal. Then he offered me a cup of coffee, and I don't even like coffee, but I said yes because it made it like two adults having a normal conversation. I know. I'm not an idiot. He's probably just really good at his job, that's what you're thinking, but I couldn't see the harm in it. And did I mention he's cute? Did I mention I noticed his eyes lingering on my hot pink C-cup running over when I leaned to put my coffee cup down? Maybe he's bored, too. Maybe he daydreams about long-legged pregnant gals who have a normal appreciation of sex. And what else do I have to do all day, besides sit around talking about my due date and knitting booties? (No! I will not knit booties!)

As relaxed as I felt with him, I'm not going to tell him the father's name. I see Robert again on Friday.

Love xxoo Jenny

P.S. I told you about The Girl who got Pregnant Without Having Sex. Now I will tell you the story of the Prettiest Babies Get Sold to Rich People. This is true, too. I know because all the girls say it's true. But I'll let you be the judge.

The story goes that if you see someone taking Polaroid snaps of your baby, you should be worried. I didn't even know that we get to see our babies after they're born, but apparently we do. Anyhow, if you have a cute baby, especially a blonde one, especially a boy, or one with blue eyes, and you want to keep it, dream on. Even if you already decided to keep it and signed the papers, etc. They will tell you that the baby is sick. Then they'll tell you it died. But really it got Sold to Rich People who can't have their own baby. And that's how the nuns keep this place going. How else could they afford to keep this big mansion and feed all these girls year after year? Not to mention the nice fresh soaps in the bathroom all the time. They don't have jobs. Makes you think.

I asked Ginger if she believes it and she said these girls have too much time on their hands. But . . . she didn't say no. Believe it or not . . .

P.P.S. (this means post-post, in case you didn't know) Do you think I could call you collect at the gas station? You work by yourself on Saturday afternoon, right? We (which actually means you, sorry) could pay Bob back. But you know I'll repay you someday when I'm a rich poet. Ha ha.

[TWENTY-TWO]

On Saturday afternoon Jenny called the gas station collect.

"Holy shit, Mag, I can't believe how glad I am to talk to you. You're not going to get into trouble, are you?"

"No, I'll pay for it. Bob likes me. He thinks Bea's a hag for sending you away."

"He knows?"

"I didn't tell him. It seems like half the town knows. I never even knew so many people around here knew our names. Vern told me Uncle Leslie heard some ladies in the grocery store talking about it. They think Bea went too far."

Jenny didn't say anything.

"Are you there?"

"Yeah, I'm here."

"It's kind of ironic, don't you think?"

"Yeah, I guess."

"What's wrong?"

"What isn't? I guess I just don't like the idea of it. Everybody talking about me."

"Well, not everybody. I exaggerated. I just thought you'd be glad that Bea's plan backfired."

"Yeah, score one for pathetic me. I really just want this to be over. Sorry, Mag. I don't mean to be such a downer."

"I guess you've got a right, Jenny."

"You're not mad at me, are you?"

"What are you talking about?"

"It's been bugging me. I screwed up your plan. I know how you worry and now you've got this to worry about."

"But you'll be back in a few months."

"Yeah, that's right."

She was quiet. I tried to think of something to say. "It snowed here."

"Yeah? It's raining here. Do you have a minute or two? I mean, there's no one waiting for gas or pickle chips or something."

"No. It's dead today."

"Do you think I should tell John? This will sound weird. Promise me you won't tell anyone."

"I won't," I said but I felt my stomach flip.

"I don't know why I say that. Who are you going to tell?"

"What is it?"

"It's about John. The reason he left town. It wasn't because he wanted to see the world. In that letter that he wrote to me? The one I burned?"

"Yeah."

"He told me he left because he's homosexual. Weird, eh? I mean you wouldn't think it somehow. I don't know a lot about sex or anything, but it sure seemed to me like he liked it. But maybe I forced him."

"You didn't force him, Jenny. You can't force a guy to have sex."

"But are you shocked?"

"I'm kind of shocked, yeah. He didn't seem homosexual to me."

There were about five seconds of silence on the phone and then Jenny and I both broke down laughing.

When she could catch her breath, she said, "Because you're the expert. You should meet Dr. Robert. But it's not funny, really. John said he didn't think he could ever be himself in Williams Lake. So even if I wanted him to come to my rescue and marry me, which I don't, that probably wouldn't work out too well."

"It's not—it hasn't crossed your mind, has it? In your letters you sounded pretty sure."

"I've got to go, Maggie—my time's up. No, don't worry, I'm fine. I just have way too much time on my hands. I'll write to you tonight. DON'T worry, okay?"

"Okay."

She hung up.

But I think we both knew how pointless it was for her to tell me not to worry. As soon as I put the phone down I felt the heaviness in my stomach rising up and tightening around my chest. Her letters had sounded like the Jenny I knew, always sunny, always righting herself, like a good canoe riding rough water. But on the phone I could hear some dark thing crouched on its haunches, calling her. She was having a hard time hanging on.

The bell rang for the gas pumps. I looked out and saw Uncle Leslie's green truck in the falling snow. The afternoon light was almost gone. He waved at me and as I went towards him, I wanted to say, "Help."

Dear Maggie,

I don't have the same memories of Dad as you do. I always thought he saw you as kind of like a son (no offence). But me he didn't get. Maybe because I was too girly. (I don't think I'm too girly, but you do. Really, I'm just a girl.)

I remember when we were little—I doubt you'd remember—we went to visit a friend of Dad's. It was way out in the bush on a very rough road. We had fun getting there. There was a tree across the road at one point and Mom and Dad had to get out and move it. They were laughing and teasing each other and I held you in my lap. How old was I? Five? Six? I don't know exactly. Old enough to remember it.

The cabin was one room, smoky and dirty. Frying pan full of grease on the woodstove, flies on dirty dishes on a wooden box. Dirty clothes in the corner. There was no running water or bathroom. There were too many mosquitoes to leave us outside. I know because Mom tried, put us on a smelly blanket under a tree and we were attacked instantly. We both cried and she brought us in. The bed you and I sat on smelled like piss and body odour.

After a while, a few empty beer bottles had been set on the floor by the woodstove, and the man, I forget his name, took Dad out to show him something. Something they had been talking about, I don't know what. When they left, the man picked up the sack of beer and took it with him.

Mom yelled after him, "Are you worried I'm going to drink it all while you're gone?"

And his voice came back, "You might just, Irene. You might just."

"Jesus Christ," Mom said. I remember being surprised because it meant she was really, really mad. She'd only use the God curses if she was super-mad. I had no idea what had upset her so much. She paced the cabin, breathing heavily like she was out of breath. When I asked her what she was doing, she said, "Trying to calm down."

Then I spit up on the bed. I mean I barfed. All over the bed. I don't know why. The man had given us some bread and jam. Maybe it was that.

Mom said, "Oh, for Christ's sake! Leave me in this shithole with the kids. I guess I deserve it."

And I started to cry. She picked us up, one under each arm and carried us out to the car and she held me and said, "Don't cry. You're my peach. You're my beautiful, beautiful girl. You didn't do anything wrong. Don't cry."

I barfed some more, I think. Then she told me she was going to look for something for my stomach. I saw her come out of the cabin with the blankets bunched up and she shook them out and threw them over a bush. After a while she came out again and brought me a cup of weak tea.

"I'm not squeamish but that's a filthy cabin," she said. "I boiled the water good and long. It'll make you feel better."

I slept a bit and some time later, I heard the car start. Mom was in the driver's seat. She drove, saying nothing, and Dad sang songs. Remember those pretty Irish songs he knew? There was the one about the belle of Belfast city—"I'll tell me Ma when I go home"—Dad reversed the words and sang, "The girls won't leave the boys alone." And the one he called the fake Irish lullaby. "Too-ra-loo-ra-loo-ra, hush now don't you cry."

I fell asleep again and woke up when the car stopped. I barfed some more and Dad looked over the seat at me. He was holding you. His lips were curled in a nasty kind of disgust. The look on his face made me cry. Mom was leaning in the back door and said, "Aren't you going to help me?" Before he could answer, she slammed the car door and went in the house. Dad said, "She's your daughter." Mom didn't hear him, but I did. He carried you in the house and left me there. I remember I felt sorry for myself, lying there in my own vomit all alone in the dark. I felt like it was a test. Would he come back and get me? I didn't wait long, but it was Mom, not him, who came with a towel and a blanket and rough, angry movements. It stuck with me, Maggie. I'd seen this secret side of Dad and he knew I had. Any time we were alone together after that, there was that secret.

Well, I was thinking about him because I was thinking about fathers. One of the girls here, she's kind of funny, but also mean and mad, she tells the Tony Orlando and Dawn girls, "If you think any fuzzy-dicked guy cares half a crap about your babies, you're so far gone there's no coming back."

That makes the girls go quiet, but after she's gone they say things like, "She's just bitter. Who would want her? I can't imagine what her baby's going to look like. She won't have to worry about her baby getting sold to rich people."

Maybe it's true, though. Girls have the babies and girls love the babies. A guy like John, he's a decent guy, but he doesn't want to know he's a father.

Hi again,

It's about one a.m. and I can't sleep. Since I was awake anyway, I thought I'd get up and write to you. It's raining again and if you didn't know, you might think something was burning, the rain hisses and crackles like that. I'm sitting at my desk and I put the quilt around my legs because the radiator is cold. The ballerina lamp is on. When we get our house, I'm going to buy a ballerina lamp.

I felt the baby move tonight. It felt like a butterfly swimming around in my belly. It started when I went to bed and I was lying still. At first I thought a bug had crawled across my stomach and I tried to brush it off. Then I realized what it was. It went on for about an hour, Maggie, like she was playing in there. It was so cool. You might be wondering why I say "she." As I was lying there I sort of felt like she was talking to me. Not really talking, but you know. And she's a girl. For sure. Bet you any money. Well, I have a 50/50 chance of being right—ha ha.

Today I went to Mass. We don't have to go, it's optional. Sister Anne said she noticed that I don't go, even though I checked off "Catholic" on the intake form. I told her Mom is Catholic, but she was pretty easygoing about it. Sister laughed, but she said if I wanted to, I could go. She said maybe I'd feel closer to Mom if I did. So I thought what the hell. Ha ha.

Do you remember that little church in Duchess Creek that was so cold in the winter? I remember lying on the wooden pew, so I must have been little. It smelled like mothballs. And I was playing with Mom's purse, opening and closing it because it made a nice snap. And a smell of spearmint gum came from it.

The priest here told the girls we should say the rosary every night and one of the prayers should be the Act of Contrition. I doubt you'd remember it. The first part goes, "Oh my God, I am heartily sorry for having offended Thee." I remembered it. I always thought of it as an exclamation, Oh My God! Kind of like Sweet Jesus! Or Bugger it! I am heartily sorry. And then it goes on about the pains of hell and whatnot.

I thought I didn't feel sorry at all, just sorry for myself, maybe. Definitely not for offending God. But right now, I do feel kind of sorry. And if I offended anyone, it's *her*, the baby. She needs me to protect her and I act like I don't even care about her.

Don't you think we're kind of a bad design? Human beings, I mean. If there is a god, he was a little too casual or absent-minded or something. He should have thought to make sure we had maturity before we were able to reproduce, especially since, according to my biology class, human beings nurture their young longer than any other species. Like about eighteen years, Sister Rosa said, and everyone in the class gasps, as if we didn't know—most of us aren't even that old yet. But then I couldn't help thinking about Mom and us. So I put up my hand and I said, "But not all mothers do it the way it's supposed to be done and yet those offspring still survive."

"Meaning?" said Sister Rosa. (She's this tall, thin nun, all business, no nonsense, cat's-eye glasses, pixie haircut, and the way she speaks makes you think she's on a tight schedule and she wants her answers the same, pronto.)

"Meaning some mothers leave their offspring to fend for themselves sooner, kick them out of the house at sixteen, or even leave them in a basket on the hospital steps."

"Point taken. The community takes over, then. Without the human community, the baby in the basket would starve to death."

"But the sixteen-year-old wouldn't. Or even the twelve-year-old."

"I get where you're going with this, Dillon." (She calls us by our last names.) Which was funny, because I didn't even know. She said something about instinct and the debate in biology about which behaviours we could attribute to instinct. But I wasn't thinking about that. I was thinking about how when Dad died, it was like a flood that comes sweeping in and knocks you down. And you think you'll just drop dead right on the spot. But you don't.

Which brings me to my recurring dream. I've been dreaming about tidal waves. I don't know where my brain got the idea of tidal waves, but I must have heard it somewhere. They do happen on the BC coast. I think I remember Mom talking about one once and how the village had to move to higher ground.

Anyhow, I dream that a big wave has risen up from the ocean and surged through the city, everything's floating, cars and trees, and it rises up right up the steps of Our Lady of Perpetual Help Home for Unwed Mothers, and it sloshes in under the door, and keeps coming, washes across the polished hardwood floor of the foyer and laps at the stairs, one by one. I pull my blankets up so they won't touch the floor, but pretty soon the water has risen so high the bed becomes unmoored and floats free. Night before last, the whole house listed and I had to hold on to the table leg to keep from washing out the window. Symbolism. If I knew what the table leg symbolized, maybe I would know what to do.

To tell you the truth, I'm starting to regret that I came here. I'm homesick, and I don't even know for what. Not for Bea's house or our crummy little bedroom there, but it's just this feeling of loneliness. Sometimes I think this feeling will never leave me. And I wonder if she feels it, wherever she is. She must think we're okay. If she knew we weren't okay, she would come back. We've been wrong, Maggie, up to now, to do nothing. We need to let her know we're not old enough to be away from our mother yet. I don't know anyone here in Vancouver and I'm surrounded by people who want something from me. They're taking my blood and asking me questions about sex and writing down the answers and staring at me sadly with these eyes that try to appear non-judgmental, but are really just dripping with judgment. I can almost hear their private thoughts: dopey girl, I never would have, your bad choices, your type, your age bracket, your prospects, your failure to plan. Failure to plan is planning to fail. (Do you like that one? I find it catchy.)

I only came here because I didn't have time to make any other decision. I thought I owed it to Beatrice, because I had so disappointed her. But what can she do to me? Shame me to death? Do people die of shame?

I will leave you with that deep philosophical question now while I go to bed and dream of floating out the window.

Love xxoo Jenny

Dear Maggie,

Sorry for that downer letter I wrote last night. I think I was trying to avoid going to sleep because I hate mornings the most. I wake up and it's all still true and I just want not to wake up, which I can do by not going to bed, if you get my drift.

Are you sitting down? Probably, since you're reading this. You should sit down, so you won't fall down. Don't be mad at me, please don't think I'm a spacey, dopey girl, I've given this a lot of thought and I've decided that I'm not relinquishing after all. I'm keeping.

What in the seven circles of hell??? (I just imagined you saying that, like Ted used to, so I wrote in your part so I'd feel like you were here with me.)

So far I've only told Ginger and she's thrilled and thinks we can get an apartment together, but I told her no, I couldn't live in the city. I want to go home, wherever that is, somewhere up there with you and the coyotes and chickadees. No, I haven't figured out a plan yet, since as I said before I don't think there's a big demand for typists in the Chilcotin, but the pioneer women managed with all their babies. I told Ginger she could come and live with us. I hope you don't mind. You'd like her. She won't anyway, so no harm in asking.

If Robert can stop looking at my boobs long enough today, I'll tell him. I have this feeling everyone is going to be disappointed in me all over again. More later.

Hi again,

Like I suspected, no one is exactly cheering my decision. Dr. Robert said, "Can I ask what made you change your mind?" I said, "Mother's instinct." He looked at me rather stupidly, I thought. (That's Ginger's expression.) He couldn't think of anything to say for quite a long uncomfortable time. He tents his fingers when he's thinking. He wrote something down. Finally, to rescue him, I said, "You wouldn't understand it because you're a man."

"True," he said. Ha ha. But still nothing. And then, "So mother's instinct, you say. And you see that as . . . ?"

"As the reason I want to keep my baby."

"I'd like to explore that a little further." And blah blah blah, it wouldn't interest you. But after a while, he said, "And in terms of a plan."

I have learned that his statements are meant to be questions. So I told him I didn't exactly have a plan yet but that I had about five months left to figure it out.

"These are big choices, Jenny. Big for anyone, very big for a fifteen-year-old girl."

"I'm aware of that."

I was impressed by my own voice, very firm, very sure. The funny thing is that I feel so much better now that I've decided. She was the table leg. All along.

Please write to me and, keeping in mind I'm not going to change my mind about this, tell me what you think.

Love xxoo Jenny

[TWENTY-THREE]

I DID WRITE TO JENNY. It wasn't my finest moment. She didn't keep the letter, thank God. She ignored most of what I had to say, which included, if I remember right, the phrase "give your head a shake." But she kept what she could use. That meant taking my advice about talking to Sister Anne, who I saw as my sensible ally.

Sister Anne surprised me by not trying to talk her out of it. I expected more from her, a persuasive argument. But instead she told Jenny, "Inform yourself." And this became Jenny's motto.

Then Jenny changed her mind about John and wrote to him care of his parents' house in Williams Lake. She made it clear that the only thing she really needed from him was money. She said she would pay him back. John got the letter eventually. He was in Northern California, picking fruit, washing dishes and playing saxophone and piano in bands wherever he could find them. The first cheque he sent was for $200. "Don't say you'll pay me back," he wrote. "I don't want you to."

Sister Anne also took Jenny to write the test for her beginner's licence, and then she took her out for drives in the evening. Jenny told me she practised parallel parking down in the shipping yards, between some big containers.

"I drove down Granville today!" she wrote in one letter and drew a little happy face beside it.

You can't die of shame, Jenny. If you could, I'd be dead. Christmas was coming and what I should have done was go to Vancouver to be with my sister. Bea was taking the bus to White Rock to spend the holiday with her sister.

"If you want to come along with me on the bus, I'll buy you a ticket," she said. "The home will allow visitors for Christmas." I didn't ask her how she knew.

"No," I said. "I'll stay here. They need me at the gas station." Not true, of course. I was just too mad at Jenny for deciding to keep the baby to make the sacrifice of riding a bus for twelve hours with Bea. And also too worried. I carried around the constant hope that Mom would pull up in front of Bea's house with her grin and her strong legs and her kiss. My fourteenth birthday had passed without word from her. But Christmas seemed like a time when she might come. We needed her now more than ever and if there was such a thing as mother's instinct, maybe she would know. I was afraid to be away and miss her. She could slip away again, not knowing that we weren't okay.

"Suit yourself," Beatrice said and went about pulling her little white suitcase out from under the bed, wiping the dust off it and folding clothes I'd never seen her wear in a neat pile on the couch. Beatrice had two sets of clothes she wore all the time, navy stretch slacks and an off-white cardigan or grey stretch slacks and a green cardigan. But it turned out she had a closet full of other things: pastel pantsuits and crepe blouses with bows and paisley scarves. She talked to herself as she packed. She had started doing that soon after Jenny left, little things like, "It could use dry cleaning." And "Where did I leave my umbrella?" It irritated me, but then everything she did irritated me, even the condiments she kept in the fridge but never used. Ancient relishes, mint sauce and HP Sauce—they must eventually go bad, like after three years. She put her suitcase by the door two days before her departure.

I should try to think of something kind to say. I should be more generous, but I was happy to see her go. Having someone else's house to yourself is not the same as having your own. Still, a stifling cloud of rage and unspoken accusations lifted from me the moment she was down the steps. I made hot chocolate and watched *Get Smart* with my feet on the coffee table. I smoked a stale cigarette, one of Jenny's. There was no alcohol in the house. I thought briefly that it might be fun to get some, then I decided it would involve talking to people, so I dropped the idea.

All the snow had melted over the previous week. Everyone who had come through the gas station said something about it being a green Christmas. But I didn't mind. I didn't want it to feel like Christmas at all. Then the morning after Bea left, Christmas Eve, it started to snow, so light that three customers in a row said, "Is that snow?" and I said *yes*, as if I was the authority. By noon, when the flakes were coming down like apple blossoms, I had to listen to every second person say that they guessed it would be a white Christmas after all.

I kept expecting Mom to drive in. Every crunch of tires on the gravel made me look up. Why I thought she would come to that gas station where I happened to be working, I don't know. I suppose I thought someone would have told her.

Bob closed up at three o'clock and I walked back to the house through the falling snow. It was sticky enough to make a snowman. I had a pork chop to fry up and I made instant mashed potatoes and a can of creamed corn to go with it. Dark already, the snow coming down steadily, I felt like I was being buried. I turned on Bea's silver Christmas tree on top of the TV, although I hated it, both its chintzy falseness and the fact that she put it on top of the TV. It just reinforced how pathetic her life was, the TV the centre of her world. Jenny once asked Mom why we didn't have a TV and Mom said, "You mean overlooking the fact that we don't have a fridge or a dryer either? We could have a TV, if it was important enough to us."

But I liked the coloured light that Bea's tree threw. Not a fire, but a memory of a fire, Christmas Eve playing cards by the light of the lantern and Mom bringing us a plate of biscuits with fresh cream and blackberry jam. Where did she get the cream? What plans did she make for the day, following some dream she had for all of us together on Christmas Eve? The woodsmoke perfume. Snow angels later, all four of us, Dad giggling. Looking up at the stars, the night so clear and cold. I don't know how old I was, but even then I knew to hold on to it. I understood how fragile it was.

I looked out the window at the quiet street. Fallen snow had turned the neighbours' cars into weird tall shapes. More was falling, and it blurred under a porchlight like a cloud of insects hovering.

I went to the phone and dialled information. "I'm looking for Our Lady of Perpetual Help in Vancouver," I said.

"I'm sorry? What is the name you're looking for?" said the operator.

"Our Lady of Perpetual Help. That's the name."

"Hold on please. There's an Our Lady of Perpetual Help church. Is that the number you want?"

"No."

"I'm sorry miss, that's the only number I have. Merry Christmas," said the operator.

Bea's backyard was a bowl of deep snow capped by sky thick with reflected light. It was only a city backyard and Christmas was all wrong but I couldn't help seeing how beautiful it was. I put on my parka and went out the door. I found the snow shovel and began a pile right in the middle of the yard. Music floated from a neighbour's house. I hoped they didn't know Bea was away and that they wouldn't see me, alone out there. I piled and packed, piled and packed, took off my parka and worked in my sweatshirt. I stopped to make hot chocolate, sat on the back step and drank it, thinking of Vern, who had gone to his Mom's for the holidays.

Voices on the street, happy shouts and car doors slamming. Then the commotion of revved engine and spinning tires and shouted directions. "Straighten your wheels. Okay, put her in reverse. Give her some juice. Again." Then quiet, deep, even here. It must be late.

I began to dig a tunnel into the pile. After a while, I got the flashlight and went to the shed for a smaller shovel. Sweeping the dark corners with the flashlight beam, I saw her travelling fast, too fast on a snow-plugged road, her muscular hands gripping the wheel, headlights cutting through thick falling snow. She'd like a cigarette. There'd be no one there to roll it for her and you couldn't stop on a road like that or you'd get stuck for sure. Her thermos of tea would be between her legs, the tea only lukewarm by now.

I locked the shed. If anything came down the street, I'd hear it. But nothing was moving. Not even out on the highway.

It was early morning, not yet light, by the time I finished the snow cave. I found a candle, stuck it on a little snow shelf inside and lit it. It was better in here. Christmas day had come. No one in the world knew how my arms ached, or how pale the light of the candle was against snow crystal walls.

I wonder now how deep a person's grief can go. Jenny never mentioned that Christmas, not in the letters she wrote afterwards, not ever. But I wonder if leaving her alone there like I did altered her, and if it led to what came later.

[TWENTY-FOUR]

There should be different words for giving birth than the ones we have. "Giving" should at least be "undertaking" or "undergoing." I remember in church how the priest said, "Mary bore Jesus," and I always thought of it as "bored." But now that I know what "bore" means, and now that I've seen what Jenny went through, it's a much better word than the passive "the baby was born," like it's as easy as growing fingernails.

Sister Anne said if men gave birth there would be different words, and we thought of some, sitting around the card table playing Scrabble and waiting for Jenny to come back from the hospital. I had left school three weeks early to be with her. Sister Anne had a visitor's room beside her own where she let me stay. We came up with "disgorge," "disburden," "unship" and, my favourite, "disembogue," which we found in the thesaurus. It means a pouring forth of waters.

Jenny was sleeping like the dead when I left her, the baby,

a girl, as Jenny had predicted, sleeping peacefully in a little plastic bassinet beside her bed. Jenny had just had time to name her before she passed out. Sunshine. That's her name. I thought it was too hippy at first, but it's the kind of thing Jenny would think of. It's what she should have been named herself. "We'll call her Sunny," she said, closed her eyes and was gone, abandoning herself to sweet relief from the drugs, the blood, the panic and the forceps.

When Jenny came back to Our Lady of Perpetual Help with Sunny, she didn't behave the way I expected. I had pictured a soft-eyed, red-haired Madonna, cooing over her baby and gazing lovingly down at her. Instead, she was nervous and irritable.

"I'm so tired," she kept saying. "I just want to sleep." She claimed she hadn't slept an unbroken hour in the hospital, and because of her complaining, they let her go early.

"They don't want someone messing up their schedules. Honestly, the nurses think if you don't wake up at seven a.m. raring to go, you're a negligent mother. They should try sleeping in a room with three other girls all snoring and crying and moaning like ghosts. And then they kept threatening to give her the sugar water if I didn't nurse her often enough. And they were yacking about bonding and whatnot. You can tell they're just waiting for me to fuck up so they can say I told you so."

"No one thinks you're going to fuck up," I told her. Sunny was asleep on her chest in the upstairs nursery and I was keeping her company. The idea was that I would stay with Jenny and, as her primary support, learn how to help her with the baby and then we'd go home together. "Home" was another story.

"Oh yes. They do think I will fuck up," said Jenny, "and they already have a list of people who want my baby. Look how beautiful she is." She moved her arm aside to let me see Sunny's face. She was beautiful. She had a fuzz of pale hair, an angelic, heart-shaped face and perfect little lips that moved in her sleep. But Jenny's voice was angry.

"Do you know I actually prayed for an ugly baby? I prayed it on my rosary. I asked Our Lady of Perpetual Help for it and look what I got. I'm being punished."

"Jenny, that's ridiculous. She's beautiful because you're beautiful. She's even got your green eyes. What did you expect? A pig nose and three eyes?"

"Very funny." She laid her head back against the rocking chair and closed her eyes. In a moment, her mouth dropped open and she started to snore lightly. I lifted Sunny gently off her chest, but Jenny woke with a start.

"Where are you taking her?"

"I'm just putting her in her bassinet so you can sleep."

"That's another thing. Why is her bassinet set off to the side like that? And why does it have that strip of tape on it?"

"I don't know. Maybe it's because she's a newborn. Why don't you go to your room and nap for a while? She's sleeping now. They say you should sleep when she does."

"Will you watch her?"

"If you want. But you know there's always someone here."

She snorted drily. "That's what I'm worried about."

"I'll watch her," I promised.

That night with Jenny in her room trying to sleep, I asked Sister Anne, "Is it true that there's a waiting list for Jenny's baby?"

"No, Maggie, it's not true. Her decision will be respected. We'll do everything we can to help her be successful."

"But who decides if she's successful?"

"She'll be fine. It's always hard at first and not just for the young mothers. She's doing fine."

I believed her, but Jenny's fears didn't seem unfounded. She was in a place, after all, where babies were regularly given up for adoption. The mothers were watched, helped for sure, but also watched. I trusted the nuns more than the social workers. We knew kids in Williams Lake who were in foster homes because they'd been taken away from their families by social workers. Mostly Indian kids, but not only.

And Jenny was not doing fine, no matter how much I wanted to believe her behaviour was normal for a new mother. She told me things that she wanted me to keep between her and me. "A girl came to my room last night," she said, one morning. "She had long black braids and she was wearing a long white nightgown. It was soaked in the front. When I turned on the light, I could see that it was soaked with blood."

"You were dreaming."

"I wasn't dreaming, Maggie, I talked to her. She even knew my name. She had been at Our Lady of Perpetual Help. She told me that her baby had been chosen, and now mine was chosen, and that I better protect her. Her baby was taken away from her because she hemorrhaged and she was too weak to care for her. She was warning me."

"That's weird, Jenny."

"I know. But this place is weird, you've got to admit that. The stories that go around. There's got to be some truth to them."

"Not really. They're just a bunch of worries. You're becoming a worrier like me."

"It wasn't a dream, Maggie, I'm telling you. I wasn't even asleep. I don't sleep. I can't."

The detail in Jenny's dream unnerved me and I spoke to Ginger about it. Ginger had a room on the third floor, down the hall from the nursery. She'd had her baby, a curly headed boy she named Jamie. She was breast-feeding him when I came to her door. She seemed older than Jenny, and completely at ease as a mother.

"Where does she get this stuff?" I asked her. "Where would she have heard it?

"Get her to talk to Dr. Robert."

"She won't. She swears me to secrecy about all this stuff. Maybe *I* should talk to Dr. Robert."

"I don't think so. You can't betray her trust."

So I kept quiet, too. But it didn't matter. Dr. Robert figured it out by himself.

"He wants to know why I didn't name the baby Irene," Jenny said to me one evening after she'd seen him.

"What do you mean? Just out of the blue, he asked you that?"

"He thinks there's something wrong with me. As a mother. I know it."

"Because you didn't name her Irene?"

"He knows about Mom."

"What about her?"

Jenny laughed, this dry laugh she had developed that was nothing like her real, happy laugh. It was sarcastic and full of bitterness and although I was trying to be mature and helpful, it hurt me. It was a "you are a naive idiot" kind of laugh.

"I'm not following," I said, with just an edge of impatience.

"I told him way too much about myself. And Ginger's in on it, too. I confided in her. I saw a file in his lap with Ginger's name on it. Everything I told her is in there."

"You're scaring me, Jenny."

She laughed again. "That's good. You need to be scared. You need to get a grip on what's happening here."

Two days later Sister Anne ushered me into the room that served as Dr. Robert's office. He looked up and smiled at me, but it was not an easy, genuine smile. It was the pained and crooked, trying-to-be-sympathetic smile of someone about to deliver bad news. He danced around with some small talk, presumably meant to put me at ease but didn't. Then he said, "Have you ever heard of the baby blues?"

I shook my head.

"Women get a little weepy and emotional after the baby is born. It's normal. Happens to seven out of ten women and usually lasts a week or so. We thought that's what Jenny was experiencing." He smiled the pained smile again. I looked at Sister Anne, who was frowning. I believe she had more respect for my intelligence than Dr. Robert did.

"It turns out that what Jenny's experiencing is a bit more severe. It's known as postpartum psychosis. Now I know that's a scary name."

I stared at him. It wasn't scary yet, since I didn't know what it meant, but when he said that, I swallowed drily.

"We don't know a lot about what causes it, but we do know how to treat it. That's the good news." He paused. I waited for the inevitable other half, the bad news. I thought he looked—gleeful. He was percolating with the scientific details he wanted to discuss.

"Now, is there any history of mental illness in your family?"

"I don't know."

"Any alcoholism?"

"No. I mean I don't think so." I thought of Dad, his quiet spells.

Dr. Robert sat back and met Sister Anne's eyes.

"This line of inquiry . . ." began Sister Anne.

"I'm trying to get a picture of the family's mental health. We know that postpartum psychosis often occurs when there's a family history of mental illness."

"Maggie's father died when she was ten. She's now fourteen." Sister Anne said my age a little pointedly, but Dr. Robert didn't seem to notice.

"And how did he die?"

"Logging accident."

"And your mother?"

"How did she die?" I said.

"Did she die?"

"I don't know. Hasn't Jenny told you all this already? What are you going to do to her?"

"Okay," Dr. Robert smiled again. "I guess we're getting ahead of ourselves. Jenny will need to go back to the hospital. We'll be able to watch her there, and treat her of course."

It may have been the only thing they could do for her, it may have been the right thing, but it was also the worst thing. It was just what Jenny feared.

[TWENTY-FIVE]

Even if Jenny hadn't asked me to, I probably would have gone looking for Mom. There was nothing I could help by staying. I couldn't soothe her agitation or persuade her that her fears weren't real. Besides, nearly everything she said had some ring of truth to it, and even as I spoke the words to dismiss it, my gut churned with the slim possibility that she was right. People were watching her, "observing," as she put it. They could take Sunny away; it's not as if it hadn't happened before. Bad things happened to people all the time. They could happen to us. They came in threes. I knew it. Jenny knew it.

But I didn't believe, as Jenny did, that her being held in hospital, given various doses of drugs, some that made her inconsolably sad, others that made her stony and blank, had anything to do with Mom's disappearance. No one knew where she was, and, furthermore, everyone seemed to take it as a given that she was somewhere she didn't want to be found. I guess there was no law against deserting your children. It was a crime only to us. And it happened gradually, like winter coming, the way you don't put your bike away until one day it's buried in snow and you realize that the days of bare legs and lung-burning speed are gone and you don't really believe they'll be back.

To an outsider, it was almost like she planned it.

"I want you to go," Jenny said to me one evening. It was June. Outside, sunlight and long shadows spilled across the green hospital lawn. Blue hydrangeas glowed with the last light. Sister Anne and I had walked over from Our Lady of Perpetual Help, through the smells of cedar and ocean air. I had told Sister Anne I was leaving.

"I think it's best, Maggie. There's nothing you can do here. Jenny's in good hands. We'll take care of both of them. I promise I'll visit her every day. She's a gutsy girl. She and Sunny can come back and stay with us once Jenny's able."

So I had been prepared to tell Jenny. But she beat me to it.

"You have to look for her. She needs to know what's going on. They won't let me out of here until we find her."

I took a breath. I was about to protest. The psychiatrist had warned me not to "indulge her delusions." But I was tired of fighting.

"I'll try," I promised.

"They won't let me nurse Sunny," she said, and the tears welled up and ran down her cheeks.

"I know, Jenny."

"It's because of the drugs. It's for her own safety."

"I know. But she likes the bottle. She's getting chubby."

"Do you think so? You don't think she'll be damaged? Sometimes an hour or two goes by and I realize I haven't thought of her at all. It's like I forget I even have a baby."

"You're a good mother, Jenny. Look at you. You're in the hospital, you're sick and still you're worried about being a good mother. That's the sign right there that you are."

"Maybe the same thing is happening to me as happened to Mom."

"No."

She cried then and all through the rest of visiting hours, even when Sister Anne brought Sunny in from the nursery and Jenny gave her a bottle and Sunny clutched her finger and gurgled happily. A little baby girl trying to soothe her girl of a mother. Then Jenny fell asleep with Sunny on her chest and the tears continued to soak Jenny's hair.

Sister Anne and I took Sunny back to the nursery, then on our way out we spoke to the nurse about the crying.

"It's not an exact science," the nurse said. "The doctors try to get the dose right. It might take another week or so. She'll improve gradually. It takes time."

—

Jenny had given me some of the money that John had sent. He had also offered to buy her a car, but that was no help to me yet. I made a list of people I could trust. It was a short list: John, Vern, Uncle Leslie. Vern had got some summer work with his other uncle near Bella Coola. John was still in California. Uncle Leslie never knew my mother, so I couldn't picture myself asking him for help.

That night I listened to the low rumble of traffic from Granville Street and I tried to pretend it was a river, the Chilcotin in early summer, rushing along with the sun glinting off it. I dipped a tin pot in the flow; it spilled onto my legs. An eagle whistled. I realized that I couldn't wait to get away, from Vancouver, from Williams Lake, and from the storm of worry that boiled and thundered in the heart of me.

[TWENTY-SIX]

A CHICKADEE SANG fee-bee below the raucous cry of a raven. A waxwing chirruped high and thin and a woodpecker hammered a nearby tree. Early morning, fresh and cool, and the bush was a jungle of sounds. The sunlight held just the soft breath of the heat it would bring later. I had only what I needed: matches, a tin cooking pot, a flask of water, some teabags, packages of Tang, a loaf of bread, a jar of peanut butter, some fishing line and hooks, a coil of rope, a sleeping bag and Dad's jackknife.

I went down to the creek and scooped a pot of water. There was no breeze and I easily rekindled last night's fire and settled the pot between two stones to boil water for tea. I had a handful of strawberries the size of my baby fingernail that I'd collected yesterday. I ate them for breakfast. They were so tart and delicious. I felt the stirrings of the same deep peace I'd felt last night by the fire, watching the constellations take shape in the night sky, the Big Dipper, Orion, Cassiopeia, Perseus. Peace seemed wrong; I felt guilty for feeling it. Still it came again with the familiarity of morning sounds. My mother had disappeared, my sister was in a mental hospital and I was sitting in the shade of an aspen, heating a pot of creek water for tea.

I had a sleeping bag, the pot, a mug and cutlery set, and a backpack to carry it all. I had money tucked away so that I could buy more food at the store in Duchess Creek. I had decided, like Chiwid, to walk and sleep out. The first day out of Williams Lake, I kept expecting someone to come after me. I didn't want them to. Mom would not be found by asking someone to lead me to her. I'd have to sneak up on her, like the man in the fir forest that night, who slipped in with the headlights off, leaving her no place to run.

After breakfast, I packed up my things, doused the fire and scattered the rocks and set out again. I was following the road. As the day began to heat up, I found the creek again and soaked my hair and shirt, let my feet cool in the fast running water. I knew the names of things out here: Canada mint, stinging nettle and horsetail by the water. Nodding onion on a sunny slope, the pale purple flower bending gently. Mallow, lamb's quarters—you can make a salad from the fresh young leaves. Yarrow for tea. Salsify, plantain, thistle, all along the roadside. You can eat the leaves and stems. Strawberries, you have to have the eye for them, the three leaves low to the ground, the tiny ruby berries. Last year's rosehips, shrivelled, but still good to chew or put in tea.

I made camp that evening near a path leading to a swampy lake. In the night I started awake and reached out for something familiar. Sand under my fingers, pebbles, twigs, the night very dark. I listened for what had wakened me. Nothing. Maybe that. That silence—not a breath, not a peep, not a stir. A quiet so soft and full I wanted to stay awake for it.

The smallest breeze rose and, on it, the scent of woodsmoke. I remembered then that I had dreamed of fire, carried on the wind, racing across the treetops. I was running with the animals, deer and raccoons and squirrels and long-legged birds, fleeing to the creek with flames thundering overhead.

And then from the woods, a single deep call, an owl. A few seconds later, an answer from another direction.

Not everything can be a sign. They're just signalling each other, calling out their territory. They don't know anything about me or my disappeared mother or how she loved the quiet of the night and sought out the lonely places.

But the worry crept into the calm of the night and down deep where I kept my darkest fears. Like the silence, there was nothing I could name, nothing that took shape, not yet, but worry billowed and gnawed, grew, and then came the drift of smoke again. That was something to latch onto, a forest fire nearby maybe, or someone camping. Which was worse? Mom feared humans more than bears or wolves or storms. "Which humans?" Jenny had asked. None in particular. Humans are unpredictable.

Leaves shivered now, softly. Nothing else, though I listened until my heartbeat galloped in my ears. I rolled to the precipice of sleep and jerked awake several times, sweating, sniffing the air, listening. When I woke to daylight, snow was gently floating down through the trees. I blew a flake from my arm. It wasn't snow, but ash, falling from the sky. Through the aspen leaves the sun was an orange smear, obscured by smoke. A breeze had picked up in the night and blew in ash and the heavy smell of pinesmoke. Somewhere north of here, the forest was on fire.

I walked through the day. Helicopters cut the quiet, flying north. A man in a big silver car pulled alongside me. His window whirred down and he offered me a ride. "No, thanks anyway," I said. Hundreds of birds rose from the telephone wire like a cloud, and turned all at once, sweeping across the road, turned again, and wheeled the other way, across the open meadow. Vehicles went by, some with an acknowledging wave of the hand. Some stopped to ask, "You all right?" or "Can I help you any?" But I didn't take any rides. I had lunch on a rock, the sun beating down on me, insect sound filling the roadside.

In the late afternoon, a truck came towards me and stopped on the other side of the road.

"We've got to stop meeting like this." Uncle Leslie smiled broadly through his open window. "I was just to Bella Coola. Smoke bothering you?"

"No. A little," I said.

"Where you headed?"

I couldn't answer, didn't know how to answer. I had not so much lied to him about my mother as neglected to tell him the whole story. The truth embarrassed me; it seemed to reflect badly on Jenny and me. The pain was a river I rode; I could not plant my feet in it or it would knock me down.

"I can take you to Duchess Creek," he said when I didn't answer.

"That's out of your way."

"Maggie," he said. Just that, but the tenderness in it took me by surprise and something broke in me. Standing there in the falling ash at the side of the road, my knees gave and I sank to the gravel. I began to cry, first like a baby and then like some kind of injured animal and I couldn't catch my breath and almost toppled over into the dirt from the weight of my backpack. Leslie caught my arm, saying, "Okay now, it's all right now. Let me help you."

He took my pack and put it in the truck then guided me into the cab and closed the door behind me.

I choked on air, and tears and snot streamed down my face. Leslie sifted through the glove compartment and found some serviettes and handed them to me, saying, "That's all I have." I wiped and choked, wiped and choked. He took my hand and held it, tight.

"It's all right now," he repeated, over and over.

His solid grasp steadied me. Slowly, slowly I returned to firs and aspen, the road ahead, hazy sky.

We drove west.

"Not to Duchess Creek," I said.

"Find a place to camp?"

I nodded. Closed my eyes.

We drove into the canyon south of the river on a lonely road. The land opened up to undulating grassland, an eerie wind slicing paths through the soft grass. Prairie birds wheeled and scolded. Hoodoos cut in sandstone climbed the other side of the river. Leslie pulled in where a log cabin had been abandoned. Its doorway, missing the door, gaped in shadow. Brambles poked up through the porch floorboards.

"The cabin's no good now, but I like the spot," he said. "The smoke isn't as bad over here."

I nodded. The river was a swift silty green and cool air rose from it.

"It might get a little bit chilly tonight. How're you set up?"

"I've got a good sleeping bag," I said.

"I put my tarp up on the back of the truck and sleep under there. Got a bit of foam for a mattress." He went about rigging it up and set his propane stove on the tailgate.

"Tea or hot chocolate?" he asked.

"Either is good."

I sat by the river. Suddenly I was so tired. This was Mom's favourite time, the space between day and night when the breeze, if there was one, died down, the sky deepened with green-tinged clarity and the clatter of day hushed. When we were at a lake, she liked to make her after-supper coffee over the fire and take it down to the beach to sit and listen to the water slap softly against the shore.

Leslie brought me a mug of hot chocolate and sat beside me. We drank in silence, watching the river. After a while, he heated up some beans over a little fire. We ate while the night darkened.

"Tell you a story," said Leslie. "How Vern came to live with me."

He'd been out to Nistsun to visit his sister and her son. He didn't like the white man Jolene was living with. "I've never liked any of them, truth be told. Superior sons of bitches. But this one was real bad. Violent. Vern had had to call my brother William one night when this piss-ant held the butt of a shotgun against Jolene's stomach. Poor little guy came running over to William's house in his underwear, yelling his head off, William said. I couldn't get that picture out of my head. I went to pay them a visit. Thought to talk some sense into Jolene and get her to turf the guy, with our help of course. What did she see in these guys? I just don't know. What did she see in herself that made her think she didn't deserve better?

"I stayed at William's place that first night. I was tired from the road and I couldn't stomach seeing the white guy when I was tired. I was sleeping in the screened porch. It was the longest day of the year. As I said, I was tired from the drive but I couldn't sleep. Beyond the pines I saw the mountains white capped and shadowed by cloud. I remember I watched the moon rise over the mountain and fill the clouds with silver light. I heard howling and wondered if it was a wolf. Something was knocking against the side of the porch in the wind. Next thing I knew, I found myself standing outside Jolene's house in the moonlight. A small blue bird flung itself against the bedroom window again and again. It was trapped inside. I moved to the living-room window and looked in. In the middle of the floor, a wolf was bent over a deer carcass, tearing chunks from her ribcage. The doe's neck stretched towards me and she opened her eyes and looked at me—not afraid but so soft and pitiful.

"I saw a shovel leaning against the step and hefted it, ready to smash the window. Then I woke up in the bed in William's porch. My heart was going ninety miles an hour. The moon had gone down again and so had the wind.

"I got up and went inside the house. I wanted to ask William what he thought about the dream, but he was asleep. So I put on my pants and shoes and I walked across the reserve to Jolene's house. I had no idea what time it was, but the reserve was quiet so I knew it must be late. She lived up close to the bush—you remember—and as I got closer, a long, lonely howl played out somewhere nearby in the hills and this time it really was a wolf. It sounded so forlorn, I felt a chill. I could see light from the living-room window spilling out on the dirt in front of Jolene's house. I heard shouting, a scream, maybe Jolene. A few vehicles were parked out front. I had a hell of a dread of what I would find. It was just like my dream. There was the shovel, leaning against the step, and I picked it up. I didn't stop to look in the window or knock, I just walked right in.

"Jeez, they were surprised. He had some other guy by the hair. White guys, both of them. Some others were half passed out at the table.

"'I'll scalp ya, swear to god you try that again, you fuck.' That was him, pardon my language. I remember the way he talked. There was nothing good in him, nothing. I held the shovel up, ready to swing. Their mouths dropped open. 'What the hell are you doing here?' Jolene said. I must have looked like a ghost. 'I'm taking the boy,' I said. No one tried to stop me. No one said anything.

"I still remember carrying him in my arms down the road. He woke up and said my name then fell back to sleep. Little Vern. God, I loved him. That wolf took up again and some others joined in and they howled us all the way home. He slept that night in the porch, curled up beside me. I worried for Jolene, but I knew I'd done what I could for her by taking her son out of there."

Uncle Leslie leaned over and put a few more sticks on the fire.

"I tried to protect him. He missed his mom, but I couldn't

let him go back there. Sometimes I wondered if I had the right. I still don't know."

After a while I said, "Jenny had her baby. She named her Sunny. She's keeping her." I told him about the nuns and Jenny's paranoia and her visions of girls with bloody nightgowns and baby-stealers. "Jenny needs Mom. She's just a girl and I don't know what to do for her. She needs her mother."

"And you're looking for her?"

"Yes," I said, and he didn't ask me anything more.

Uncle Leslie put out the fire and I tucked my sleeping bag alongside a boulder near the truck.

"You're going to be okay there?" he asked.

"Yeah. As long as it doesn't rain."

"It won't rain tonight. You sleep well, then, Maggie. If you need anything, anything at all, just call out. I'm not a heavy sleeper."

"Okay. Uncle Leslie?"

"Hmm?"

"Thank you."

"You're like my own niece. Sleep well."

I thought I would be able to sleep. I wasn't afraid and I wasn't cold, at least not at first. The stars were bright in spite of the smoke; the rhythmic rushing of the river drowned out any other night sounds, except the higher pitch of crickets singing from the grass. But my mind ticked and twitched at the edge of sleep. I had a picture of Uncle Leslie carrying little

Vern through the wolf howls. I saw the little body curled into the protective arms of the bigger one. Then it was me carrying Cinnamon, her tiny body warming me. Each time I opened my eyes, the moon was a little higher and the air a little colder. Something large was down at the river, splashing and huffing. I was cold now. I got up and went to the tailgate of the truck. Just stood there.

"Cold?" Leslie said, as if he'd been awake the whole time too.

"Yes."

"Come in here, then."

Leslie made room for me beside him and I crawled in with my sleeping bag, firewood and lawn chairs on one side of me and Uncle Leslie on the other.

"Go to sleep," he said and his arms folded over me like I was a little girl.

[TWENTY-SEVEN]

SMOKE FROM THE forest fire had settled over the region. There was no wind and the sun hung above the trees, a pale orange disc. Leslie stopped at the end of the driveway of our old house in Duchess Creek.

"Doesn't look like anyone's living there," he said, and we laughed. The porch had caved in on one side and the window of Jenny's and my room was broken. The hydro wire looked to be sagging almost to the ground.

I lifted my knapsack and got out.

"I'll make a few inquiries, if it's okay with you," Leslie said.

I nodded, set off down the driveway. When I looked back, he was still sitting there. He waved and put the truck into gear.

I left my pack near the spruce tree. What had once been a scraggly front yard had been returned to the wild. Deer scat nestled in tufts of grass here and there. They grazed here, on the wild rose bushes. The roof that Mom and Rita and I had once fixed was missing shingles; those that were left had rotted in the heat and cold of the seasons.

It wasn't a house built by people who meant to stay, as Mom used to say.

The door was unlocked. Inside, the house still smelled of old wallboard and mouldering insulation. But our family's smell was gone. The house had been scavenged of almost everything. The Formica table and chairs were gone; so was Dad's green chair and the beds in our room. The only thing left was the woodstove and Mom and Dad's bed. I pushed open the bedroom door. A film of dust coated the mattress. On Mom's side, a blood stain the size of a quarter. Spiders had stuck the folds of the curtains together with their webs; they crackled as I parted them to look out the window.

And then I caught a whiff of her lipstick, the briefest breath of that drugstore cosmetic-counter sweetness. I raised my head to breathe it in deep. Then the acrid scent of the forest fire billowed in on the breeze. Except there was no breeze. I turned to see if I had left the door open. I hadn't.

I swear she was there. I know that sounds crazy, but it felt as though she'd taken my hand in hers. It felt so good, I started to cry again and I heard her voice, telling me to shush now, Maggie-girl. I sat on the bed and it stayed with me, that feeling of her being there with me. I thought of phoning

Jenny to tell her, but I thought, what would that do, two of us off our rockers and hearing things?

I slept that night in that haunted house. I know that sounds crazy, too, but I wanted her to come back. Any minute she would be real, her footsteps crunching in the driveway.

But in the morning it was Agnes who came, in a sky blue cotton dress dotted with red flowers and wearing jeans underneath it, just like she used to.

She said she had wondered if she'd ever see me again and then she swallowed hard and her eyes glistened. "I'm getting so old, I cry when I'm happy now," she said. She wiped tears from her cheeks.

"You're not old," I said and hugged her. She felt thin in my arms and she held on after I went to pull away. Her chest heaved with the effort of not crying. It felt strange, me comforting her as if she was a child. But I wasn't comforting her, really. I was thanking her, though I couldn't say the words.

"I'm canning fish," she said, ducking her head to try and hide new tears. "Come over and help me."

We drove over to her house, and I watched her graceful gait, maybe a little tentative and pained as she climbed the steps, though she wouldn't be forty yet.

"I've got a touch of arthritis," she said, feeling my eyes on her. "I'm too young for that!"

In the house, she put the kettle on. "Have you come to make an honest woman of me?"

"Honest woman?"

"How many years ago did I promise to take you to Potato Mountain?"

"Four or five."

"Let's go tomorrow then," she said. "We'll have to put together a few things. We can take some of this fish."

"I don't want to mess up your plans."

"You're not going to believe the flowers we'll see up there. This is the time of year to go."

"Really, Agnes? Are you sure?"

Agnes started to laugh. She picked up the teapot and carried it to the sink and she stood there looking out the window, her shoulders shaking.

"Do you have a sleeping bag?" she said, still looking out the window.

"Yes."

"Good." She wiped her eyes and turned to me again. "We'll just take one little bag each. Sleeping bags. Some food, some water. Matches. A little tarp. Who did I lend that tarp to? Oh, you're going to love it up there. I haven't been in three or four years, I don't know why. You just forget how much you need to go."

When we got to the end of the road in the cool morning, a horse stood waiting, tethered to a fence. She flicked her tail and whinnied softly when she saw us.

Agnes patted her nose and fed her an apple. "This is

Linda. She'll carry our gear for us. You can ride her for a while if you want. Gotta watch the steep parts, though."

I shook my head. We left the sunshine and headed into the shade of the trees. We walked in single file, the horse snuffing her breaths and her tail swishing softly. We passed a big old pine and stopped to stare up at the deep fissures of its orange bark. The purple of Jacob's ladder pushed through ferns. Grasses poked from rock and, in breaks in the shade, patches of yellow balsamroot glowed in the morning sun. We climbed and the pines grew smaller, the aspens brushier and the meadow opened up, green and awash with flowers. The sun poured down, lighting the Indian paintbrush, the balsamroot and silver skeletons of pines, twisting amid the grass.

Agnes stopped to rest on a rock beside the trail. Warm now, I took off my jacket and looked out across the valley and the snow still lying on the mountaintops, white blending to ragged white cloud. But above us, farther up the trail that wound through the meadow, the sky was friendly, unforgettable turquoise brightened by sunlight, and the mountain was softened and gentle. Wild onion tanged the air. Agnes named the plants for me: violet, speedwell, buttercup, saskatoon, kinnikinnick, saxifrage, meadow rue, foxglove, columbine, strawberry, arnica, forget-me-not, soopollalie.

Soopollalie, soopollalie.

"We make Indian ice cream from that one," Agnes said. "The berries whip up like soap suds. That's the name, I guess."

A spell had been cast, or had one been broken? Here on the mountain, the sun pouring down, birdsong, wild onion and pine, among familiar flowers, things I could name and words I understood.

We had lunch on the mountaintop, looking out across the valley and the lake below. Later, settled around the fire in our little camp, Agnes told me the story she knew.

"I met your mother in Williams Lake when we were teenagers. Her mother had died—I don't know when—she was little, I guess. Her father was a cowboy. He came up from the States somewhere, didn't know a thing about ranching—that's what people said. But he was a fast learner. My dad and him worked some ranches together. He came to love that life, I guess. But he never knew quite what to do with Irene. Especially when she grew to a teenager. She was a little wild, you know. And beautiful. You know that. Her dad sent her to high school in Williams Lake and she didn't see much of him after that. I know, because holiday time everybody went home, but Irene stayed, and if there was no car at home, I stayed, too, with my old aunty. She was kind of dotty, sat in a chair in her room all day long, looking out that window at the mountains to the west. I suppose she was homesick, too, come to think of it. I made her meals, brought them to her on a tray. It was lonely sometimes.

"It was a Friday after school. Irene was walking behind me. I knew she was there. That was a holiday weekend, Thanksgiving, a long weekend. You didn't like those too much if you couldn't go home. 'You have beautiful hair,' I heard her say. I didn't turn around right away. What if she was talking to somebody else? But I knew it was me she was talking to. I was older than her—we weren't in the same grade. She ran to catch up with me. 'You have beautiful hair,' she said again. 'Do you do use something special on it?' I told her it was eggs. She looked at me with this funny look, like she thought I was kidding. Then she burst out laughing. I just stared at her, and then I started laughing too. My god, we laughed. Laughed till we cried. What was so damn funny, I don't know.

"But I invited her to my aunty's house in town. We made a big turkey dinner for just the three of us. My old aunty ate like a bird, just a bit of white meat and a tablespoon of mashed potatoes. So really, it was just for your mom and me. We made the stuffing, we made a mountain of potatoes, turnips, cranberry sauce, cauliflower with the cheese sauce. Pumpkin pie and whipped cream. Spent my aunty's money on all those groceries. We put a white tablecloth on the table and used my aunty's good dishes. We had to wash them first, they hadn't been used for so long—you know, the gravy boat, the platters, she had all of that. I don't know what possessed us, just the two of us and all that trouble, all that food. We were at it the whole day and night. We were still doing dishes after midnight. But, boy, we sure had fun. Your mom, she had that spirit in her—just up and do something, just because."

"I remember," I said.

"We stayed friends after that. But we didn't run with the same bunch. Irene was in with a drinking crowd. Not that she did much of that herself. But she tolerated it. I couldn't stand to be around it. Look what it did to so many of our people. Just wrecked them. Wrecked plenty of whites, too, but there's more of them, so you don't notice so much."

The fire had burned down so I put on more wood and poked it to life again.

"Can I ask you something, Agnes?"

"Yes, you can."

"Was my dad a drinker?"

"I didn't know your dad too well." She stared into the fire and I thought that was the end of it. She took up a stick and rearranged the embers so the fire flared and lit up her face.

"Some men think if they don't do anything bad, you know, like beating the wife or kids or yelling at them, where's the harm? Some men just open that bottle and in they go. They disappear. Maybe that's worse. Maybe harder for the women."

We sat in silence. The fire popped and spit bright embers on the ground and we stomped out the big ones.

"Your mother didn't finish high school. She didn't like living in town. She took off halfway through grade eleven. I heard she went to Bella Coola, got a job in a restaurant or motel or something. She was only sixteen or so. She met a man there."

I felt my stomach tighten.

"Name of Emil Deschamps. Métis fellow from the Prairies. He had a fishing boat and she got a job fishing with him."

Agnes laughed. "Imagine that. That's going to go one of two ways. I guess they fell in love. I guess maybe Emil was in love with her when he asked her to go out on his boat. I saw him once in Duchess Creek on his way through to Williams Lake or somewhere. Irene told me who he was. He was a handsome man, shiny black hair, curly, kind of tall, nice smile. Had a big old car. Maybe a Pontiac."

"Was Mom with him then?"

"Not at that time, no. But she told me they took that boat out and went to the most beautiful places, islands and beaches. She told me I would love to see it. She told me we should go sometime and I thought I might, she made it sound so good. But I didn't. She didn't either, as far as I know. She was married to Patrick. She had little Jenny. That would have been 1959, because my dad died that year. Irene loved being a mother."

I looked up at the sky and there was the riot of stars that my grandmother had missed so much.

I spoke slowly. "She did love being a mother, didn't she?"

"She told me so, Maggie."

"Well then I don't understand."

"No," said Agnes.

"I'm looking for her. I'm out here looking for her. Jenny needs her. But I don't really want to find her. I know that's a terrible thing to say. But what would it mean if we found her, alive somewhere, living her life?"

"No," said Agnes again.

A star shot across the sky just above the trees. I breathed in quickly. Then another followed, a brightness disappearing.

"You need to go see Rita," said Agnes.

[TWENTY-EIGHT]

UNCLE LESLIE WAS waiting for us when we got back to Agnes's house.

"I found her car," he said.

"Come on in," said Agnes, and we went inside where she made tea. She brought out biscuits and homemade jam and we sat at the kitchen table.

"I asked around about your mom," Uncle Leslie began again. "A fellow over here said, 'That lady with the red hair that drove the Chevy station wagon?' He said he knew a guy who bought the car about three years ago. Over near Dultso. So I drove over to see him. He said he bought it from a man, dark-haired guy, maybe Japanese, he said. Told him the car had been well cared-for by his wife. And it was. Still in beautiful shape. I bought it from him."

Agnes started to laugh.

"You what?" I said.

"You in need of another car?" Agnes said.

"I bought it for you, Maggie. You're going to need a car, you and Jenny and the baby. You can't be hitchhiking around the countryside with a baby."

"Uncle Leslie, I . . ."

"No, don't say anything. I don't want to hear it. By rights the car is yours. And I got it for a song."

I called Jenny from Agnes's house. She sounded so much better, the worry that clutched my stomach uncoiled a little.

"She's a happy baby," Jenny said.

"Like her name."

"It makes it easier for me. Sister Anne got us a stroller. Ginger calls it a pram. We've been out walking. The roses are all in bloom. But I can't wait to come home."

I swallowed. What did she mean?

"Mag?"

"Yeah, I know, Jenny. Hey, you won't believe this." And I told her about the car.

"That old car," Jenny said. "I loved that car."

Driving in that car with Mom always felt like escaping. We hit the road with no one to answer to. We were unaccountable and unaccounted for. There were strings of days when even Dad wouldn't know where to find us. Powdered milk and canned meat, no toilets, no beds or doors.

I used to pity the people we passed along the way, especially the women. I pitied Mrs. Duncan yawning behind the counter at the Nakenitses Lake store. As I paid for my Orange Crush, I could feel in her eyes that she wanted to escape, too. Sometimes I said to Mom, "Do you think she's jealous?"

"Sure she is. Who wouldn't be?" she always said and I wonder now if she was serious. I should ask Jenny, but at the time, I believed her.

We napped under the sheltering branches of giant spruce trees and made tea from rosehips and spruce needles, and sweetened it with honey. Mom kept some one-gallon glass jugs in the car and she knew where there were springs grown round with graceful willow. We knelt in the thick moss and caught the water in the jugs as it bubbled out. We swam naked in remote lakes and creeks. We sunbathed on warm rock, like wood nymphs, Mom said. Sometimes she called Jenny and me "the little people."

"Who are the little people?" Jenny asked.

"They're the secret ones who live in an underground world that can only be entered at the water's edge. They like it if you leave them little gifts of candy and cloth." Sometimes she gave us a bright kerchief to tie to a branch near the water.

"But you don't want to get too friendly with them," she warned. "If you do, they'll steal you away to live with them for seven years."

And then, when we returned to the car, there was the sun-baked vinyl smell of it, the warmth, like a nest.

Uncle Leslie brought the car over to Agnes's. I wanted to be happy to see it, but any trip we made now in the station wagon would not be an escape. A net of memory was tightening around me.

FIRE

[TWENTY-NINE]

THE YARD WAS THE SAME as I remembered it—chickens scattered as we drove in. The grass was as green as it would get all season. In the shade of a row of crab apple trees, Rita looked up from digging and rested her foot on her shovel. I thought her mouth fell open a little when she saw the car. I waved and Uncle Leslie cut the engine. My stomach twisted.

I got out of the car.

"I'll come back in a while," he said, and I almost laughed. Was he scared of Rita, too?

As he pulled out of the driveway, Rita ran her hand through her hair then thrust the shovel into the earth and came towards me.

"Aunt Rita," I said, before I thought about how it would sound.

She breathed in sharply. "Margaret," she said. She stood there in the sun, dumbfounded and flustered. I thought to hug her but I was waiting to see which emotion her clouded face would settle on.

"It's been a long time," I said into the awkwardness.

She laughed drily. "Bit of an understatement."

"Who's your driver?" she asked, but she was looking over at the shovel sticking up in the dirt.

I had the urge to back up slowly, the way you're supposed to if you meet a bear, throw something down to distract her, run.

"He's from Williams Lake."

"Does he have a name?"

"Leslie. Leslie George."

"I guess I could use a break. Would you like some coffee?" she said, finally turning her head to me.

Inside, the house was the same. The woodstove that separated the kitchen and living-room areas, kindling neatly stacked in a box beside it, the same big old dining room table cluttered with mail and newspapers, where Jenny and I had done our homework, the sagging couch, the braided rug. So much had changed for Jenny and me, but Rita had settled into her life a long time ago. I envied that. Change would be an irritant to Rita now, and I was bringing it, like a cold wind funnelling up the valley.

Rita went to the kitchen cupboard and took down the coffee tin.

"Where are you staying?" she asked.

"I'm camping."

She hesitated, just a second too long. "Stay here."

"I don't want to be any trouble."

"Oh for god sakes." She rattled the coffee pot on the stove. "I meant for the night, not forever."

"I know," I said. No excuse came readily to mind and there was no turning back. The last time I'd seen Rita, we'd left in a hurry in the middle of the night. She had not forgotten.

We took our coffee mugs and sat in lawn chairs on the porch. The boards had that soft silver sheen I remembered. I had sat here watching for Mom and brushing my fingers back and forth along the grain of the weathered wood.

A clumsy silence wrapped us. Rita looked out at the road, I looked at her. Her mouth seemed tighter and the skin around her eyes and neck looser. Her fine blonde hair was shorter, but cut in the same plain way, straight bangs, the rest just grazing her shoulders. I tried to remember the way she had been, the face that had drawn Mom to her—a wide-open frankness and a crease of mischief around the eyes.

"Where are you living?" Rita asked.

"Williams Lake. But Jenny's in Vancouver." I was about to blurt it all out, but Rita cut me off.

"Good for you." Her voice was flat, just a semi-tone off a taunt. "How long have you been there?"

"Let's see. I guess it's about three years."

She looked surprised. Was it possible that she knew nothing about where we'd been since we left her? I decided not to tell her about Jenny right away. Maybe I wouldn't tell her at all.

"I've got some horses since you were here last. Would you like to see them?"

"Okay."

"Listen Margaret," she said. "I can't stand the polite chit-chat. You came here for a reason, and soon enough I'll find out what it is. But for now, let's cut the crap and go see some horses."

Ten deep breaths, I heard Dad say, to keep from panicking in a survival situation. I breathed deeply.

Rita took an apple from her jacket and handed it to me. "Last year's," she said. "They'll take it." And so we walked down to the corral and I fed the horses and they nuzzled their soft noses against me.

When Uncle Leslie came back, I told him I'd stay a couple of days. He nodded to Rita and she nodded back. As he drove away again, she said, "Family friend?"

"My friend," I said, and it was only then that it dawned on me that Rita was waiting for me to tell her about Mom as much as I was waiting for her to do the same for me.

I helped Rita finish transplanting some lilacs, while the afternoon sun brightened the snow that still held high in the mountains across the lake. Then she said, "I've got about two cords of wood to stack. When's the last time you did any hard work?"

"It's been a while."

"Then I'm doing you a favour."

We bent and tossed, bent and tossed and I remembered those fall days after Dad died, Rita and Mom stacking wood and singing. I had the feeling I was walking backwards through our lives and that I would knock up against something suddenly that would make sense.

Later, we fried a chicken and ate that with mashed potatoes and peas.

"Everything on the table is grown here," Rita said.

"Good for you," I said, in the same tone she'd used with me. And she smiled.

When the light began to fade, uneasiness seeped back into my body. The day had been nice and I was afraid of the talk that was to come. After the dishes, we went out to the porch again.

"I love this time of day," Rita said. "My muscles are aching, so I know I've done something. And there's the moon rising. It's so peaceful. I think about the work I did, what I'll do tomorrow. I wouldn't change it, you know."

"I want to have a farm someday."

"You do?"

"Yeah. With Jenny and her baby. My niece."

"Huh," she said. "Jenny had a baby?"

"Yeah."

"Huh."

Some bats dived in the dark, and the dog lifted his head to look up then settled back into sleep. The lighted house cast a glow into the yard.

"Maggie," Rita said. It was the first time she had called me Maggie in a long time. "You might as well tell me why you came and get it over with."

I considered ways to begin. But there was really only one question. "Do you know where my mother is?"

"No. Where?" said Rita.

"No. It's a real question. I want to know if you know where she is."

"Why on earth would I know where your mother is?"

I didn't answer. Agnes had said I should come to see Rita and I hadn't thought about asking why.

"You were best friends."

"Were we? Oh god, Maggie, this is so unpleasant. What's to be gained by dredging it up?"

"What's to be gained?" I felt my face burn. "Maybe you didn't understand my question."

"Maybe I didn't."

We sat there, the house, the porch, the moon, the trees, and I burned and she burned and my heart beat furiously and I thought of leaving, on foot if I had to, then thought how ridiculous it would be to replay that scene.

After a few minutes, I calmed enough to think of a new tack. "Why did you and Mom fight that night? Why did we leave?"

Rita didn't speak and when I looked over at her, she appeared to be crying. "Christ I need a scotch," she said. She got up, and went into the house and came back with a large glass.

"The problem is I'm going to come out looking badly in this. No way around it." She sipped the scotch. "Forgive me if I'm not too enthused about dragging myself through the mud."

I almost said, "I'm not asking about you." People who live alone become selfish, I thought. Bea was selfish in the same way, even though she wasn't exactly alone. Maybe it was because Bea and Rita had no children. Mothers give and bend, even when they get nothing in return. At least, that's the way it's supposed to be.

"What do you remember about that night?" Rita said, after another swallow of scotch. "What did Irene tell you?"

I was momentarily confused. Irene, the woman who was my mother.

"I was sleeping in the car that night."

"I'd forgotten that."

"You and Mom fought earlier in the day."

"She'd been out all night. I hadn't had a moment's sleep. I was worried sick. I mean the gall of it just sent me. You might not want to hear this, Maggie, but it was so irresponsible. She's a mother and she's got two little girls and she's off gallivanting all night. The only reason she could get away with it was because she trusted me to cover for her. And she was just so smug, coming home in the middle of the afternoon with her clothes all wrinkled. I could smell the stink of that man on her."

I felt like I'd been punched. "That can't be right."

"Damn right. It wasn't right."

"Who was he?"

Rita sipped her scotch and stared out at the night. The silence yawned. A bird called in the woods, and another answered.

"Who was the man?"

"She was pretending, that's what she was doing. And she was cowardly. I couldn't forgive her."

"Rita, who was the man?"

She didn't answer.

I got up from my chair and went inside. In the bathroom I splashed cold water on my face. Rita's anger had smouldered all this time and I was poking it back to life. Whoever the man was, he was getting Mom's attention, and Rita wasn't.

I settled back into my chair. The bottle of scotch was now sitting beside Rita's lawn chair.

"I loved her," she said.

"What?"

"You heard me."

"You mean, like. . . ."

"Yes like that."

"I . . ."

"Maybe you've never heard of such a thing. Well, it's more common than you think. I'm just a normal woman who loved a woman, who just happens to be your mother."

I couldn't have said anything if I'd tried.

"I told her that night. That's why she ran. But she knew long before that. She just pretended she didn't. It was more convenient."

I didn't know what to say. My head was buzzing like the bugs crowding around the porch light. Rita sat there sullenly nursing her scotch. She was still angry, after all this time.

"But did you see her again?" I finally asked.

"She sent me a letter. A fucking letter. Not even a page long. I opened it, hoping maybe she had come to her senses. She would apologize. But no, it was excuses, 'if I understood et cetera, et cetera.' Why bother? Why bother to write someone that kind of letter? Why bother to read it? Waste of paper. Today, when you drove into the yard, I thought for a minute that it was her, at last. Pathetic."

She was drunk now and I supposed it would all come out, all the bile. Maybe it would be good for her.

"I'm going to tell you something you don't seem to know," I said.

"All right."

I had scared her a little. I could hear it in her voice.

"The last time we saw Mom was the day after we left here."

"What do you mean?"

"That night you fought. We drove away. We went to Williams Lake and she left us there."

"With your father's friends."

"That's right. The Edwards. We haven't seen her since. She sent some letters, some money, but then even that stopped. For all I know she's dead."

Rita seemed suddenly sober. She shook her head. "That's not possible." She stared at me as if I'd take it back. When I said nothing, she got up and lurched inside. I could hear her through the screen door, in the washroom, vomiting.

Minutes passed. I began to feel a chill in the night air.

I went inside and put the kettle on. Muffled noises came from the bathroom. In the cupboard I found a box of tea. I warmed the pot and dropped in the bags. When she still didn't come out, I went to the door and knocked. "Are you okay?" I said. "I'm making tea."

"Thanks," I heard. I went to get the kettle.

Several more minutes passed before she came out.

She lowered herself into a chair at the table and I put the tea in front of her. She inhaled the steam, her hands wrapped around the mug. I sipped mine and could think of nothing to say.

"Maggie," she finally began. "I didn't know."

"But you know more than you're saying."

"Yes, you're right. I do."

It was my turn to be scared.

Her hands shook as she lifted the mug to sip the tea. "She came to see me one more time. It was January. I'd got the letter in October and then she showed up one day in January. It was stinking cold. Deep snow. The roads were in no shape. I hadn't even cleared my driveway. She was driving a pickup truck. She didn't have the station wagon any more. She said she'd sold it. The truck wasn't that good, that's why I remember. I was worried about her driving around the freezing countryside in that hunk of junk. The battery was for shit. I gave her jumper cables. Well anyway," Rita waved her hand. "She was pregnant, Maggie."

Something happened next, but how can I tell it? Something,

nothing, I don't remember. I believe I did nothing. I believe I sat. Some storm raged inside me, lightning, treetops exploding in flame. The cage of my body somehow contained it.

"She asked me to take in you girls," said Rita. "She said it would be temporary, but she'd left you too long at the Edwards. She didn't know them well and she'd never meant it to be that long. She offered to pay me. I said no. Or wait. Let me think now for a minute. What I said was, 'Am I just your pal who helps you out whenever you have an emergency? Is that all I'm good for?' And she said, 'I don't know why I imagined you would help me. You're a selfish woman. A selfish, lonely, bitter woman and that's what you'll always be.' If I'm remembering right."

"But why did she have to leave us?" My voice was someone else's. It hovered high above my body and drilled and drilled like a woodpecker and I had the strangest feeling, my body a shaking whirling blizzard, and I thought of Jenny—that maybe that was what it was like for her now.

Rita said, "His name was Emil. She said he needed her."

"What about us? We needed her," I said. It croaked out of me like the squawk of a broken bird.

I found myself out on the Nakenitses Lake Road, howling. It was getting light in the east. I was suddenly just there on the road, walking hard and howling. I don't know how I got there but I had covered quite a bit of ground. I saw headlights coming towards me. A woman picked me up, not Rita. She had a blanket and she wrapped me and she spoke softly.

She was kind. I don't know who she was. Still don't. She took me back to Rita's and Rita thanked her. Rita put me in her own bed. She gave me hot milk and she sat with me while I drank it. Then she turned off the light and left me.

[THIRTY]

What I couldn't get over when I listened to the story Rita told me the next day, what I can't get over still, is that she would know this at all, and we wouldn't. How could a stranger come into our mother's life and, after just a few months, know more about her than her own children? I had this image of Mom as a lake, with Jenny and me bobbing around on her surface, never dreaming, never even wondering about the green depths beneath us.

Rita had brought me a cup of tea when I woke up and said, "Breakfast is on the table." We ate in silence. When we were done, she said, "After you're cleaned up, come on outside."

I could hear the ring of the axe as I stepped onto the porch. She was splitting wood. I joined her at the woodpile and she handed me a pair of gloves, then looked across the meadow at the mountains and said, "It's beautiful, isn't it? I often think how lucky I am to have this piece of land, and when I wake up in the morning the most complicated thing I have to do is split up a pile of wood. Did you know I used to live in the city? I was a teacher."

"You?" I said.

"You're shocked, I see." She drove the axe into the chopping block and took off her gloves. "Well, I don't blame you. Obviously, I'm not doing it anymore. But yes, I went to Teachers' College in Saskatchewan. Then I taught up north for a year and I hated every minute of it. So I applied for another teaching job in Vancouver and I got it. It was such a change from northern Saskatchewan, and at first I liked it. I went out to plays and movies and I spent a lot of time at the library.

"But then I started to miss the north. I read books about it. I read this one book called *Driftwood Valley*. I'll lend it to you if you want. It's about a woman and her husband who go into the wilderness in British Columbia. Just north of here. And they build a cabin and live there. I decided I wanted to do that. Without the husband. I could see my life, ten years, twenty years of it day after day and only the summers to do what I wanted. I realized I didn't really like kids. It just infuriated me how little sense they made. No offence. But you're not really a kid anymore. I wanted to get away. I wanted to be left alone."

"Why did you become a teacher in the first place?" I asked.

"Survival. I had to survive. It was that or get married and there was no way I was going to do that." She put her gloves back on. "I found this place for sale. It came with the mail delivery job. It seemed made for me. Come on Maggie, help me stack this pile. I've had the night to sleep on it and I've decided to tell you everything I know. You and Jenny have been fending for yourselves all this time—you're old enough to know."

We worked through the morning, as the sun beat down on us, growing hotter as it rose overhead. Dust and bark chips clung to the glaze of sweat on our arms. I tried to focus on stacking, fitting each log neatly into the pile, and not on the image I kept getting of Mom sitting in a cabin somewhere feeding lunch to a baby, a baby who would be about three years old.

Then I latched on instead to what Rita had said about the crappy old truck with the bad battery. Maybe she had had an accident. Maybe she'd gone off the road, been buried in snow and never found. Or maybe the truck had stalled out somewhere in the middle of nowhere. She'd been driving to us, after she left Rita, and when she couldn't get the truck going, she'd broken the golden rule of survival: leaving the shelter of the truck and trying to walk out.

I stopped to drink the mug of water Rita brought. The more I thought about it, the more sense it made. I wanted to tell Rita to forget about telling me what she knew. I wanted to call Uncle Leslie and get the hell out of there, go back to Jenny and tell her a story that would protect her, instead of destroying her.

—

"I know we must seem old to you," Rita said. We were eating our lunch in the shade on the porch. Rita had poured herself a glass of berry wine. "I'm a bit older, but your Mom is only, what, thirty-two?"

"If she's still alive," I said.

"What do you mean?"

"She could be dead. For all we know."

"Don't even think it, Maggie. Don't think the worst."

I wanted to say, "That's not the worst." But I didn't.

"My point is, when Irene got pregnant with Jenny she was sixteen."

"Jenny is sixteen."

"That's right and you see how young she is, and probably scared."

"She's in the hospital."

"With the baby?"

"She had the baby a month ago."

"So why is she still in the hospital? Don't play guessing games with me, Maggie. I'm trying my best."

I told Rita what had happened to Jenny and after she heard it, she said, "So. It's even more important that I tell you."

She refilled her glass. "You need to know about Emil. I'm not going to hide anything from you, but you'll have to be patient, Maggie. I'm going to tell it in my own time, the way I remember her telling me. She told me once that she wanted to tell you girls someday, when you were old enough. I think that ship has sailed." This is what Rita told me.

—

Irene had met Emil in Bella Coola. After she quit school in Williams Lake, she headed west until she couldn't go any farther. She got a job in a café. She didn't know anyone. The cloud in Bella Coola was depressing, hanging low like smoke in the valley if there was no wind. To Irene, coming from the dry sunny plateau, it seemed like there was always something coming from the sky, rain or snow or just the feeling of rain sometimes. Sometimes the east wind howled down there like they'd all be swept out to sea. She was probably lonely.

Emil came in for lunch every day. He was from the Prairies and must not have known very many people himself. He always came in alone. He always had the same thing, the homemade soup and a grilled cheese sandwich and a pot of tea. They had this routine, where she'd say *the usual?* And he'd say *the usual.* It was a little game they played.

Emil talked to her, but his talk was a bit odd, it didn't seem ordinary and yet in some ways, it was dead ordinary. He'd comment on what she was wearing, even when she rarely wore anything other than flannel shirts and jeans. He'd comment on the folds of the shirt, for instance, the way the fabric fell softly from her shoulders, maybe the pattern of the plaid. He'd notice the way the cheese melted in his sandwich and spilled over the bread. When she brought him his order he'd point that out. And he'd say, *This is the best sandwich ever.*

I think you are the queen of grilled cheese sandwiches. The queen of grilled cheese sandwiches, of all things. But she was sixteen and his oddness appealed to her. That and the fact that he was so interested in everything she did.

He told her about the places he went in his boat, the *Elsa.* A white-shell beach with old totem poles hiding in the trees. You could pick clams and mussels and feed yourself on salmonberries and trout. *When the tide is out, the table is set,* that was the expression he used. Old Indian villages, no one there in the summer, just the ravens and bears and once in a while a cougar. That appealed to her.

Of course when Irene told Rita the stories, Rita thought Emil was long gone out of the picture. She'd been out on a boat around there once, and had often thought of going back. But it had scared her a bit, the ocean. She didn't think she was the coastal type.

Irene didn't know anything about boats or the ocean either. She didn't know a clam from a mussel.

What she liked about Emil was that he was kind. She talked about his eyes. How soft and kind they were, his long eyelashes. He was older than her by about ten years, in his mid-twenties. At first, she didn't think of him romantically. But she liked his stories and the intensity of him. He wasn't like anyone she'd ever met. *Come and visit me on the* Elsa, Emil said one day. And one day she went.

They walked down to the dock where he was moored. He had restored the boat himself. It struck her that it looked fresh, like it hadn't been out on the water much, painted white with a fresh blue stripe and *Elsa* lettered on the hull. He kept herbs in clay pots on the deck and she noticed that. She noticed his clothes drying on a line. Maybe she fell in love with the boat first.

Emil told her he had first seen the boat for sale at the dock in Bella Coola—it was a thirty-five-foot gillnetter, in need of repair. Someone had brought it up from Steveston and then run out of money. But Emil's father was a carpenter and he'd worked at that himself for a few years. He liked that kind of work. So he'd bought it and done the repairs, then added his own touches. He'd built a cabin behind the wheelhouse. He'd made a narrow table and shelves and polished the wood to a gleam. Everything had a place. There was a little oil stove and a row of four green mugs hanging on hooks. She fixated on the mugs for some reason. They were translucent green, the colour of seawater, and every time she used one she thought how ordinary and beautiful they were. She loved the compact order of that little boat, and she imagined how it would be, bobbing in the ocean at night, snug in the cabin, drinking tea from a sea-green mug.

The cabin smelled of turpentine. He was an artist. On the shelves, held in place by a thick strip of elastic, were tubes of oil paints, brushes, and palette knives. His art was fastened to every available space. He painted recognizable things like cedar trees, totem poles, birds, but some were just triangles and squares of light and shadow.

How did you end up here? she asked him that first day. He said it was a long story, asked her how much time she had. *I better make tea,* he said and that was the start. She was giddy with the attention he showed her, tucked away in the cabin of his boat with the rain pecking the windows and a man making tea for her. What had she known up until then? Cowboys her age who wanted to rope her like one of their calves and grab her tits.

I could see what Rita was doing. She was trying to build my sympathy for Mom for something else that was coming, and that worried me. She had relaxed into the story; she was enjoying it. We were facing west, and she kept raising her eyes and gazing out towards the mountains, as if she was watching it unfold over there. I thought about lying side-by-side with Vern in our tree fort and I missed him intensely.

Irene said that Emil was gentle and slow in all his movements. He had long slender legs and arms, long brown fingers. He was graceful, always touching things, stroking them. He liked textures, noticed them in a way most people don't. She figured that was the artist in him. He made tea, not from teabags, but with leaves measured from a tin, poured the water over it, gave it a stir, timed it steeping. Sugar, milk from a can. He peeled an orange and put the segments on a plate. It became one of the things she loved, watching him make tea for her.

He gave her a pillow and helped her tuck it behind her back. She could sense his desire, but said she ignored it. She was flattered by his attention.

Emil told her he had inherited money from his aunt, lots of it, not that there was much left by the time she met him. He'd gone to New York, to art galleries, art shows, talks, coffee houses. He'd travelled, gone to Europe to see the masters. He was admitted to art school in Toronto on the strength of his work.

Art school changed his life. When he returned to the Prairies, the landscape felt claustrophobic. He had the feeling all that sky was closing in on him. He began to have what he called visions. Weird visions, like dreams, but they happened when he was awake—intense and very real. He had a recurring one he told Irene about. Birds of prey were following him, hawks and falcons and eagles. He saw them everywhere, perched on fences, store roofs, signposts, in the tree outside his bedroom window. He'd done a series of drawings of them and he showed her. Two whole sketchbooks full.

He had another aunt who lived in Bella Coola and he came out to visit her, to get away from the Prairies and the visions.

That's when he decided to buy the boat.

Irene's visits to his boat became a regular routine and, eventually, he asked her to go out on the boat with him. He said he wanted to fish and he needed a partner. This was a pretence and they both knew it. But the idea of bobbing in the ocean with Emil looking after her was too appealing to resist. Irene had been on her own for quite a while already by then. Her dad had left her to go to school in Williams Lake while he was out cowboying around the countryside. He seemed to think she could take care of herself. Which was probably true. He didn't even know she'd gone to Bella Coola and it was a long time after that when she found out he'd died of a heart attack way out in the woods, looking for horses.

Anyway, one day in the café, Irene was serving a group of men, and after Emil left, they started to talk about him. They didn't seem to care if she overheard, in fact she thought maybe their talk was partly for her benefit:

He knows fuck-all about fishing.

He's from the Prairies. He knows prairie chickens and deer.

His boat looks good.

Sure it does, he's a carpenter. Not a fisherman.

I don't think he cares much if he catches anything or not.

He'll get himself drowned.

Long as he doesn't take anyone down with him.

It should have made her uneasy, but being sixteen going on seventeen, she just thought they didn't understand Emil. He wasn't just looking for fish; he was looking for experiences. He was an artist.

They went out the first time in June. They didn't take the nets and gear. Emil said he wanted Irene to get used to the *Elsa,* learn how to use the tide charts, all of that.

The cliffs rise straight up from the water out there and they stretch down into the water just as far, like there are two worlds, and you're in between them. Irene had to surrender to the mountains and the bald eagles and the wind, and to Emil. That started to dawn on her as she watched him steering the *Elsa*—she was in his hands.

Everything about this world was unfamiliar to her. The words *galley* and *deck* and *dinghy* and *bunk*. Emil on the bunk in his blue jeans and bare feet, eating a plate of fish that they'd caught with handlines off the boat, and watching her. It was so intimate, to see his feet. She had never seen his bare feet. And the way the boat was called "she." The engine was called *Vivian*. Emil would say, *I better tend to Vivian*. And he'd go down below and start her up and then chuff, chuff, chuff, off they went up the inlets. Irene found out later that Vivian was the engine make, and not a name he'd made up.

A couple of days out, Emil came up behind her on the deck, pulled her close and kissed her neck. She had a moment of fear, but it burned off in the heat of his touch.

Rita stopped.

"What?" I said. I almost shouted it.

"I need a little break."

"Now?"

"I'm going to get some crackers. The wine's going right to my head."

I had been thinking that Mom then had not been much older than I was now, and that Vern was gentle like Emil.

And that Rita's voice had grown tender as she talked and I supposed she missed Mom, missed staying up through the night with her, talking and giggling over the things they'd done when they were younger.

When she came back outside, carrying a few crackers, she said, "Let's walk. I can't sit the way I used to. I must be getting old."

"You're not old."

"No. But telling this story makes me feel ancient."

So we headed across the meadow. The sun wasn't as intense now, and the heat felt comfortable on my shoulders. Rita kept her head down, as if she was considering where to start again. We wound through a few scrub trees then into deeper shade.

"Let's just say Emil was a kind and gentle lover, too," she finally began again. "I give the guy credit. He had studied it. Read books about it."

"There are books?"

"Sure. And he was very patient. They didn't even make love that first day when he kissed her. Or the next. It was a few days later, I don't know how many. I guess he wanted her to want it as much as he did."

So he'd do things like take her clothes off, slowly, piece by piece, but stay fully dressed himself. And then maybe he'd trace her body with his fingers. He'd take a smooth stone and place it at the hollow of her throat, find the places of her pulse with it and let her feel how warm the stone would get. He made sure she was comfortable on the bunk and he did charcoal drawings of her. She grew to love his eyes on her. He was systematic about winning her over. And she was the one finally who knocked him down on the bunk one day and made him take his pants off.

Life on the *Elsa* was sweet. They put in at little bays and took the dinghy ashore to explore. They swam in warm tidal pools at night with trails of shining phosphorescence dripping from their bodies. Every few days they looked for a mooring where they could find fresh water to wash off the salt that dusted their skin and caked their hair. Irene had had no idea how salty the ocean really was.

They had their daily domestic tasks, crab traps to drop over the side, dishwater to heat on the Coleman stove on deck. But Emil wouldn't let Irene play the housewife. He snatched a shirt from her hand when she went to wash it one day. *Don't do that,* he said. *Why?* she asked. *That's not what you are to me.*

"I like him for that," Rita said.

I did, too. I could see myself in Mom's place. Nothing to worry about and all the time in the world.

One morning, Emil ran them into a little white shell beach. They anchored the *Elsa* in deep water, and took the dinghy in. The terrain can be rough going as soon as you try to go inland. It's rainforest, lush as it gets, like a tropical jungle. They bushwhacked through thickets of wild roses and devil's club as tall as Irene, leaves as big as her head, and spiky stems. The only sound, other than the ocean, was the ravens heckling them. Before they saw it, she could hear the rumble of a waterfall, then feel the coolness.

She said it was like an Eden, the water tumbling straight down from the mountains and at the bottom, a series of pools. She couldn't wait to strip off her salt-stiff clothes. She and Emil stood naked under the cascade of water. It was very cold but it washed the salt away. Afterwards they lay on the warm rocks and Emil fell asleep in the sun.

When he woke, he said, *Do you see that?*

He pointed through the trees at a pole with a bird carved into it, his hooked beak overlooking the forest and beach beyond. Irene noticed boxes in the spruce trees that she hadn't seen until she looked carefully. They were tied with strips of cedar, and some had come loose and were flapping in the breeze.

What is it? she asked him.

They're graves. The dead are tied into trees with their possessions. If you walk through there, you can find copper bracelets, necklaces, maybe some skulls.

She wouldn't touch any of it.

He said, *No. You shouldn't take what belongs to the dead. The ravens are watching.*

Seems like you've been here before, she said.

I like it here. It's peaceful.

It was peaceful. Still beyond still. Even the ravens had left them.

Emil suddenly jumped up, said *I'll be back in a while.* Before Irene could ask any questions, he was gone.

She wasn't worried. She lay in the sun daydreaming, listening to the water spill over the rocks. She slept a little. When she woke up, she passed the time as she waited for Emil by looking for nice stones in the stream.

She kept looking over to the beaked pole and the graves like clusters of nests in the trees. She wanted to go search for bracelets in the grass, not to take them, but just to see proof that someone had been there once, led a life from start to finish there. But she wouldn't go alone.

Two ravens came back and talked to her, back and forth, know-it-all remarks, like ravens do. *All alone? All alone. Where did he go? He took off. He took off.* They laughed about it, she swore they did.

The afternoon wore on and still Emil didn't come back. She began to get annoyed. The ravens cackled: *Scared? Scared?* Then she heard movement in the brush, branches cracking, and she saw a large shape slip among the trees. Emil had warned her about bears, but this moved too swiftly and smoothly to be a bear.

She called out. *Emil! I don't like your jokes.* She thought he was playing a game with her.

But the shape moved past her and the sound trailed off.

She shouted his name over and over, scared now, and the ravens seemed to mock her openly. Finally, in the distance she heard, *I'm coming!* Then she felt the pounding of his feet approaching.

He appeared through the trees, two lovely trout hanging from his hand.

Of course she was so relieved she cried.

And he said, all innocence, *Was I gone too long?* Like he had no idea.

Let's just go, she said.

I want to make a fire on the beach to roast the trout.

She said no. She wanted to go back to the boat.

It was the first time he'd seen her angry and Emil, apparently, didn't like anger. He never got angry himself, didn't have it in him. When he saw it in her, he turned away, like he was embarrassed for her.

They rowed back to the *Elsa* and Emil cleaned the fish and fried it up. But Irene was uneasy. It was partly the place. From a distance, the totem pole looked menacing. The beak seemed like a warning. Later, when they'd eaten the trout, Emil presented Irene with a bowl of red huckleberries. And then it was hard to stay mad at him. She told him she'd been scared and she told him about the shape she'd seen in the trees.

When he didn't seem surprised, she left it alone. It was night by then. The tide was out, and a stink rose up from the mud flats and it drifted over to the boat. She was glad not to be on shore. The *Elsa* seemed like a haven of safety against the dark forest and mountains rising up out there. She missed her mother, even though Emil was there, sitting on the deck, smoking, leaning against the cabin window. It occurred to her how little she knew about him and how utterly she depended on him out there.

Rita stopped talking for a minute as she scrambled up the side of a large boulder and patted it. "Come and join me. I love sitting here. This time of day, the sun slants through here and warms it up."

I climbed up and sat beside her.

"I once found a crab claw on top of this rock. Strange, eh? It was just the end part. I kept it. I've always meant to ask someone how a crab claw could end up on a rock in the interior of BC, a couple hundred miles from the ocean."

"A bird?"

"That's probably it."

The way Irene described Emil, he sounded soft. Like the stroke of an eyelash. He would never mean any harm. But after the trip to the waterfall, she started to sense that there was something dark that had power over him. It came in spells, and when it came, it took him away from her.

If the water turned rough, they'd have to wait it out somewhere. One day, they'd anchored in a sheltered bight out of the worst of the weather, but the cliffs were too steep to allow them to go ashore. A couple of days passed and they ran out of fresh water. They didn't even have enough to make their morning coffee. So they decided to make a run for a nearby bay they saw on the charts.

After some hard going, they ran in and dropped anchor at another white shell beach. It was an Indian village—she could tell by the thick white midden, discarded shells of generations of families living in the same place. There wasn't much left of the village itself, just a leaning totem pole and the remains of some houses near the shore. But at the edge of the beach, almost overgrown by salmonberry bushes and stinging nettle, they saw a house that was still standing. They took their water jugs and coffeepot and two crabs they had caught and rowed over.

They had to beat down the nettles with their oars to get to the door that was watched over by a carved post of a big-beaked bird with outstretched wings. Inside, the house was empty. A low bench ran around the room. A few cooking pots hung on the walls. There was an opening along the roof rafters for smoke to escape and a stone fireplace in the middle of the floor. No sign of anyone, but Irene felt uneasy. She felt a presence, like they were being watched. It could have been that the village wasn't abandoned, just not being used right then. Maybe it was a winter village and the people were out fishing for the summer.

Still, it was good to be on dry land and out of the rain. They got some water from a stream coming off the mountain and Emil went looking for wood dry enough to make a fire.

He was gone a long time and she started to worry. But finally he came back and they built the fire and made coffee and cooked the crabs.

They fell asleep on the floor near the fire. When Irene woke up, the fire was out and Emil was gone. She could see pale light through the roof hole and she could hear the surf rushing into the beach. She had been dreaming about drums and a dancer wearing a mask that opened up to reveal another mask inside it. Once she was awake, she could still hear the drumming. She went to the door and looked out. No sign of Emil. But the dinghy had been carried out into the water and was slamming up against the rocks, making a knocking sound. She had to wade out and tow it back up the beach.

Mist hung in the trees. It burned off through the morning while Irene sat on the beach and waited for Emil. She didn't have matches, Emil had them, so she couldn't even make coffee. As the tide went out, she realized they had miscalculated and brought the *Elsa* in too close to shore. She was caught in a little pool, while around her the bay emptied out. There was nothing Irene could do about it, so she dug clams for lunch with a spoon.

You get a real sense of time passing when you're sitting on a beach waiting. The weather had calmed. The *Elsa* sat squat and helpless and behind her nothing moved out on the ocean. After a while, Irene got up and fought her way through the nettles to the edge of the forest to have a look, but it was so thick with brambles she didn't go any further. She slept a little and when she woke it was late afternoon and the tide had begun to slop back in.

She couldn't stand the sense of waiting around, being helpless. She wanted Emil to come back and find her, a vision of self-sufficiency, cooking clams on the beach. Barely noticed he was gone.

When the tide was full, she thought she should row out to the *Elsa* and try to move her to deeper water. She had never started the engine herself. It was a one-cylinder gas engine with a flywheel that had to be cranked. It could be tricky if you weren't used to it.

She took the coffeepot full of water, rowed back and climbed aboard. She was burning to do this right. First she had to turn on the magneto switch. Then, open the petcock and figure out where the cycle of the engine was: on intake or compression. You had to turn it until it was on intake; you'd hear the suction noise. Then you poured a little gas into the petcock. Stick the starting bar in the flywheel, give it a crank. The first time she did it, she forgot to close the petcock and gas blew all over the place. So she had to clean it up and try it all over again. She cranked and cranked, but she couldn't get Vivian to spark for her.

She felt helpless, bobbing in the chop, miles from anywhere with no sign of Emil and a boat she couldn't operate. Rock cliffs on one side, a wall of forest in front of her and a rough sea out beyond the shelter of the bay. She wouldn't let herself panic. She started the Coleman stove that they used on the deck when the weather was nice, and she boiled her clams and made coffee. But she vowed to pay more attention to what Emil was doing to the engine.

Rita swallowed and had a hard time getting the next words out. "She had learned something and she told me she never forgot it. She said she tried to teach you girls, too."

She seemed to be struggling to keep from crying.

"What was it?" I asked.

"She wouldn't ever put herself in someone else's hands like that again." Tears ran down the side of Rita's nose and she brushed them away. "You should never do that. End up at someone else's mercy. She knows it. I know it. You have to look out for your own safety." She breathed deeply. "I think you probably understand this, Maggie. You, me, Irene, we're all a bit like that. We protect ourselves. You even more than your mother. You can take that as a compliment. But it makes us difficult to live with. Irene decided that from then on, whenever they went to shore, she'd make sure she had everything she needed—matches, a knife, and food."

It grew dark and the tide went out again. She heard something big splashing around out near the cliffs. An owl called. You know what the owl call is supposed to mean, right? It's just silly superstition, but try to convince yourself of that when you're grounded in a tide pool in the dark, with just a mast light and an oil lantern.

The owl call made her think suddenly that she should be out there looking for him. He must be cold and hungry. Maybe she should have gone looking hours before. It hadn't even occurred to her.

She couldn't see anything on the beach now. She considered slopping through the shallow water in her rubber boots to the shore. She could take the big flashlight and try to signal him. But her anger returned and instead she went below deck and crawled into the bunk. She didn't expect to sleep, but when she next opened her eyes, an orange light was flickering on the porthole.

When she went up on the deck, she saw a bonfire burning on the beach. She climbed down the ladder and into the dinghy. She couldn't call out to him. She didn't know what to say or what she would find. The tide was coming in and light was starting to show over the trees. It was near dawn. When she pulled the dinghy onto the beach, he didn't get up from where he sat by the fire. He looked strange and distant. Her first thought was that he was mad at her. Maybe she really didn't understand how things worked out there. There was something she was supposed to have done, and she missed it and now he would take her back to Bella Coola and drop her off.

She said his name. She asked him if he was all right.

He didn't answer. A shiver ran through her. She really didn't know much about him at all, and she was out there in her rubber boots and pyjamas with only a flannel jacket over top.

Let's go, she said. *Put out the fire. Let's go back to the boat.*

He looked behind him at the woods as if he had been followed.

What is it? she said. Finally, he stood up and began to walk to the dinghy. She kicked some sand into the fire and hopped into the dinghy and, since he was making no effort to move, she took the oars and rowed them back.

He was covered in bleeding scratches and deeper cuts. Leaves and bits of bark and twigs were tangled in his thick curls and his shirt was ripped to shreds. When she saw the state he was in, she forgot her anger and her fear. She helped him take his shirt off and she boiled water and tried to wash his cuts. But he turned away from her. He wouldn't let her pull out the thorns and nettles that had made burning rashes on his skin. So she made him tea and a can of beans. He ate without looking at her.

What happened? she kept asking. He finished the food and lay down, turned his back to her and fell asleep.

"It's getting chilly. Let's go back."

"What?" I said.

"Back to the house. The sun's gone," Rita said.

"Oh, I thought Irene said that."

We jumped down off the boulder and headed back through the woods to Rita's.

"I have some deer sausage," she said. "We can have that with potatoes."

We ate on the porch, watching the light disappear behind the snow-topped mountains. We didn't talk much; I was still out on Emil's boat, waiting to hear what had happened to him. I only wanted things to turn out well if I could think of this Irene as someone who was not my mother. I wanted everything to be okay with Emil; I didn't want him to drop her off in Bella Coola. They might be out there still, roasting fish on the beach and chugging into civilization only to grub up and get gas.

It seemed to me that Rita could do that, separate the Irene she knew from this girl she was telling me about. She wasn't angry as she told the story. There was no jealousy or bitterness in her voice.

"It took several days before Emil was anything close to his old self," Rita began again.

It was as if he'd been under a spell, and one morning it lifted. They were drinking their tea in the silence that Irene had stopped trying to fight when he said, *I'm sorry. I know I had no business leaving you like that.*

Then he told her in a rush all the things he loved about her: the noise she made when she sipped her tea, her strong hands, the way she frowned when she was concentrating. He took her hands and kissed her neck and repeated that he was sorry, he didn't know what he had been thinking. She was the best thing that had ever happened to him. He promised to do better. And Irene was relieved. He was the Emil she loved again. She assumed it had been an aberration and she forgave him.

They ran into Namu for gas and grub. That night was behind them. Nothing had happened. They slipped down the ladder to swim in the sea. They gathered sea urchins and dug clams, tried drying seaweed and sprinkling it on their eggs in the morning. Emil's cuts healed. They made love with the hatch open and the stars shining on them.

But in the evenings, he told her bits and pieces of the most fantastic story.

You should know, he said. *I don't want to scare you, but you may have noticed the birds following us. They've been following me since Winnipeg.*

That's what he said.

Just when I think I've escaped them, they come back. I'm not saying they're the same birds.

Irene had noticed the birds, too. Had they been there all along? And he'd say, *There are things we don't understand, things that happen that we can't explain rationally.* Irene knew that to be true. He'd say, *You don't think I'm crazy, do you?* She said no. She began to watch the cormorants that hung around the *Elsa* and the bald eagles that gazed down on them from the branches of spruce trees. But she also noticed that Emil's eyes had a bright restless sheen she hadn't seen before.

The other morning in the old village house, he said one evening, *I heard them. They were outside, but I knew it wouldn't be long before they figured out how to get in. I waited until they were in the trees by the beach and I ducked out of the house and ran for it. That's how I got all cut up. It wasn't that I was deserting you.* It was important to him that she understood that. *It's me they're looking for.*

He told her he managed to evade them for a while. But when he had to stop and catch his breath, he heard them in the tops of the cedars, their wings beating the air. They were screaming down at him.

He warned her that she'd find it a little hard to believe what happened next. He saw a huge feather lying on a rock. It wasn't an eagle feather, or a hawk's; it was about two feet long. He thought it might be an offering of some kind, or maybe some kind of protection. So he picked it up.

I would never trust anyone else with this story. I'm not making this up.

And Irene saw that he believed every word of what he told her.

He lowered his voice to a whisper. *When I picked up the feather, I became a bird. A giant one, about the size of a human. I lifted on these huge wings and I rose above the tops of the cedars and I just kept going. I broke through the low cloud. The sun was shining up there, but the world beneath had disappeared, the ocean, the forest, everything was gone. Then I saw mountains, snow-topped, almost silver and I found myself landing at the foot of one, in front of a large black bird who was surrounded by other, smaller birds. How did you get here? he asked. His voice was weird, like a crackly radio.*

I picked up a feather, I said.

You're lying.

I'm not.

Where is it then? Give it to me.

I don't know where it went. I must have dropped it.

You're lying.

I don't know what happened to it.

That's what you always say, isn't it?

No.

It's never your fault, is it?

Then Emil told Irene there was something he had never told her, never told anyone at all. He needed to tell her. The bird knew it. He didn't know how, but he knew.

Irene wasn't afraid of what he would say. All she wanted then was to be worthy of whatever secret he told her.

The bird said, *I know all about your brother and what you said and what you didn't. You told yourself it wasn't really lying if you didn't tell everything. Humans don't know how to lie. You could learn a lot from us birds. We don't feel guilty. You start to feel so guilty, you erase all the benefit you got from lying in the first place.*

The bird offered Emil a deal. He'd keep Emil's secret if Emil kept his. The bird's secret was that place. He called it his kingdom. He said Emil had to find the feather he'd dropped and bury it. Not just shallowly either. He wanted it at least three feet underground. Emil said he would do it. Next thing he knew he was lying on the forest floor again. He looked for the feather. He must have looked for hours, until it was too dark to see. Then he came back to the beach and lit the fire.

So you never found it? Irene asked.

Emil said no. But he thought maybe it was a trick. Maybe the bird already had the feather. He probably got a good laugh at his expense.

Irene said that in spite of how crazy the story sounded, she believed him. Or she didn't believe exactly what he had said, but she believed the essence of what he had told her, that he had had some strange encounter. And she was nervous about the fact that he hadn't found the feather like the bird asked. She thought this would haunt Emil. She asked him if he thought they should go back and look for it.

He said no. He thought it was best to stay away from there.

"What about the brother?" I asked.

Irene didn't push it, and for a while it seemed as if Emil had forgotten about it. One afternoon, a wind kicked up. It looked as though it might blow for days and they needed to find shelter before it really blew up. But they'd left it a bit too late, I guess.

The *Elsa* pounded into giant waves that broke over the deck. The chart showed a bay ahead, but all they could see, when they cleared a bit of window, was a choppy foaming white sea. The wind kept pushing them back and little by little the *Elsa* had edged close to the high cliffs. They had to worry about not only the cliffs, but what might be near them, under the water. Irene steered while Emil poked his head out and shouted directions.

They were being hammered by the wind, not making any headway. The cliffs were drawing closer. Emil thought they might be smartest to try and tie up to a deadhead rising straight up out of the water. He went out on deck with a pole and tried to keep the *Elsa* from smashing into the rocks. It was a terrifying couple of hours. Irene could hear things scraping the hull. Rocks or submerged trees or something else, she didn't know. Water crashed over the *Elsa* and she dipped and plunged like she might go down for good. Finally, out of the storm, a bigger fishing boat came alongside. They tossed them a rope and towed the *Elsa* in behind the shelter of a kelp bed.

The water suddenly flattened out. She said it was the strangest thing to see. Emil told her he'd heard that the Indians used to slide their dugout canoes up on top of these kelp islands when the water was too rough. They even built fires on them and rode out the storms there.

The fishermen told Emil there was a good chance they'd damaged the *Elsa*'s propeller or cracked the hull since there were mountain peaks of rock under the water where they'd been tied up. He went below to check, but could see no sign of cracks. The fishermen said they'd let someone know to check on them when the weather let up.

That night, with the waves crashing into the kelp bed and the storm lashing rain against the portholes, Emil handed Irene a photograph of a boy, about her age.

That's my brother, he said. *That picture was taken in high school. He was beautiful.*

Irene agreed. He had thick black hair like Emil's, and dark spirited eyes. His smile was a grin, all confidence.

His name was Edward and he was a year older than Emil. Everybody loved him. He was always happy, a practical joker. He had a beautiful voice, sang in the church and school choirs. Most people didn't know that he had a mean side. Emil said he may have been the only one who knew about that.

Socially, Edward was at ease in a way Emil never was. He liked people, he knew how to like them. He hated how nervous Emil was. What did he have to be nervous about? Sometimes, after they'd been somewhere together, he'd just open a valve and let all his hate pour out on Emil. Why couldn't Emil ever say the right thing? Didn't he realize he insulted people? He was embarrassed to be seen with Emil. He said that often. He told Emil he should go live like a hermit in the bush since he couldn't learn how to act properly in public. He'd rage and roar like a wildfire you couldn't stop until finally he'd start to sputter out.

Emil said that everything Edward said was more or less true so he didn't know how he could defend himself. He didn't even try.

But one day after school had ended for the year, they went out to a bush party. Everyone got drunk, Emil included. Edward didn't say anything to him that night as they were walking home and Emil was relieved. The next day they went fishing, just the two of them. They went down to a bridge over a creek near their house. They drank some beer to take the edge off the night before. But Emil knew there was something coming. There was always something coming.

His brother had this way of clearing his throat before he spoke. It was a kind of warning. And he finally heard it, the throat clearing. Edward was good at finding Emil's most vulnerable places. Some people are like that. Siblings maybe most of all.

You were an embarrassment. That much he remembered, but that was nothing new. *That girl you were chatting up thought you were an idiot. I saw her laughing it up with her girlfriends after you walked away.*

He'd heard worse before, but Emil liked the girl and that day, he'd had enough. He shoved Edward so hard in the chest, he went down on the bridge on his back. His head hit something, hard, and he kind of bounced back up. He was surprised. Emil had never fought back.

Edward sat there rattled for a few minutes while Emil brought in his line. The day was ruined. He was going home. Edward caught up to him and said, *So you do know how to defend yourself.* His voice was a little slurred. Emil thought he'd bitten his tongue when he hit the bridge.

That night Edward didn't come down for supper. He told their mother he had a headache and wasn't feeling well. He stayed up there all night. When Emil went to bed, he thought Edward was pretending to sleep so he wouldn't have to talk to him. Edward wouldn't apologize—he never had—but something might have to change, now that Emil had stood up to him.

When he woke up the next morning, he turned over and saw Edward still sleeping. It was late and he wondered what kind of game Edward was playing. But something made him uneasy. Maybe he was too still, or maybe it was too odd, Edward sleeping in on a beautiful Sunday morning when he usually met his friends in the park for rugby. He went to Edward's bed and leaned over him to get a look at his face. His skin was the colour of ashes. He put his hand on his arm to nudge him. He was cold.

"Oh my god," I said.

"Yeah," said Rita. "He called for his mother. She came running. When the doctor got there, he focused on that headache Edward had complained of. Emil didn't even know if his brother really had a headache or if it was just something he told his mother. But the doctor went from there. He asked about what Edward had been doing the day before and Emil told about the party on Friday night, told about the fishing, and the beer they'd had to drink. He just didn't tell about the way he'd shoved him so hard he'd slammed his head into the bridge."

"Poor Emil," I said.

The stars had come out. Rita carried our plates into the kitchen and put the kettle on to make tea. I stepped off the porch to get a better look at the sky. I could see Cassiopeia above the house. I wondered if Mom was out on the *Elsa* again with Emil, looking at these same constellations. Maybe they'd both been lost at sea. It could have been an accident. But I couldn't go from the last time Rita had seen her to an accident on the *Elsa* without a lot of time in between that I couldn't account for.

"I'm almost at the end of what I know, of what she told me," Rita said when she came back with steaming mugs.

When the weather calmed, Emil went underwater to look at the propeller. Sure enough, a blade had been sheared off. They hailed a passing boat and were towed into Namu.

The wharf was busy with boats coming and going. That was 1958, the year of the record salmon run. Seine boats were coming in loaded down with all this fish. People made their fortunes that year. The village stank of fish. Boats were tied to the float six deep. At night the tires that kept the boats off the dock creaked and rocked, the wind rang through the rigging, and voices carried across the water. Irene wanted to leave as soon as possible. But Emil seemed in no hurry. He struck up conversations with the fishermen and drank beer and tinkered with the boat while he waited for the propeller. He said he planned to get in on the salmon run and needed to refit the boat for it. Not wanting to feel like a prisoner to his plans, Irene went for long walks along trails in the bush, picking berries.

One day she came back to the *Elsa* after a walk and he was gone. He had left his tools on the deck, along with an opened, warm bottle of beer. She expected him back any minute. She thought he had gone to the store to pick up something for the boat. But night fell and the noise of the wharf rose and floated over to where she made her coffee on the Coleman and tried not to worry.

Days passed. In spite of her best efforts to keep busy, to pretend not to be bothered, her anxiety grew. She couldn't eat, could barely sleep, and in the mornings, she threw up.

There was a doctor at the cannery in Namu. Irene sat outside the office for two hours and watched people come and go. Finally, she made herself go in. The doctor was a white-haired man, kindly. She told him she thought she was pregnant. He asked her some questions and examined her. He said a blood test would confirm it, but he was pretty close to sure already and by the time he got the test results back, she'd already know herself.

He called her *dear*. He said *Dear, who are you living with here?*

Irene was afraid to tell him.

He said he wasn't there to judge her. He was seventy-five years old, something like that, and he'd seen it all. But he told her she was going to have to start looking after herself. She was too thin. He wanted her to put on a good twenty or thirty pounds. He told her she'd be okay to work for a few months, so she might look in at the cannery. He said, *You think about yourself and that child you're carrying. That's all you need to worry about now.*

She didn't do anything right away, but as the days turned into two weeks, she realized that Emil might never come back. Her first job was mopping the floor of the cannery. But after a couple of weeks, when they could barely keep up with the volume of fish coming in, she moved to filling tins.

Each night, she returned to the *Elsa,* made supper on the little stove and wondered when Emil would come walking back up the wharf. The weather was turning and she knew she wouldn't be able to tolerate the boat all winter long. She was dying for a hot bath. At the end of the day, her hands and feet were so cold, she had to boil hot water and soak them before she could get to sleep.

"Was it Jenny?" I said. "Was she the baby?"

"Let me finish, Maggie," Rita said. Then more softly, "Okay? But I wonder if you can guess what happened next."

Irene was making good money at the cannery. She decided to look for a decent place to live. On her next payday, she went to the general store and bought some dishes, pots, a cast iron frying pan, some towels.

She had put on a few pounds, but she wasn't showing.

There was a redheaded man working at the cannery. His name was Patrick and he was as sweet as peaches. The older Indian ladies Irene worked with liked to tease him. They called him Salmonberry. He even blushed like one, they said. He'd made friends with some of the Chinese men who worked on the cutter. One of their parents ran a Chinese restaurant in town. At lunch break one day, while they sat outside catching the sun before it disappeared for the winter, Patrick invited Irene to come with him to the restaurant that evening. She hesitated about ten seconds, maybe fifteen. Not only had she not eaten in a restaurant for several months, and never in a Chinese one, she liked Patrick. When he smiled, her heart skipped a beat. Later, when the Indian ladies saw them together, they nudged each other and said, *Two salmonberries. They belong together.*

Rita stopped. We had both heard an owl calling, very close by.

I had been trying not to let Rita see I was crying. I didn't want her to soften it for me. I wanted to know. But my breath had caught and I had to wipe the string of snot hanging from my nose.

"I often hear owls here," she said.

"I know."

"It's just a superstition."

"I know."

"I'll get you something for that runny nose."

The night was clear. It was getting late, but pale purple light still showed in the west.

Two salmonberries. That was the story Mom and Dad told Jenny and me. Jenny was born in May 1959. So there was no way there could be another baby. It was Jenny. And Dad was not Jenny's father. Emil, poor, romantic, beautiful Emil was Jenny's father. I couldn't imagine telling her.

Rita handed me a roll of toilet paper and a glass of water.

"Thank you," I said.

"I hope I haven't been mistaken, telling you all this," she said. "It can't be wrong to tell the truth, can it? I've always believed that."

"Will you tell me about Dad? After they met."

"I think you've heard most of it."

She didn't tell Patrick everything right away. She told him she was living on a friend's boat, but looking for a place for the winter. He told her there was a nice little room for rent in the house he was living in. After they ate their chow mein, they walked over to see it. It was on the top floor and had a window overlooking a creek. There was a bed, a hotplate, and best of all, a private bathroom with a bathtub. Irene was so excited, she told Patrick she wanted to meet the landlady right away. She rented it to her that evening.

That weekend she packed her things into a child's wagon that one of the fishermen lent her, and she hauled them up to the house. She left the *Elsa* shut up against the weather as best as she could. She considered leaving a note for Emil, but when she tried to write it, nothing would come. If he wanted to find her, she would be easy enough to find. The rest was so obvious, it didn't need to be said.

She waited until October to tell Patrick she was pregnant. By that time, she had a sense of how he might react. She told him during lunch break at work. That way she didn't have to answer a whole lot of questions. He was too nice to reject her outright. He was surprised, she could see that, but his only question was, *What will you do if he comes back?*

She said, *I'll keep doing what I'm doing.*

That night after work as they walked home from the cannery, he asked her to marry him.

"And, as you know, she said yes." Rita stretched her arms over her head. "Too much sitting."

I was relieved to know that Dad had known. I didn't want to think of him being fooled. I didn't want to think there had been that secret between them all those years.

"The rainy season had started on the coast, so they went to Williams Lake shortly after. Irene was glad to be back to sunshine. Patrick got a logging job and he was away quite a bit. But he was there when she had the baby. When Jenny was born, Patrick said, *Another salmonberry*. Irene told me that was when she knew she loved him."

Rita went in the house. She was gone for quite a while. When she came back she had two glasses and the berry wine. She poured some for each of us and raised hers.

"To . . ." she began, but then she choked up. We clinked our glasses and sat looking out at the night and wondering where she was.

[THIRTY-ONE]

WHEN MOM'S STATION WAGON pulled into Rita's yard Saturday morning, it was Vern who was driving it.

"Who's that?" Rita asked, her voice teasing, as he stepped out of the car and smiled at me.

"Vern!" I almost ran to him.

"Uncle Leslie had to go clear a rockslide somewhere. He asked me to pick you up."

"You got your driver's licence," I said.

"More or less."

Rita gave us the lunch she had packed and made me promise to call her.

"I will," I said, but as I waved and smiled, I felt relieved to drive out of her yard.

"You look pretty comfortable behind the wheel," I said to Vern.

"Thanks."

"How long have you been driving?"

"About two weeks. I had to get to work."

"How come you're not at work now?"

"I've got a few days till they need me again."

He also looked good, in his white T-shirt and worn corduroys. His skin had darkened from working outside and the muscles of his forearms were taut as he held the wheel.

"When do you have to be back?"

"Next week," he said.

We drove the Nakenitses Road with dust flying up behind us and a cooling breeze from the open windows. Vern put the radio on and the rhythm of the road made me sleepy. When we got to the stop sign at the crossroads, I said, "Let's go to Bella Coola."

"What's in Bella Coola?"

"Maybe someone who knows about Mom."

"I'm game," said Vern.

"Really?"

"Sure."

"Should you ask Uncle Leslie?"

"I know what he'll say. So not asking will save time."

"Will he ream you out?"

"Doubt it. Unless we don't come back. Just jokin'."

"I've heard the road's kind of hairy."

"The Freedom Road," said Vern.

"Have you been on it?"

"Oh yeah. On it, up it, down it." Vern giggled.

"Are you nervous?"

He started to sing. "I've been everywhere, man. Breathed the mountain air, man, travelled I done my share, man. I've been everywhere." He giggled some more and so did I. "No, not nervous at all."

"Maybe we should stop and eat lunch first."

"Good idea."

Vern pulled the car to the side of the road and we got out. The sun was hot so we made our way down the ditch to a rail fence that was shaded by fragrant pines. Perched on the fence, we ate the egg sandwiches Rita had made for us. Something large was walking down the highway, coming our way.

"I hope it's not a bear," Vern said.

"Are you afraid of bears?"

"I have an average, normal fear of bears."

"Lightning, bears . . . I wonder what else you're afraid of. Look, they're horses."

"Phew," said Vern.

Two horses walked single file and riderless along the side of the road, heads down, as if they'd been travelling all day and were getting tired. One was a bay and the other was a beautiful brown and white pinto. They were sleek, well-cared-for horses with combed tails. They stopped parallel to us and observed us, then munched some grass, and moved on.

Across the road in the distance, mountains rose up blue and snow-topped and a small blue lake interrupted the green of the meadow. Vern noticed it at the same moment I did.

"It's probably full of weeds."

"But it looks so tempting."

We straddled the rail fence and ran for it. As we got close, our feet sank in the boggy ground.

"It's mucky," Vern said.

"Yeah, but the water looks nice."

"I dare you."

"What'll you give me if I go in?" I said.

He laughed as he took hold of my shoulders. "My admiration?"

"No way," I said and grabbed him around the waist. We struggled into the shallows and then we both went down.

"It's cold!" Vern yelped.

"I'm wet," I said, pushing myself onto my hands and knees.

"That was the idea."

"Your idea," I said and tackled him again.

Reeking of muck, and snuffing boggy water, we struggled out of the lake and picked our way through the meadow and back to the car.

"That was refreshing," said Vern.

"I have a change of clothes." I smiled at him. "Do you?"

"I have my dirty laundry I was taking to Uncle Leslie's. You won't mind if I put on my dirty work jeans?"

"Go right ahead." I laughed.

Vern and I changed on opposite sides of the car. It felt good to stand for a minute with the sun on my bare damp skin and to know that I was with Vern, driving west as far as we could go. I looked over and he was looking at me.

We left the plateau at the same place a large roadside sign read, Chains must be carried by ALL vehicles.

"Does that mean us?" I said.

"It's just in winter. Chill out, Maggie. Vern George is at the wheel."

Another sign, just after the other but bigger: Steep grade ahead. Test your brakes.

Vern looked at me. He made an elaborate show of pumping the brakes. "Brakes—functioning. Gas tank—on half. Oil—present, as far as I know. Everything's copacetic."

The blue mountains that lay ahead were wilder, more remote than the ones we were used to. The snow on their tops was such a vibrant white, they looked pretend, like a magical land lay at the end of the road.

"No turning back now," Vern said.

To the south, the mountains repeated themselves to the limit of our sight. There seemed to be no habitation in there, no roads, no towns. The forest thickened, spruce and firs with shreds of black moss caught in their branches, interspersed with ponds and bogs. A small black bear was eating by the roadside. Vern looked at me pointedly, but didn't comment. A light rain began to dot the dusty windshield. We had begun our descent.

Along the roadside, wild roses bloomed luxuriantly and we cracked the windows to catch their scent and the hint of rain. We crawled along. The edge of the road, which dropped off into trees and canyon, was less than a car width away. The road was built for escape, a way to get out when the rain and the mountains were getting to you. It must not have seemed necessary to have two lanes. Maybe the road builders had ploughed through in a frenzy, not thinking about the traffic that would eventually have to travel back in.

A pickup truck was approaching.

"Oh boy," said Vern.

"Just stay on the inside," I said.

"Don't worry. I'm not going anywhere near that edge."

Vern tucked in close to the mountainside to let him pass. The truck was thick with mud, and the driver waved and went on, leaving us alone again. Moments later, we drove into the rain.

"Shit," said Vern under his breath. Then, "Fear not, Maggie! Vern George is in control."

"I'm not afraid," I said.

"Good, because you shouldn't be afraid. What's there to be afraid of?" He kept his eyes straight ahead as he talked, and his knuckles were pale with tension on the steering wheel. "Besides the fact that we're sliding down an eighteen percent grade, five feet from plunging into the abyss? I'm not afraid either. It's all downhill. Nothing to it."

I smiled at him, though he didn't see it. I had the strangest feeling, not fear, but surrender, like the road was swallowing us, our tires barely clinging to earth. I was grateful to Vern, in this car, in the rain, him cracking jokes.

Our windshield wipers moaned as the downpour came full force. The road became a slime of mud. The tires slid more than rolled. Vern pumped the brakes and steered to the inside. There was no need to touch the gas pedal. He did everything he could to slow us down for the curves.

"Smells funny," I said.

"It's the brakes."

"Should we stop?"

Vern laughed weakly. "I don't think we can."

There was nowhere to stop anyway, and if we did stop in that mud, we might not get going again.

It was hard to tell how many feet deep the canyon was, maybe a thousand, and how many rusted-out car bodies might be at the bottom.

"How deep is this mud?" Vern asked.

We were creeping along so slowly, I opened the door to check. We were about six inches deep in thick sticky ooze, being sucked downhill by gravity. "Deep enough," I said.

We could see the height we were at, hills and mountaintops at eye level. We went down and down, and then the road spit us out into a broad green valley with trees towering over us and the mountains so close. Vern pulled over and dropped his head to the steering wheel.

"Holy shit, I wish I had a smoke right now," he said.

He began to giggle. Then we both giggled ridiculously till tears streamed down our faces and the adrenalin had been evenly shaken throughout our bodies.

"I don't ever want to drive that road again," said Vern. He looked out the window. "This looks like a pretty good place to live, right? We can just stay here forever."

We had driven back into sun. Vapour rose from the road. Everything looked incredibly green and vibrant and I didn't want the day to end.

We drove along Highway 20, looking for a good road. When we found one that looked promising we took it. Deeper into the woods, the land rose up and closed in around us.

"Bear shit," said Vern, pointing ahead of us. "We're not alone."

We stopped beside a scree that left a little room for us to pull off the road. A stream ran beside the road, and there looked to be a path leading into the forest.

"Want to see where that goes?" I asked Vern.

"Looks like up this mountain."

"We might find berries."

"And the source of the stream. Maybe hot springs."

We set out, the path quickly disappearing among the thick trees. We kept going, climbing gradually and steadily. Moss and rock and huckleberry bushes, their delicate leaves catching the sunlight. I tried a berry but it wasn't ripe enough yet. The trees thinned and the wind picked up. Coming out onto rock, there were just a few scrubby trees to break the wind. We had been breathing heavily with the effort of climbing and when we stopped, I had the feeling someone was watching us. We sat looking down on the tops of trees, as the wind swept over the rock. Animal paths wound through the bushes.

"There's something eerie about this place," Vern said.

"Maybe it's the wind."

"Yeah, maybe. Let's get out of it."

Back down in the trees, the wind seemed to grow even stronger, but it was high in the treetops, which were beginning to sway wildly. We weren't paying a lot of attention to retracing our steps and we found ourselves walking in swampy ground with tall ferns growing from rotting, moss-covered stumps. Through the wind, I thought I heard a voice call out a single word.

"This terrain isn't familiar," said Vern.

"Did you hear that?"

"What?"

"It sounded like someone calling."

We both stopped to listen. Nothing. As we began walking again, I heard it again, a two-syllable word that sounded a lot like my name.

"I heard it that time," Vern said.

"What did it sound like to you?"

"A woman's voice, calling someone."

"Yeah." I tried to shake the feeling of anxiety that had overtaken me. Who would be looking for me? Who would know I was here?

Suddenly a shape burst out of the trees from behind us and streaked off leaving a wake of shaking underbrush.

"Jesus Christ," said Vern, his hand to his heart.

"I think it was a dog."

"How could you tell?"

"I just got a glimpse of the tail."

Then in front of us appeared a woman in a raggedy leather jacket, jeans and rubber boots. A rifle hung from a strap over her shoulder.

"You better get in out of this wind," she said. "Storm's coming. You never know what trees might come down."

Vern and I were so surprised we both just stared at her.

"Just looking for Laddie, my dog."

"He ran by us," I said.

"Chasing something," she said. "There was a small plane went down in here a few days ago. Wreckage still hasn't been found, but I saw it come down. Did you come across anything?"

Vern and I shook our heads.

"If you do, come and let me know. I'm camped down the road about a mile. You'll see it. Blue tent."

"Sure," Vern said.

"Some government people on the plane, the RCMP said."

A gust of wind piled into the woods and the treetops bent to their limits.

"Better get inside," she warned us again and disappeared into the trees.

"The road's got to be close," Vern said. We hurried ahead, and he was right.

The car was nowhere in sight at the spot where we came out, but we were pretty sure we were too far south.

"That way?" I said, and Vern nodded.

After about five minutes, we could see the scree piled at the bottom of the mountain.

"Thank god," said Vern.

Once we were safe in the car, Vern said, "That was kind of weird."

"She didn't look like the official search party."

He turned on the car and cranked the heat. "For a minute there, I thought someone was calling your name."

"Really?" I crawled over the seat to get my sleeping bag.

"Cold?" said Vern. He helped me spread the sleeping bag. There was something in his manner, some restraint that I recognized in myself.

"You?" I said.

He nodded and I spread the sleeping bag to cover both of us. The wind hammered the car and whistled at the windows. There was too much to say, so we said nothing.

Vern put his cool hand at the back of my neck. I turned to him. He pulled me close and I felt his warm lips on my neck. Then he cupped my face in his hands very tenderly and kissed me. Like sliding down that mountain road, the surrender.

The windows fogged over. The car had stalled. Vern shut it off. His hands travelled from my neck to my shoulders, down my arms to my hands, which he held for a moment. Then he slid his fingers up under my shirt and cupped each breast gently. He fell against me with a moan. Ignoring the buttons, he pulled the flannel shirt over my head and halfway off my arms. His mouth moved down my neck and his tongue touched one nipple. I breathed in sharply. Vern made a noise like a small animal, pressed his hips against me and bucked and shuddered in my arms.

We lay there like that, damp and hot under the sleeping bag, as dusk dimmed outside the fogged windows.

"Maggie," Vern said.

"Yeah?"

"I've been wanting to touch you so bad. I'm sorry if I . . ."

"No. Me too. I'm glad. I mean I liked it."

He cleared a patch on the windshield and through it we saw a sliver of moon showing over the ridge.

We put the back seat down and made pillows from our clothes and pulled the sleeping bag over us. Vern fell asleep right away. But I lay there listening to two coyotes barking close by and I worried. I couldn't see how I would tell Jenny that Dad was not her dad, that we were only half-sisters and that Mom had a life we never knew about. I couldn't think of a way to soften it. I decided I wouldn't even try to tell her over the phone. I'd wait to see her in person, and even then, I'd wait. But when I thought of telling her in person that meant I had to think about where we would be, where we would live and whether I'd have to quit school or not.

Whispering. "Maggie." Louder. "Maggie!"

I struggled to open my eyes.

Vern was bending over me, his voice thick with sleep.

"What?"

"You were dreaming. Are you okay?"

"Mom was calling me. I heard her. Just like today—*Ma-ggie*. She was standing there, holding Cinnamon and calling me. But when I got closer, it was that old lady from the woods and she was pointing her rifle at me."

"You're crying. Don't cry." Vern put his arm under me and pulled me to him. "Don't cry. Maybe we'll find her. Maybe she's in Bella Coola."

What would he think of me if I told him that the absence I felt right then like a hole scooped out of my stomach was not for my mother, but for my white and orange cat with her soft little chin and her purr like a tractor.

[THIRTY-TWO]

Bella Coola lay drenched and grey in the late morning light. Rain soaked a small white church, a faded totem pole and the paint-peeling houses of the reserve. We found a store and I went in and bought a can of beans, a loaf of bread, and a few barely ripe bananas. An older man was at the till. As he put my groceries in a paper bag, I said, "Do you know a Deschamps in town?"

"Alice Deschamps? I know just about everybody, darling. There might be a few names I forget now and then, but not too often."

"Older woman, from the Prairies?"

"That's her. Her house is the red brick-sided one over by the river."

"Thanks."

We found the red house by the river. It was small and neat, with fake brick siding, sheltered by lilacs and with catmint and daisies drooping in the rain around the front step. I knocked at the screen door. No answer. I knocked again. The front drapes were drawn, but I thought I saw them move gently. Just beyond the edges of trimmed lawn, a dense forest of cedars and firs towered. I knocked once more, then went back to the car where Vern and I sat, ate our lunch and waited.

When no one came after a couple of hours, we drove down to the docks. Rain pitted the water and soaked the cedars. Moss ate at the old silvered wood of a rotting pier. Blue, green, grey, greyish green, greenish blue, bluish grey. Only the orange, rusted tin roofs of the cannery buildings and the docked boats with blue and yellow and red trim interrupted the monochromatic landscape. A man in a pickup truck pulled over by the side of the road and sat with the engine idling. The cannery roof slanted at the same angle as the deep green mountain behind it and the snow-covered far blue mountains behind that. This was the end of the road. To go any farther, we'd have to get in a boat and wind our way along the river, through cloud-shrouded mountains and out to the ocean.

Vern and I decided to make phone calls. Vern called Uncle Leslie, but there was no answer. I called Sister Anne.

"She's out of the hospital, Maggie. She's staying here for now with Sunny. They're both doing very well."

"So she's better?"

"She's much better. They're monitoring her medication, but she's been clear-headed. She's taking good care of little Sunny. Do you want her to call you?"

"I'm in Bella Coola," I said. "She could call me at the pay phone, I guess."

I gave her the number and we arranged for Jenny to call at five o'clock. The rest of the day, as Vern and I took muddy back roads and poked around dripping rainforest and fast-flowing creeks, I thought about what I could say to her.

But at five o'clock when the phone rang right on time, I didn't need to say anything.

"Maggie, you wouldn't believe how cool Sunny is. She's got these serious green eyes and she's always watching everything. The nuns say she has an old soul. They don't think she'll give me any trouble. I'm so glad I named her Sunny—it's perfect for her. And she smiled at me the other day, I forget what day that was, when she was feeding. And she's growing like crazy. You've gotta see her. We've been out in the stroller. I'm starting to like Vancouver. You can just walk to the store and buy flowers and all kinds of fruit. What are you doing in Bella Coola?"

"Wow, Jenny, you sound really good," I said.

"I feel so much better. That was pretty weird for a while there, eh? You must have been freaked out. But this is the best thing that ever happened to me. I mean, not the freaking out part, but Sunny. When I think I almost gave her up, it makes me cry. I look at her and I just start bawling my head off, thinking what an awful thing that would have been. She'd never have known her mother."

"That's great, Jenny. So, I'll call Sister Anne again in a few days, okay?"

"Wait. What have you found out about Mom?"

I hesitated. "I told you about the car."

"Yeah."

"Not too much more yet. But there's someone in Bella Coola who might know something. That's why I'm here."

"Maggie?"

"Yeah?"

"Now that I'm a mother, I can't believe she'd just walk away. I hope you know what I'm getting at."

"I think so."

"Okay. Well, see you soon then. You won't believe how big Sunny's getting."

"I can't wait to see her." I hung up. I was glad that I had not said anything to disturb Jenny's joy.

The next day, while Vern went to the docks to try some fishing, I walked over to the red house and knocked again. This time, when the curtains moved, I saw a cat poke her head around the fabric, her little white paws clinging to the window ledge. She looked at me furtively and disappeared. I tapped the window with my fingers. I wanted a good look at her face, but it couldn't be a coincidence. It was Cinnamon.

I pounded on the door. No one answered. I felt the tears rising. My cat. Who was this woman who had my cat? I went around the house and tried the back door. I thought of looking for a screwdriver, popping the lock. I even checked the windows, after first making sure no neighbours were watching me. Then I sat on the step and waited until I got too chilled and wet to sit there any longer.

Vern and I had made a little camp down a logging road that night. We built a fire in the evening and watched the sky finally clear above the woodsmoke and trees. When I stood to stretch, Vern stood too and took my hands. I moved into him and felt him stiffen against me. He unzipped my jeans and slipped his hand inside. When my knees gave a little he caught me by the small of the back. It was glorious to be standing by the fire with the stars shining on us, the lonely road, the fragrance of the towering cedars and Vern's hands moving over my body.

"Don't worry," he whispered. "I know we can't go too far."

And so I didn't worry. We opened the back door of the station wagon and stretched out on the sleeping bag, our heads hanging out to look up at the stars. Our skin was as moist as the air and dimpled with the pleasure of fingertips mapping muscle curve and nipple and smooth line of dark hair on belly.

[THIRTY-THREE]

"CINNAMON," I SAID and bent to pat her. She was sitting right at the door when it opened.

"What did you call her?" the woman said.

"Cinnamon. Isn't that her name?"

She studied me. "I didn't name her. My nephew gave her to me. She's an old cat."

"She's not that old. She'd be about five. She's my cat. I named her Cinnamon."

"Who are you?"

"My name is Maggie."

"I don't know you."

"Margaret Dillon."

"I'm sorry, no. I don't know the name. Who are you looking for?"

"I'm looking for Emil."

She studied me again. "You better come in then. Sit.

You can move those buckets. I've been out picking berries."

She looked nervous. She wiped her hands on her apron. "Would you like some tea?"

"Please," I answered. When her back was to me, I said, "Is he still alive?'

She turned to me abruptly. "You're going to have to tell me who you are."

"My sister is Emil's daughter."

Alice, Emil's aunt, piled the counter with potatoes, onions, carrots, and celery as I sipped my tea slowly, waiting.

"I'm making fish soup. I could use some help." So, while she cleaned and cut up the salmon, I chopped the vegetables. Cinnamon came and sat patiently waiting for her share of the fish trimmings. Alice made up a small plate and handed it to me. I set the plate on the floor, smoothed Cinnamon's fur and watched her eat.

"She was the runt of the litter," I said. "I had to feed her goat's milk with an eye dropper to keep her alive. She was just tiny. I got her just after my dad died. My mother is Irene."

I could feel Alice stir at the name.

"Do you know her?" I asked. I handed over the chopped celery and she put it in the soup.

"I know the name. I never met her. I didn't know she had children."

"I haven't seen her in three years."

Again Alice bristled, then sighed.

"Emil is my brother's son. He's artistic, always was. Grew up kind of a quiet boy, very serious. Not like his brother. I think that was hard for him. Edward was everyone's favourite. He died suddenly when they were teenagers and Emil never really got over that.

"I always had a soft spot for Emil as a boy. He used to climb into my lap and sit watching the world. That was when he was really little. But I didn't really know him as an adult until I moved out here. He came out to visit me and he ended up buying a boat. I understand he met Irene around that time. I didn't see him again for many years. A couple of years ago now, late summer, he showed up at my door in the middle of the night with the cat. Your Cinnamon—I just call her Puss." She looked at me apologetically. "Emil didn't tell me her name. He was in no state."

He had been thin and wild-eyed, barely recognizable. He had only come to ask her to take the cat. He had not even spent the night, only left the cat after making her promise she would take care of her and then he had gone. It was months more before she learned where the cat came from and the story it was a part of.

Alice promised me she would tell me all she knew. But she said it was a story that should be told in safety and that she wanted me to spend the night and the next day with her. I said I would.

I walked down to the dock to find Vern and we drove back to Alice's house together.

"You sure, Maggie?" he said.

"I'm sure," I said.

"I'll come round here tomorrow afternoon." He had a hold of my hand and seemed reluctant to let go. "Sleep well," he said and leaned over to hug me. "It'll be just me and the bears tonight."

All that evening, Alice and I kneaded dough, rolled out pie crusts and cleaned berries.

Alice told me she had left Manitoba in 1955.

"I ran away," she said.

"Ran away from what?"

"My husband. I had inherited some money from my sister. She knew what was going on in our house and when she died she left money to me and to Emil. I didn't actually have the money yet, but I couldn't wait. I had enough for a bus ticket to Calgary. Then I hitchhiked. I wanted to go somewhere my husband would never have heard of. I got a ride from a logger who was heading to Bella Coola. He told me about this road that had been pushed through a couple of years before. Told me it was called the Freedom Road. And that convinced me that it was the place for me. Mind you when we drove that road, I didn't think I'd live to enjoy my freedom."

"I know what you mean."

"Oh, it's nothing now compared to what it was."

Before bed, the counter was laden with fresh buns and berry pies.

"You need to get some sleep," Alice said.

I had waited this long and I would have to wait some more. I could hear the river from the spare bedroom where Alice had made up the bed for me. The room was chilly and I pulled up the extra blanket. I heard the rain coming down hard again. Vern would be listening to the steady rhythm on the station wagon roof. In the middle of the night I woke hot and tangled in the sheets, dreaming that Vern was touching me. A sweet ache spread from my centre out to my limbs, my fingers, my toes. I tried to open my eyes, to remember where I was, but I was held on that warm, soft edge of sleep. There was a sound, familiar and comforting, in the room. It was Cinnamon, purring beside me, her warm body curled against my back.

In the morning, we didn't eat breakfast. Alice gave me a cup of weak tea. She led me to the edge of her property and into the bush. We followed a muddy path through the trees to the rocky river's edge, then down along the riverbank until we saw smoke rising from a fire on a strip of pebbly beach. Two young women were tending a fire. They smiled at me as we approached. Not far from the fire was a shelter made of a frame of bent branches covered with blankets and canvas. The rain had stopped in the night and the mountains and sky were bright-washed blue. The river tumbled cold and clear over rocks. One of the young women dipped a pot into the flow and scooped the fresh water into a barrel. She did this several times. Cedar smoke scented the air. The other woman gave me a flannel nightgown to put on and asked me if I was wearing any jewelry. I wasn't. The women and Alice put theirs on a bench beside the fire.

When everything was ready, we went into the shelter. Blankets were pulled down over the door. The darkness was total. Water hissed and a blanket of steam enveloped us. My heart slowed. My eyes closed. The heat burned the surface of my skin, then seeped still deeper into my bones and loosened them.

A story rose in the darkness, a story of a man who lived in the shelter of a burden so huge he was impervious to ordinary fear. He wasn't afraid of grizzlies or cougars, lightning strikes or snowstorms or the birds of prey that made their nests in the trees beside his cabin. Sometimes when his aunt took the motorboat up the inlet and hiked in to see him, she found him outside his cabin in the clearing, his hands red with cold as he sat in the drizzling rain drawing birds in charcoal on damp cardboard.

She stoked his fire and made him soup and pan-bannock and stayed to make sure he ate it. He had been scraped clean—there was nothing more for loss to scavenge from him. Guilt had spread in him like rampant stinging nettle and choked out every other thing so that he no longer felt it like other people did, because he had no other feeling to compare it to. It was only because of this that he could live at all.

This is a sad story. Don't think about approaching him gently like a wild, cornered animal. Don't think about holding out a hand to him. This will not be allowed.

After some time, we emerged into the sunlight, splashed ourselves with river water from the barrel and listened to the birds scolding each other as they built their nests in the trees on the far bank.

When we went back inside, the rocks hissed, steam rose and the heat deepened. Hooves rushed past outside and thunder rumbled. Stories peopled the dark.

A woman named Irene in a cabin in the bush with the snow just melting and the Solomon's seal blooming under the trees and the tender turquoise broken shells of hatched birds' eggs cushioned in the moss. Irene, our mother, who had beautiful red hair and legs as shapely as a fawn, labouring in childbirth with only a man who loved her and a self-help book several years old. The sun shone on the cabin floor and moved up the walls, then the shadows lengthened and the windows darkened and the fire popped and crackled, the water boiled again, steam rose and still she laboured and the baby refused to come.

He offered to carry her to the truck and she spat at him and called him an idiot. But he'd read about that. How mothers could turn ugly that way. It didn't stop him from trying to massage her with olive oil, which didn't stop her from slapping his head and telling him to get away from her.

The story, you have to understand, is told by a man who loved our mother to the woman who was his protector who told it to me to protect him. But I suppose that most of it is true. When he could see the crown of the baby's head, Emil held a mirror for Irene to see and when the head refused to budge any further, Emil tried to help it out. Irene was worn out from pushing so long and couldn't do much more. It was dark outside. An owl hooted at the window and Emil felt he was being taunted. Sometime after midnight, Emil finally pulled the baby out. He was a boy and he was blue. At the same moment, from somewhere deep within our mother's body, blood began to flow in a torrent. Emil had never seen a torrent of blood like that.

It gushed onto the floor while Irene lay spent and asking for a blanket. Emil didn't know whether to tend to the baby or Irene. He stuffed towels between Irene's legs and tried to get the baby to breathe. The books said you weren't supposed to spank the baby, but in desperation he did it anyway. It didn't help. So he put the baby in the basket they had prepared for him and he turned to Irene and the blood.

She had stopped asking for the blanket but he tucked it around her anyway and kissed her forehead. The colour of her skin was like the inside of a mussel shell, luminous gray-purple. The towels were soaked through and there were no more, and when he tried to look, the blood just gurgled out, a viscous gelatinous purply red. He thought of cold water, to stop the bleeding, but he had only hot water.

The owl was hooting and Irene was still and cold to the touch, her breathing barely discernible. So he ran outside to the woods and found some snow and scooped it into a clean pot and carried it back into the steaming, bloody house. He kissed her again but by then she was dead. The cat, Cinnamon, hunched in the chair by the stove.

He spent part of the night in the rank-smelling bloody house while the fire cooled. Then as dawn came, he carried the cat outside in his arms, took a can of gasoline and splashed it on the front door, on the walls, at the four corners of the cabin and he lit it. He stood in the trees and watched it burn to the ground with both Irene and the baby inside. He himself disappeared with the cat and was not seen for a long time. When he surfaced, he was not a man anyone who had once known him would recognize. His aunt Alice saw the ghost of him that one night when he brought her the cat. Then she did not see him again until she heard the rumour of the black-bearded rake of a man living in the bush drawing birds on cardboard. She knew it must be him and she went to find him.

The heat had laid me out flat on the ground. A baby wailed. Snot streamed from me and into the cool mud under my cheek. The light, when I crawled out of the heat, stung my eyes. Sun and turquoise sky. Steam billowed from my body as a woman rinsed me with cold river water.

We ate salty salmon soup and buttery rolls. Berry pie. Sweet tea. Birds hopped from branch to branch, chattering, working on their nests.

"There's a piece of land up the valley," Alice said. "Emil has the deed for it. He told me it's in a safety deposit box somewhere. He meant it for Irene. I think he will want Jenny to have it now."

The fire snapped and smoked with the rich scent of cedar. We watched the shadows change; sunlight striped the ferns and fallen trees. And then it was time to go back.

In the morning, when the sun came over the mountains, Vern and I packed up the station wagon and drove out of the valley. We saw two bears, three deer, and wild roses blooming everywhere. I held Cinnamon, who watched out the window, alternately meowing and purring, then climbed into the back and curled up on the floorboards in the same place she used to. Alice had insisted I take her. "She's all I have of her to give you," she said.

I closed my eyes and slept. I dreamed of Mom, and in the dream I was cradling her in my arms.

ACKNOWLEDGEMENTS

I wrote the first draft of *Shelter* in 1992, five years after my mother died, and shortly after I'd met my husband, David. David told me stories of his childhood, some of which took place in the Chilcotin where he had lived for a short time on a wilderness ranch about an hour from Williams Lake. The first summer after we met, we travelled Highway 20 and the back roads between Williams Lake and Bella Coola in David's indestructible Volkswagen Scirocco, and it was on that trip that the two sisters, Maggie and Jenny, and their missing mother, began to haunt my imagination.

I finished the novel a year or so later and sent it to a publisher, where it was rejected. So I put it away and began work on other things. But a few years after I became a mother myself, Maggie and Jenny's story drew me again and I began rewriting it completely.

I mention this because there are people I would like to thank who supported me in various ways through those first drafts in the early '90s: Jay Draper and Barbara Johnston;

Allan MacDougall of Raincoast Books; and my colleagues at UBC where I was finishing my MFA.

For the current *Shelter,* I owe thanks to the Saskatchewan Arts Board for initial financial assistance. I am grateful to Okanagan College for supporting the research and writing of the manuscript. My talented colleagues in the Okanagan College English department inspire and sustain me. Anne Cossentine, Deborah Cutt and Surandar Dasanjh in the Penticton campus library went out of their way to chase down microfilm of newspapers from the 1960s and '70s, as well as any obscure articles I needed. Stan Chung talked to me about growing up in Williams Lake in the 1970s and I consulted his book of essays, *Global Citizen*. Sage Birchwater's beautiful book, *Chiwid,* gave me insight into the people of the region, as well as the inspiration for the fictional Chiwid in *Shelter*. Mr. Birchwater also met with me and answered my questions about the Chilcotin area during the 1970s.

While researching the novel, I stayed at Bracewell's Lodge in Tatlayoko Lake twice. My thanks to Connie for making me welcome. The hike from the lodge up Potato Mountain in June is unforgettable. My generous hiking companions on the second trip were Al, Jesse, Jack, Lynn and Maggie, our guide. They named the wildflowers for me as we climbed.

The Cowboy Museum in Williams Lake provided historical details. Gaines McMartin answered my questions about logging. My father-in-law, Dan Joyce, was an invaluable source of information about fishing and boating on the BC coast. He told me stories of fishing in the 1950s, and read parts of the draft and corrected details.

Although I have tried to incorporate all the information that I received, any inaccuracies are mine. People who live in the region will notice that I have fictionalized most of the smaller place names, out of respect for the people whose histories are intertwined with the names.

Thanks to my very good friend Rozanne Haddad for inviting me to stay with her at Nimpo Lake, where she worked one summer as a baker for a fly-in fishing camp. Her effervescent personality helped introduce me to a side of the Chilcotin I wouldn't have seen otherwise. In the novel I've given a tip of the hat to Fred (whose last name I still don't know), who drove me to Bella Coola on the Freedom Road and showed me "the good place" that I've tried to re-create here.

I want to thank the Naramata Centre, where I stayed on several occasions during the writing of the manuscript. The peaceful setting beside Okanagan Lake allowed me quiet, uninterrupted working hours. Melanie Murray and I shared manuscript drafts while staying at Naramata. Anne McDonald encouraged me at various stages along the way. I appreciate their ongoing interest and support. My stay in the Henriquez boat studio at the Leighton Artists' Colony, Banff Centre, provided inspiration for the *Elsa* in *Shelter*.

Denise Bukowski is not only an indefatigable agent, she also offered advice on my initial rewrites, advice that I took, and that strengthened the novel considerably. I thank Louise

Dennys for her enthusiastic response to the manuscript. My editor at Random House Canada, Anne Collins, seemed from the start imbued with the spirit of *Shelter*; her editorial suggestions were both insightful and exacting. Thank you to Angelika Glover for fine and careful copy-editing.

I am so grateful for the unflagging encouragement that comes from my family, siblings Anne, Mary, Pat, Barbie and Neil. My father, Arthur Greenslade, died before *Shelter* was published, but he never failed to ask me, each time we talked, "How's the writing going?" As I write this, David is in the kitchen cleaning up the breakfast dishes and my son, Khal, is playing a tune on the harmonica in the living room. Having them in my life gives me the joy and sense of security that make my writing possible. I thank them deeply.

FRANCES GREENSLADE was born in St. Catharines, Ontario, and has since lived in Manitoba, Saskatchewan and BC. She has a BA in English from the University of Winnipeg and an MFA in Creative Writing from UBC. Her first book, a travel memoir called *A Pilgrim in Ireland: A Quest for Home*, won the Saskatchewan Book Award for Non-Fiction. Her second memoir, *By the Secret Ladder: A Mother's Initiation*, was published in 2007. Frances teaches English at Okanagan College in Penticton, BC.

A NOTE ABOUT THE TYPE

The text of *Shelter* has been set in Adobe Jenson (aka "antique" Jenson), a modern face that captures the essence of Nicolas Jenson's roman and Ludovico degli Arrighi's italic designs. The combined strength and beauty of these icons of Renaissance type result in an elegant typeface suited to a broad spectrum of applications.

The display titles have been set Sackers Gothic Light.

BOOK DESIGN BY CS RICHARDSON